"I WASN'T GOING TO DO THIS, CORA."

"I wasn't going to start this between us. I know that's not why you're here," he said, his voice full of grit.

"I wasn't going to start it, either," she said, her heart pounding in her chest—from his closeness, from the way he was holding her, from what might be happening, and from the honesty she was about to let loose from her lips, "but I can't help that I want it. Want you."

"Jesus." He was almost shaking with restraint. "I'm worried about you not feeling good," he said.

"With you looking at me like that, I feel better than I've felt in a really long time."

"Cora—"

"Slider, just this once," she whispered, desperate for his touch, desperate for a connection, desperate for *him*.

It was as if her words snapped something inside him, because suddenly he was kissing her like she was the water and he was a man who'd been lost in the desert.

By Laura Kaye

Raven Riders Series

RIDE WILD
RIDE ROUGH
RIDE HARD

Hard Ink Novels

HARD TO SERVE
HARD EVER AFTER (novella)
HARD AS STEEL
HARD TO LET GO
HARD TO BE GOOD (novella)
HARD TO COME BY
HARD TO HOLD ON TO (novella)
HARD AS YOU CAN
HARD AS IT GETS

LAURA KAYE

A RAVEN RIDERS NOVEL

AVONBOOKS

An Imprint of HarperCollinsPublishers

RIDE WILD. Copyright © 2017 by Laura Kaye. All rights reserved. Printed in the United States of America. No part of this book may be used or reproduced in any manner whatsoever without written permission except in the case of brief quotations embodied in critical articles and reviews. For information, address HarperCollins Publishers, 195 Broadway, New York, NY 10007.

First Avon Books mass market printing: November 2017

Print Edition ISBN: 978-0-06-240340-7
Digital Edition ISBN: 978-0-06-240341-4

Cover design by Nadine Badalaty
Cover photographs: © Wander Aquiar Photography (portrait); © DenisTangneyJr/Getty Images (street); © Roman Samborskyi/ Shutterstock (man's hair)

FIRST EDITION

17 18 19 20 21   QGM   10 9 8 7 6 5 4 3 2 1

To anyone struggling to break the habit.
Don't give up.

I want to find something I've wanted all along
Somewhere I belong
—"Somewhere I Belong," Linkin Park

CHAPTER 1

It was their normal routine, and it was awkward as crap.

Cora Campbell bit back a smile as she sat in the passenger seat of the beat-up pickup truck. She didn't think Sam Evans, her boss-of-sorts, would appreciate her humor. Or, like, *any* humor. He filled the driver's seat beside her, his big hands on the wheel and black tattoos snaking all down his lean, muscled arms. From the corner of her eye, she sneaked a glance at his face, and one word came to mind.

Wild.

Longish wild brown hair, like he couldn't keep from raking at it in frustration. Wild brown beard that Cora sometimes imagined chopping off just so she could better see the face it seemed like he purposefully hid beneath it. Pale green eyes, mesmerizing in their uniqueness, but also wild with emotions at which she could only guess . . .

"So, um, Slider," she said, her use of the nickname his motorcycle club had given him slicing through the uneasy silence, "anything special I need to know about Sam and Ben for tonight?"

That pale gaze slashed her way, and she felt the chill of it into her bones. Slider didn't scare her—he was too good to his boys for that. But it was entirely possible that his glances appeared in the dictionary next to *Intimidating as Fuck*. And maybe even *If Looks Could Kill*. And definitely *Like, Whoa*. It was a good thing he paid her so well to babysit his sons. In truth, he was doing her a pretty big favor giving her a part-time job while she figured out her life, so she put up with his . . . moodiness.

He huffed out a breath, as if mustering the energy to reply sucked vital life force from his soul or something. "Sam has homework he wants your help with," he said, his tone almost apologetic. "And Ben . . . is Ben."

Cora nodded. Having babysat the kids four or five days a week for the past three months, she had a decent idea what Slider meant. At six, Ben was a sweetheart of a boy, but nightmares and monsters under the bed gave him more than a little difficulty sleeping. "Okay."

They came upon the two-story white farmhouse where Slider lived and Cora sometimes worked. Empty, overgrown flower beds. A misshapen wreath on the door, so bleached from the sun Cora could no longer tell what color it'd originally been. Shutters hanging at odd angles from years of neglect. The house had an abandoned, decaying feel about it, and Cora didn't really have to wonder why that was.

Slider hadn't even parked when the front door exploded open, the creaky screen door wobbling like it might just give up and fall off its hinges. A little boy darted out next to the gravel driveway, hopping excitedly as if the grass hid a trampoline. Except for the lighter brown hair and happiness shaping his face, there was no denying Ben was Slider's kid.

Cora stepped out of the truck into the warm early September evening wearing a smile. "Hey, jumping bean."

"Name's Ben, not Bean," he said, his grin all the cuter for the big gap where his front teeth should've been.

"You sure? I could've sworn it was Bean." She hugged him as he threw his arms around her waist. Where Slider was a walking, talking wall that kept all his emotions barricaded, his younger son wore every single emotion on his sleeve.

"No." He laughed. "It's *Ben!*"

"Okay, Bean." Hiking up the backpack that served as an overnight bag, she glanced at Slider and found him watching her through narrowed eyes, like maybe she was a foreign language he couldn't decipher. Tall and broad-shouldered, he had a ranginess about him that, like the house, spoke of neglect. She'd seen him sit with the kids at meals, sometimes even with a plate of food in front of him. But it was possible she'd eaten more watching movies in bed with her friends Haven and Alexa last weekend than she'd seen Slider eat in the past three months combined.

The youngest Evans let loose a long-suffering groan. "No, Cora, it's *Ben*," he said, pronouncing her name more like *Coowa*. It was so cute it almost killed her.

"Finally, you're here," Sam called from the front door. At ten going on eleven going on thirty-five, the kid was the definition of an old soul. It was in his eyes, the seriousness of his personality, the way he took care of his little brother, as if, without being asked, he was trying to relieve some of the burden of being a single parent from his father's shoulders.

"I am, in fact, here. Now the party can begin," Cora said, ruffling the older boy's hair as she stepped into the neat but shabby living room. Sam tried to hold back his smile as he dodged her hand, but didn't quite manage.

"Wait. We're having a party?" Ben asked as she dropped her bag on the couch.

Sam rolled his eyes. "No, doofus, it's an expression."

Ben's shoulders fell, and now Cora was the one

holding back a smile. "If two certain someones I know take their showers without any complaints, maybe, just maybe, we can have a party." The littler boy's grin was immediate, but what really caught her attention was the way that Sam's attention perked up, even though he tried to hide it. "Deal?" she asked.

Just as both boys agreed, Slider cleared his throat.

Cora turned to find him shrugging into his button-up uniform shirt with its *Frederick Auto Body and Repair* logo, the movement causing his T-shirt to ride up his side. Just a momentary glance. Just of one small part of his body. But it revealed two things that stole her breath—more ink, and a frame that was all raw muscle and sinew.

Like a wild animal.

The comparison should've been alarming, but for some reason, that wasn't how her body interpreted it if the flutter in her belly was any indication. Never in a million years would she have described Slider as attractive, but there was something unquestionably *attracting* about him, even if she couldn't quite articulate what that was.

"Leaving?" she managed.

He nodded. "On seven to seven," he said. "You have my cell."

"We'll be fine," she said, bracing her hands on Ben's shoulders. "Won't we?" she asked, hugging him against her as she peered down into his little face.

"Yeah," he said. "Don't worry, Dad."

Slider gave a single nod as his gaze skated between Cora and his sons. "See ya later, alligators."

Sam rolled his eyes, but Ben grinned and said, "After while, crocodile."

Slider winked at his youngest. Just a single little wink. But, together with the way he said good-bye to the kids every time he left, it proved to Cora that there was a sweet, playful man in there somewhere. Or at least there used to be.

Either way, it was clear that what Slider had left of himself to give, he gave to his boys. And given what a miserable piece of crap both her dad and her best friend's father had been, Cora knew how much having a good father mattered. It mattered a lot. She had to respect that much about Slider, whatever else his faults might be.

The door had barely closed behind her boss when Ben whirled on her. "Is it time for the party yet?"

"No," Sam said, looking a little nervous. "I, uh, I have homework first."

"Later, kiddo. I promise. Why don't you watch some TV while I get dinner on?" When Ben made for the family room at the back of the house, Cora eyeballed Sam. "Your dad said you wanted help. That right?"

"Yeah." He shifted feet, like something about wanting her help made him uncomfortable.

"Okay, well, why don't you work at the table while I make us some food?" she suggested, leading them into the kitchen, where the neat but shabby theme continued. "How's pasta sound?"

Sam shrugged as he slid into a seat and slapped a worn-out backpack onto the table, appearing every inch like a prisoner being led to the gallows.

"What's up with you?" Cora asked as she crumbled ground beef into a frying pan to brown. Next, she filled a big pot of water to boil.

He sighed. "I have to do an interview."

Frowning, she pulled a jar of sauce and a box of noodles from the pantry. She was going to need to ask Slider to grab some groceries soon, a chore that would be so much easier if she had a car of her own. As would getting back and forth to watch the boys. Cora sighed. Just one more thing to add to her list of stuff she really needed to make happen in her life. "Of?"

"Someone I admire." He stared at the page in his hand.

Wiping her hands on a towel, she turned to him. "Okay, and did you have someone in mind?"

He looked up at her. And even though he didn't say a word, his eyes held the answer.

Suddenly, Cora was the uncomfortable one, which had her rambling. "Um, maybe, like Doc? Or Bunny? Or even Dare?" The Raven Riders Motorcycle Club's founder; the founder's sister, who'd escaped an abusive marriage and recently survived an attack on the club; and the club's current president all seemed like good choices to Cora. Much better than . . . the person Sam was currently staring at.

He shrugged with one shoulder. "I was hoping . . . you'd let me interview you."

"That's, um, really flattering, Sam. But . . ." Geez, how embarrassing was this to admit? "I'm not all that admirable."

In the positive column, she was a high school graduate, had turned out to be pretty good with kids, loved animals, and could concoct a good runaway plan when necessary. Cora rated herself as a better-than-average friend, and seemed to be able to make people laugh. In the negative, she'd recently been kidnapped by a gang and rescued by a biker club, and now resided with that club while she figured out what the heck to do with her life. And that wasn't even considering what'd happened with her father, back before she'd run . . .

Which she refused to let herself think about just then.

"To me you are," Sam mumbled, suddenly fascinated with the surface of the table.

What the heck was she supposed to say to that? When it was possibly one of the nicest things any human being had ever said to her . . . She eased into a seat. "Really?"

He nodded and finally met her eye. "You're kinda funny," he said.

"Just kinda?" She winked.

Sam's grin was reluctant in that preteen way of his. "I mean, you have your moments."

Cora smirked. "You're really selling my admirable qualities here, Sam Evans."

He shrugged again. "Okay, fine. You're funny. You take good care of us. And you make Ben happy. And I heard you're the one who helped Haven escape from her dad. That was pretty hard core."

"We did it together," Cora said, nearly glowing from the praise. Kids' willingness to just lay their truth out there was one of the things she absolutely loved about being with them. Even if Cora couldn't really agree with Sam's view of her. "That's what friends do for each other." Especially best friends, which Cora and Haven Randall had been since grade school, back before Haven's father had become so possessive that he'd withdrawn her from school to control everyone she saw and everything she did. Cora's father was exactly the opposite—he hadn't cared less what Cora did, where she went, or who she saw—as long as she didn't need his time, attention, or money, which he drank or gambled as fast as he made. She and Haven had sometimes debated which more deserved the *Worst Dad of the Year* trophy. It varied from day to day.

"And you make our house feel . . . alive again," Sam said more quietly. "Like Mom used to."

It was such a stunningly beautiful comment that emotion knotted in Cora's throat. Sam's mom—Slider's wife, Kim—had died young from breast cancer over two years before. The boys rarely mentioned her, and never in Slider's presence. At least, not that Cora had ever witnessed. "Sam," she said around that knot. "That's the sweetest thing anyone has ever said to me."

He blinked up at her, like he wondered if she was teasing him. And she so wasn't. Instead, she was wondering what she could possibly do to actually deserve that kind of compliment. "So, is that a yes?"

Man, she hoped Slider realized how awesome his kids were, because she would give a lot to have children this amazing. Maybe someday that would happen for her. Though, given that people generally preferred to use her rather than keep her, not to mention how much of a mess her life was right now, she was certain that someday was at least a million days off.

"Yeah, that's a yes," she said. "What exactly do you want to know?"

RETURNING FROM HIS only call of the night, Slider parked the tow truck in the lot at Frederick Auto Body and Repair just as the sun turned the morning sky gray. Once, he'd been a master mechanic contemplating owning this place, and now . . . now his life was just like his night had been. A whole lotta nothing punctuated by the occasional unexpected emergency.

He wasn't sure if that was better or worse than the

slow, plodding slog of the fourteen months he'd spent knowing catastrophe was coming right at him and his boys, yet unable to do a goddamn thing about it.

But that was cancer for you. Fuck you very much.

Sad truth was, though, that catastrophe had been coming for the Evans men one way or the other, hadn't it?

Damn it all to hell.

Slider punched out. Drove home. Heaved a big breath before he went inside.

God, he hated this house.

Its ghosts, its memories, Kim's touch in every room and on every surface. He couldn't breathe inside this house.

He went in anyway.

Noise. Voices. Laughter.

He found the source of it all in the kitchen.

Sam and Ben sat at the kitchen table with the baby-sitter, who was demonstrating how to hang a spoon from her nose.

The babysitter.

That was how he thought of her. How he *had* to think of her sometimes. Because if he thought of her as Cora, then he might think of her as a woman. And if he thought of her as a woman, he might take note of the soft waves of her sunny blond hair, or the flare of her hips, or the way the playful glint in her bright green eyes matched the mischievousness of her smile or the sarcasm in her voice.

And Slider couldn't do any of that.

Not when the last time had gone so very wrong—and in ways no one else in his life even knew.

"Dad!" Ben called, shoving up from his seat and sending milk and Cheerios sloshing from his bowl. He rounded the table.

"Little man," Slider said, giving him a squeeze when the boy's body hit him at full speed. "Sleep okay?"

"Yeah," Ben said. "We saved you ice cream."

"Hey, Dad," Sam said, taking his bowl to the sink and cleaning up his brother's mess—without having to be asked. Sometimes Slider had to wonder which of them was the adult around here anymore, and didn't that make him feel like fucking Dad of the Year.

"Ice cream?" he asked, eyeing the babysitter where she stood at the sink rinsing the breakfast dishes.

She threw a tentative smile over her shoulder. "I promised them a party, so I texted Phoenix and asked him to bring over a couple half gallons and all the fixings for a sundae-building party."

"Phoenix taught me how to make a banana split," Ben said, talking a mile a minute. "Except marshmallow goop is gross. And cherries stain the ice cream and make everything red which is even grosser."

Cora chuckled. "I didn't see any ice cream left in your bowl, Bean."

The boy turned a smile on her that was gonna break hearts one day. "Well, no . . ."

"Go brush your teeth and put on your shoes," she

said, shaking her head with an indulgent smile. "Bus will be here in ten minutes."

Slider watched the series of exchanges like he was merely an observer. Like he was on the outside looking in. And it was an apt description, wasn't it? The babysitter was the one giving his kids a reason to smile and be happy. And his club brother, Phoenix Creed, had apparently had a hand in that, too.

It should've all struck him as completely normal. A happy, functional family. But normal . . . Jesus, normal killed him these days. It really did. He was glad for it, for Ben's and Sam's sakes. But otherwise, normal felt a whole lot like trying to swallow crushed glass. It'd been like that ever since Kim had told him what had been going on with her . . .

Cora's voice forced away the thoughts. "Can I make you something to eat?"

He slanted a glance at her, studiously ignoring the little intimacies of her appearance—like that her makeup-free face and cute pigtails revealed that she'd woken up in his house, like that the oversized sweatshirt she wore over a pair of boxers likely covered the clothes in which she'd slept, like that she'd painted the second toenail on each foot a different color from the rest.

None of which he had any business noticing. "I'm good," he said, the lie obvious to both of them, but what the hell did that really matter? "Thanks," he forced himself to add.

Sam returned first to the kitchen, and Slider was grateful for the interference.

"Finish your homework?" he asked his boy.

"Yeah," Sam said, throwing a shy smile at Cora—who was suddenly blushing a beautiful, brilliant cherry red that made Slider pull a double take. It was on the tip of his tongue to ask, but then the whirlwind that was his six-year-old came into the kitchen, and, after a couple of quick good-byes, Cora was bustling them both out the front door for the bus.

The house resoundingly quiet now, he glanced out the front door. And found Cora walking up the driveway while holding the boys' hands—both of them, even Sam, who hadn't offered or sought a hug in . . . well, just over two years. The kids' laughter reached him even from this distance, their body language relaxed, happy, and open despite the fact that the gray morning had turned drizzly.

Damn, there was no denying this woman was good with them. Even more, she was good *for* them. Much better than the older neighbor lady had been, with her smoking and bad knees and dislike of noise.

Slider had gotten lucky finding Cora. Once, he might've thought that she'd come along right when they needed her, as if the universe had personally done him a solid by dropping Cora Campbell in the Ravens' lap. But Slider didn't believe in luck or fate or divine providence, and he knew one day, Cora would leave him, too.

Everybody did.

They were just using each other in the meantime.

Been there, done that, got the motherfucking T-shirt.

When Cora returned five minutes later, he stood at the kitchen counter chugging a glass of water.

"So, I'll get changed," she said, thumbing over her shoulder. He gave her a nod and tried not to let his gaze connect the rain droplets that darkened her sweatshirt and slicked the exposed skin of her legs. "But I wanted to mention that we need to go grocery shopping."

We. The word was a total sucker punch.

And it made him need to get her the hell out of his house. At least for a few hours. Because the only *we* Slider did now was the kind he'd created with his own blood. "I'll get on it."

She didn't leave to get dressed like he expected her to. Instead, she lingered, then finally said, "I know you're on again tonight and need to sleep. Maybe . . . I could get Bunny to take me and we'll drop everything off here later."

"That's okay," he said, shaking his head.

"Or, if it's easier, I could even hang here today and you could take me when you wake up. God knows I don't have anywhere special I need to be, so it wouldn't be a problem . . ."

He pictured her staying in his house in a sudden flash of images—her making lunch, her cuddled into the corner of the couch watching TV, her stepping out of the bathroom, hair wet from a shower, and the sweet-smelling scent of her lotion trailing after her . . . Twin reactions coursed through him. A yearning for the companionship of another adult sharing his space and his life. And a kneejerk fight-or-flight *hell no* that both left him unsettled and pissed him off.

All of which meant she had to go. Now.

"Jesus, I said I'll take care of it. I don't need you." Something akin to panic had the words coming out more harshly than he'd intended, and his brain was already scrambling to clean up the mess his mouth had made. "To do it, I mean. I don't need you for shopping. Okay? I got it."

"Right. Of course," she said, backing out of the room, green eyes flashing with an emotion he couldn't name.

Annnd he was a giant asshole. He scrubbed his face on a long sigh and waited for her to come back so he could drive her home. And apologize.

He waited. And waited.

What the hell?

"Uh, Cora, you ready?" he called out, making sure his tone lacked the frustration he felt with himself. Two-plus years of withdrawing from the world around him had left him all kinds of rusty at interacting like a normal human being.

When there was no response, he waited a few more minutes. Guilt a weight on his shoulders, Slider finally went back down the hall toward the family room, where she slept on the couch because she'd long ago refused his offer to use his bed on nights when he wasn't home. The downstairs bathroom was empty. And so was the family room. A creeping apprehension squeezed his chest when he noticed that her bag was gone and the blankets she used were back in their neat little stack, too.

No. No, no. Shit.

His gaze lifted to the door to the back porch, and that was when he knew.

She'd left.

He'd been an asshole, and she'd left. And now she was out on the street.

Sonofabitch.

Slider imagined telling Sam and Ben that Cora wasn't coming anymore, that he'd upset her and chased her away, and something close to horror flashed through his gut. He had to fix this. He had to fix it now.

CHAPTER 2

I don't need you . . .

The words were dickish, but that wasn't why Cora had gotten the hell out of there.

She'd grown up hearing one variation after another of that from her father.

You think I need you around? I don't need your shit. I need you here about as much as I need another hole in my head. On and on and on.

And then . . . that night.

She'd thrown it back in her father's face.

I thought you didn't need me, Dad. Remember that?

Backing her into her bedroom, the one still decorated in teenagerish pinks and purples, he'd leered at her, his words slurred by alcohol. *Maybe I need you for this . . .*

The memory had broadsided her out of nowhere, stealing her breath and making her panicky until she'd felt like she might crawl out of her skin. No way could she have faced Slider that way, so she'd thrown on a pair of jeans, jammed everything into her backpack, and fled out the back door and up the driveway to the rural road in front of the Evans house.

It was maybe two miles to the racetrack that the Raven Riders owned and operated as their main business venture, and maybe a half mile up the mountain from the track to the clubhouse Cora called home. Walking wouldn't have been that big of a deal if it hadn't been raining. But what had been a drizzle fifteen minutes ago was now a steady and cold autumn rain that was going to leave her soaked before too long.

Fine. Whatever. She'd survived worse.

But five minutes later, it was as if the universe was sticking out its tongue at her, because the skies erupted into a downpour.

Walking faster, she pulled out her cell and debated, then shot off a text to Phoenix, her go-to guy when she needed something with no questions asked. Any chance you're around for a pickup?

One minute passed, then another. The sound of a car's engine approached, and Cora stepped into the wet weeds on the edge of the road to make sure she was out of the way. Stupid driver didn't even swerve to give her a little leeway. She frowned down at her cell. Phoenix was usually quick to respond, but it wasn't even eight in the morning.

On a sigh, she wrote to Haven next, fully aware there would be *all kinds* of questions asked. I know it's early, but any chance someone is around who could come get me?

Her phone rang immediately. That was a best friend for you. "Hey," Cora said by way of answering.

"Where are you? Are you okay?" Haven asked, her words a little hard to hear with the rain pounding the ground.

"I'm . . ." She looked at the tall stalks of corn growing in the field along the right. There was no answer she'd give that was going to make Haven believe she was okay. "I decided to walk home, but then it started raining."

Silence. Like Haven was trying to sort out all the ways that her answer was weird, because, well, it *was* weird. "You're walking? Why are you walking?"

On a sigh, Cora decided to brazen it out. "Just felt like it," she said instead of telling the truth. But she didn't want to have to explain her panic attack . . . because then she'd have to explain the memories that'd caused it. And Haven didn't know about any of that. It was a secret Cora hadn't shared with another soul. At first, she'd kept what'd happened to herself out of shame and the desire to focus on just getting away from their evil fathers, not to mention the gut-deep belief that Haven's home situation was so bad—and had been for such a long time—that Cora didn't want to give her one more thing about which to worry. Now, all that was behind them and Haven was happy. Really happy, with Dare. And the last thing Cora wanted to do was mar that happiness with her own problems.

Problems that were all in the past now that her father was dead. And the ironic thing about his death? He'd died helping Haven's father try to kidnap Haven, but hadn't tried to nab Cora while he was at it. What kind of fucked up did she have to be that, on some seriously twisted level, it bothered her that he hadn't wanted *her* back, too? When the last thing she'd wanted was to ever see him again . . .

"Are you still there?" Haven was asking.

The words snapped Cora from her spiraling thoughts, which was when she heard another car engine approaching behind her. "Yeah, sorry, car's coming." She stepped into the weeds again.

"Dare's gonna come get you. Tell him where you are," she said, not waiting for Cora to answer.

"Cora," he said in that serious-as-a-heart-attack way he had. "What's going on?" But she didn't have a chance to answer, because just then, Slider's pickup truck came alongside her, the passenger window down.

"Cora, get in," Slider called out, crawling along beside her as she kept walking.

For a moment, Cora felt trapped between the two men, which in another situation she might've found funny or arousing or both.

"Um, hey," she said, not really sure which of the men she was talking to . . . because she was surprised as hell that Slider had come after her.

"Where are you?" Dare asked through the cell.

Slider's icy green eyes bored into her. "Get in. This isn't safe."

"With Slider," she mumbled unthinkingly.

"Slider's there?" Dare asked, all kinds of other questions in his tone. "You still need me?"

The truck had been rolling beside her, but now it jerked to a stop. Slider got out, left the driver's door open, and stalked around the front of the old Chevy. She stepped back as he came at her, until her spine bumped into the faded blue metal next to the passenger door. "I guess not, Dare, thanks," she managed.

Nailing her with a stare that made her suddenly warm despite the chilly rain, Slider took the phone from her hand and pressed it to his ear. "Dare?" Pause. "I have her." Pause. "Yeah, I'm fucking sure." He signed off the call and tossed the phone through the open window and onto the passenger seat.

And then it was just the two of them. Standing nearly chest to chest in a downpour. Not speaking. Not moving. And Cora felt torn between the desire to hug him for coming after her and hit him for provoking the anxiety she managed to keep battened down tight ninety-nine percent of the time.

"I was a dick," he said.

"Yep," she agreed.

He stared at her for another long moment. "I'm kinda fucked up over here, Cora."

Her lips almost twitched in humor, but she bit back the impulse, because those seven words were quite possibly the most honest, personal thing he'd said to her in three months of working for him. And it felt . . . important, like some wall had come down between them. Or, at least, started to. "I know, but on some level, aren't we all?"

He didn't answer, but what he did say still hit her square in the chest. "You're the best thing that's happened to my boys in years. I don't want to mess that up for them. I'm sorry if I have."

"You haven't," she said, shaking her head, rain catching on her eyelashes as she peered up at him. "But don't do it again."

Slider gave a single nod, then leaned forward, his face coming close and then pausing a hairsbreadth away. For a moment, Cora was sure he was going to kiss her, but then he grasped the handle and yanked open the squeaking door. "Now get in."

Shaking a little—from the chilly rain, she told herself—she climbed onto the old bench seat. The rain had plastered Slider's T-shirt to his chest, giving her a pretty clear view of the lean, muscular frame beneath. And she found herself wondering what kissing him might be like. How hard his body would be against hers. How far she'd have to tilt back her head to meet his mouth. How ticklish his whiskers would be against her lips.

The wondering made her shiver.

He slammed his door and frowned at her. "You okay?"

"I'm wet, cold, and irritated, but sure. I'm great," she said defensively. Because she was still a little miffed at him for making her freak out—*and* for making her feel curious about kissing him.

Just a little curious. Hardly at all, really.

Damnit.

The corner of his mouth lifted. Not much, but the movement was there. And it made Cora stare. Because the change in his face, small and fleeting though it had been, made the corner of his eye crinkle a little, too. "Well, I think I can help with two of those," he said, putting the truck in gear and swinging a hard U-turn.

"Wait, where are we going? The clubhouse is the other way."

"Uh-huh," he said, slanting her another glance. All the amusement was gone this time, though, and in its place was something intense she couldn't name. "I'm taking you home."

SLIDER WASN'T SURE what the hell he was doing taking Cora back to his house. But after his words had chased her away, potentially endangered her, and caused her to get drenched, he couldn't *not* bring her home.

She'd just looked so lost, so young, so . . . fucking pretty pressed up against his truck. Green eyes like jewels, bright blond hair turned dark from the rain, wet lips like candy he'd wanted to taste. For a split second, the urge had been so damn strong he wasn't sure how he'd resisted.

Which was probably a reason to take her back to the Ravens' clubhouse. To put some distance between them.

Instead, his gut demanded he take care. Of her.

Just a little quid pro quo for how good she'd been taking care of his kids these past three months. That's all it was. Nothing more.

It took only a few minutes before he parked the truck and both of them were getting out in the rain and dashing into the house. Then they stood dripping on his living room floor, staring at each other, chests rising and falling from the sprint across the yard.

A sudden urge sucker punched Slider. To take Cora in his arms, press her against the door, and claim her with his mouth while his hands stripped her bare of the sodden clothes. And then he'd carry her to the shower and warm both of them up with the hot water before making them even hotter when he took her to his bed . . .

The idea—the sheer clarity of it in his head— nearly took him to his knees. Because if it'd been a damn long time since Slider had felt anything besides anger and emptiness, it'd been even longer since he'd felt the soul-deep lust suddenly scorching through his blood.

"So," he said, because the unusual emotions were short-circuiting his brain.

"So . . . are you going to sleep?" she asked.

"Oh. Yeah. I should . . . do that." He thumbed toward the staircase and tried not to imagine what it would feel like if she came with him. Christ, this was why he'd been trying to keep her at arm's length all these months. "And then if you're still open to it, we'll do a grocery run."

"Yeah, of course," she said. "Do you mind if I throw my clothes in the dryer?"

He shook his head and took a step backward toward the staircase. Because *now* her words were very unhelpfully adding her nudity into his runaway thoughts. "All you've done for my boys," he said, emphasizing that for his own good. *She's here for my boys. She's here for my boys.* "Consider yourself welcome to use anything in the house, Cora. Always."

With a nod, he turned and climbed the steps, not looking back and not pausing until he was in his blinds-darkened bedroom with the door closed between his newly awakened libido and the beautiful blonde standing in his living room. And then he stripped down until he wore nothing but his ink, leaving his wet clothes in a pile on the old hardwoods, and sprawled facedown in bed.

He wasn't aware of falling asleep. He wasn't aware of anything, actually.

Until a commotion jolted him awake, his heart racing, his brain disoriented.

Cora was at the side of his bed, her mouth moving, her hand on his arm, her expression filled with bad news his mind wasn't quite processing.

"—wake up, Slider," she was saying. "School called. Ben's on his way to the hospital. There was an accident on the playground."

He shoved upward onto his arms. "What?"

"Ben. He's hurt," she said. "They're taking him to Frederick Memorial Hospital."

Not Ben, Slider thought, flying out of bed and tearing clothes out of his dresser. Not his innocent little alligator. "Jesus Christ," he growled in frustration and desperation as he struggled into a pair of jeans. He turned when he finally got them up over his ass. "What else did they say, Cora? How is he hurt?"

For a moment she just stood there staring at him, mouth wide and eyes wider, like maybe he'd grown three heads while he was asleep, which was when he realized he'd just walked across the room butt-ass naked. "Um," she finally said, blinking out of her surprise. "They, um, said he fell from the monkey bars and that he'd lost consciousness but was awake when the ambulance came. Other than that, I'm not sure how bad it is, Slider. I'm sorry."

He shook his head and tried to focus as he jammed

his feet into a pair of boots and stuffed his arms into a T-shirt. Only one thing mattered here. Ben, being okay. God, he had to be okay. "Let's go," he said.

"Wait. Me?" she asked, hugging herself. For the first time, the gesture made him notice that she was wearing one of his T-shirts. And, possibly, nothing else. The white cotton V-neck hung wide on her shoulders and long on her body, the hem hitting her just low enough to make it unclear whether she wore panties. Under any other circumstances, he wouldn't have been able to think of anything else but the picture of her that way, in his clothes, in his room . . .

"Yes. Ben will want you there." *And so do I.* Because he wasn't sure what he was walking into, or how bad it was going to be. Jesus, the thought of his boy being hurt made him want to vomit. "Get dressed," he said, manhandling her toward the stairs.

"But what about meeting Sam off the school bus?" she asked, peering up at him as they raced down. "He's gonna be freaked out."

She was right about that. "I'll get one of my brothers to bring him to the hospital," he said, hoping someone would be willing to do that for him after Slider had pretty much gone ghost on the club after Kim's death. They all thought that was because he was wrecked with grief, when really it was because her cancer had made it so he could never reveal all the ways in which she'd given him cause to grieve. And the more he'd dwelt on her lies, the more he hadn't known who or what he could believe in—even the club. And that had killed him even as he hadn't been able to stop himself from pulling away from his brothers.

Nothing like betrayal to shut you down and make you unsure who or what in your life was true, was real, was worthy of your trust. Sonofabitch.

"Okay," she said dashing toward the laundry room. "I won't be thirty seconds."

True to her word, Cora returned quickly, dressed again in the same clothes as before, his white T-shirt hanging out under the sweatshirt as if she hadn't wanted to take the time to change out of it. "Ready," she said, stuffing something into her purse.

The hospital was only a fifteen-minute drive across town, but it felt like a fucking lifetime until they were pulling into the lot at the emergency department. Slider cut the engine and jumped out in one frantic motion.

And then they were inside, waiting in the line to talk to someone while Slider lost his ever-loving mind. *The smell*. The fucking smell. It took him right back to Kim's illness. The countless visits. Those final days when her death was simply a matter of *when* not *if*. His sons' heartbreaking good-byes.

And now Ben was here all by himself. Was he re-membering all of that, too? The thought made Slider want to tear down doors and walls to get to him.

But he could hardly blame the tall, bald guy in

front of them for being in the way when his blood had soaked through bandages he wore around his left wrist. "Got bit by a dog," he told the intake nurse. "Pit bull."

"Was animal control involved, sir? Do you know if the dog had rabies?" she asked. It was the first of about a half-dozen questions she asked him, and Slider's patience significantly decreased with every one.

Finally, it was their turn. "My son, Ben Evans, came in by ambulance from his school," Slider said before he and Cora even made it all the way to the counter. "He's only six."

"Of course, Mr. Evans," the woman said, her fingers flying over the keyboard. "You can come right back."

Finally. *Thank fuck.*

The receptionist's gaze cut to Cora. "Are you family, too?"

Slider saw it. The little step backward Cora was about to take as she bowed to the hospital's rules. But he wasn't having it. Not for a second, not when Ben might need every bit of combined strength they had to offer. So Slider took Cora's hand in his, and the tiny catch in her breath just made him hold tighter. "Yes," he said. "Now, please take us to him."

CHAPTER 3

As bad as Slider's earlier words had made Cora feel, his actions now made her feel more important than anyone else ever had. Except Haven, of course, who never once let Cora believe she was anything less than her best friend in the world. Slider's behavior was confusing as hell, but Cora went with it, because she was worried out of her mind over Ben.

And given how scared she was, she couldn't imagine how Slider was feeling. Not after having lost a wife.

So Cora was determined to be there for both of them. In whatever ways and for however long they might need her. Because it was good to be needed.

And no one else seemed to need her except the Evans men. Not even Haven anymore, who now had a man who was absolutely devoted to her. After everything she'd been through, Haven deserved that devotion—and every bit of the happiness she'd found with Dare Kenyon.

But it left Cora more than a little adrift in her own life.

"The doctor will be in to see you soon," the nurse said as they arrived at a curtained exam room.

Slider nodded, and then his pale gaze cut to Cora like he was looking for something from her. But she didn't know him well enough to do more than squeeze his hand in reassurance. "I can wait here until you've had a chance to see him."

"I want you with me. He's, um, going to want to see you, too." His hand still around hers, he pulled her inside.

Whatever pleasure she'd felt from those declarations quickly fell away when she took in Ben's little body, looking so small in the big hospital bed.

Slider's face was a stone wall, but she felt the jolt of his reaction where they were connected. "Hey, Benji," he said, his voice strained.

The boy's eyes swam open and finally focused. And even though his forehead was bruised, bandages covered the side of his head and one arm, and an IV ran into his other arm, the kid's face still managed to light up when he saw his father. "Dad, I got to ride in an ambulance," he said with a hint of his usual exuberance.

Slider managed a chuckle as he eased onto the edge of the mattress and took Ben's hand. "Yeah? Did they turn on the siren for you?"

"It was loud," Ben said, eyes wide. "And everything inside was shiny. And the man told me knock-knock jokes the whole way here." Cora heaved a relieved breath. Hearing the kid talk gave her hope that he'd be okay. "He was almost as funny as you, Cora."

She smiled at the sweet compliment. "No one's as funny as me, Bean. *No one.*" Even though, just then, humor was eluding her in favor of bone-deep relief. This kid had lost a mother at the age of four. The last thing he needed was any kind of permanent injury at the age of six.

He rolled his eyes. "*Coowa*, it's *Ben!*"

Happy tears threatened. "Yeah? Well, *Ben*, how's that noggin feeling? Is it true you dented the monkey bars with it?"

"Noooo," he said with a giggle as he nodded toward the bed opposite from where Slider sat. Even though the man had made it clear he wanted her there, she couldn't help but feel a little like she was intruding, so she'd hung back. But now she made her way to Ben's side. "I have a headache. And my elbow hurts. And I might need a case on my arm. But I didn't break the monkey bars. Or, at least, I don't think I did."

"I think it's called a cast, buddy," Slider said.

"Oh, yeah. And they said I could pick the color of it," Ben said. "Isn't that cool?"

Slider nodded, his eyes suddenly blinking fast. "Really cool," he managed.

Seeing the normally stoic man struggle with emotion almost brought tears to Cora's eyes. "Definitely the coolest," she added, admiring the kid's positivity. He'd been hurt, taken a probably scary ride by himself in an ambulance, and been poked with a needle, yet what he focused on was how fun the ride was and that he'd get to choose the color of his cast. She pulled a stuffed animal out of her purse. "Brought someone for you."

"Blue Bear!" he exclaimed, grasping his favorite toy, lumpy and misshapen, into his hands. Belying its name, it was more gray than blue from being washed and loved on again and again.

"I knew he might worry about you," she said, "so I thought he should come."

"Yeah, he does worry sometimes," Ben said, rubbing the bear's face against his own. "But I'll make sure he doesn't get scared."

Just then, the doctor came into the room and detailed more specifically exactly what Ben's condition was. He had a broken elbow, for which they were waiting for the orthopedist before they set it and put on the cast. His bandage hid a cut on the forehead, which had already received five stitches. And he had a concussion that required some scans and overnight observation because Ben had briefly lost consciousness.

But he would be okay.

That left Cora feeling like she might float right up to the ceiling. She'd known him only a few months, but she'd become really fond of Ben. Of all the Evans men, if she were honest. Even Slider. For all his brooding reserve, he was a good dad. And the way he'd come after her this morning proved that, on some level, he cared about her, too. Even if it was just because he valued her as a caregiver for his kids.

That was more than she'd ever gotten from most people.

When the doctor left, a nurse ducked in. "Your other son is here, but only two visitors are allowed in the room at a time."

"Oh, okay. I'll go so he can come back." Cora pressed a light kiss to Ben's forehead. "You just concentrate on getting better."

"Don't leave," Ben said.

She smiled. "I'll just be in the waiting room. Don't worry." Cora made her way around the bed, surprised when Slider reached out and grasped her hand.

"Thanks," he said, pale green eyes peering up at her from underneath the long strands of brown.

Nodding, she left and found Sam waiting at the desk with Haven and Dare, along with Dare's cousin and the club's vice president, Maverick Rylan, and his girlfriend, Alexa. Phoenix and a few other Ravens were there, too. They weren't all related by blood, but this was still every bit Cora's idea of what a family was. People who cared. People who showed up. People who claimed you, no matter what.

In his agitation, Sam looked like he might vibrate right out of his skin. "How is he? They wouldn't let me ride with him, Cora. It was so unfair."

She grasped his face in her hands. "He's going to be fine. He was super brave. But he'd love to see you."

Swallowing down his fear, Sam nodded. "Are you gonna leave now?"

"No. I'll be right out here."

His shoulders relaxed. "Good. Okay." He went with the nurse through the double doors.

And that left Cora alone with a whole lot of bikers wearing their leather-and-denim club cuts covered in patches and the Ravens' colors.

"What happened?" Dare asked, expression fierce. Everyone else gathered around.

"He fell off the monkey bars at school and broke his elbow and hit his head. He's going to be fine, but between the tests they have to run and his concussion, they have to keep him overnight," she said. Their collective sighs of relief mirrored the way she was feeling herself.

"This is the last thing Slider needs," Dare said, raking his hand through his dark brown hair. Ruggedly handsome, her best friend's man looked older than his late thirties, as if he carried the weight of the world on his shoulders. And in a way, he did. The weight of the Raven Riders' whole community, *and* the responsibility for the people they helped in the club's mission to stand up for and defend those who couldn't do it for themselves. Given the way Cora and Haven had arrived on the club's compound, and knowing all the Ravens had done—and been willing to do—to protect them and try to give them new, safer lives, Cora knew firsthand exactly how great a responsibility that was.

And it made her feel fiercely loyal to the Ravens, even if she didn't belong to that community the same way her bestie now did. As the club president's girlfriend—not to mention as a fantastic baker who'd baked her way into most of the men's hearts—Haven unquestioningly belonged with the Raven Riders.

But Cora? She wasn't sure she belonged anywhere. One more thing to figure out about her life.

"What can we do to help?" Maverick asked, standing at Dare's side. With blond hair and deep blue eyes, Mav was almost pretty in an utterly masculine way.

"I don't know," Cora said. "I guess Slider will need to stay here overnight with Ben. So maybe nothing in the short term."

"Is he supposed to work tonight?" Mav asked.

"Yeah," Cora said, glancing at the wall clock. Hard to believe it was only two o'clock in the afternoon. Standing on that rural road in the rain with Slider seemed like a million years ago. "He's on at seven.

We were going to go grocery shopping beforehand," she said, her brain slowly recalling what the day's plan was supposed to have been.

"Who knows exactly how long Ben will end up in here," Haven said, looking from Dare to Cora. Once a pale blond, her friend now wore her hair in a wavy light-brown-to-warm-blond ombré that looked so pretty with her blue eyes. Watching Haven come out of the shell built by her past these last couple months had been like witnessing a butterfly unfurl from its cocoon. And it made Cora so damn proud. "Make me a list and I'll do the shopping. That way every-thing they need is there when they get home."

"I can help you with that," Alexa said.

"You sure?" Mav asked, tucking a strand of Al's brown hair behind her ear. "I don't think you should be carrying heavy bags yet."

Alexa glanced down at her hands, mostly healed now from having been burned in a fire that had nearly killed her and Maverick and left her mother comatose in a long-term rehabilitation facility. "I can at least drive and help shop," she said.

Cora watched the couples interact with more than a little envy curling through her belly. She hated feel-ing jealous of women she considered her friends. Not just Haven, whom she'd known forever, but Alexa, too. All in their early twenties and having recently survived harmful relationships of one sort or another, the three of them had discovered a lot in common and become close over the past couple of months.

"Phoenix, would you be willing to help them?" Cora asked. "Slider kinda needs a lot of stuff from the store and Alexa really shouldn't be carrying anything."

"What am I, the manservant?" he asked with a smirk.

She gave him a once-over. With his short brown hair and always-mischievous brown eyes, there was no denying he was cute, even with the jagged scar that ran from his eye to his ear. They'd hit it off right from the start, their sarcasm and sense of humor good for sparring and banter. Once, Cora thought she could maybe even be into Phoenix. But the more time they'd spent together since she arrived, the more Phoenix had started feeling like the big brother she'd never had. Which meant she lived to give him a hard time, and he gave it right back. "Yes, Jeeves. Exactly."

He rolled his eyes and feigned annoyance. "Fine. Whatever. But I'm gonna make that manservant shit look good."

Mav slapped him on the back. "You keep telling yourself that, Creed."

Everyone laughed, then Cora typed out a long text message of groceries for Phoenix and the girls. Finally, they took off, but not before Haven made Cora promise to call and catch her up on everything that'd been going on. No doubt, had she returned to the clubhouse this morning, Cora would've been due for a full-on grilling for calling for a ride when Slider had never before failed to bring her back and forth.

But that would have to wait, because just then, Cora was focused on taking care of the Evanses. "Can one of you call the garage and let them know what's going on?" she asked Dare and Maverick.

"I'll do one better than that," Mav said. "I'll cover his shift for him. I know the owner well, and I've helped out over there before."

"Wow, okay. I'm sure Slider will really appreciate that," Cora said. Maverick was, as far as she could tell, a pretty well-known custom motorcycle builder, and she'd heard him talk about growing up in his father's auto body shop, so no doubt he knew his way around cars, too. But it was still impressive to watch everyone pitch in the way they were doing.

When all those arrangements were straight, Dare turned to her. "And how are you?" he asked.

"Me? Oh, totally fine," she said.

He tilted his head and stared at her. That dark gaze always felt just a little too observant, too perceptive for her liking. "Yeah? Then why were you calling from the side of the road this morning, Cora?"

She shifted feet and resisted cupping her hand to her ear and saying, *Oh, I'm sorry, I think I hear Ben calling for me . . .* Yeah. No. That wasn't going to fly. "How about this," she said instead. "It's all over."

His eyebrow arched, just a little. Enough for her to know he was calling bullshit even if he wasn't vocalizing it. "Haven worries about you, so that means I do, too. Actually, I would anyway, because you're part of the Ravens' family now." He kept going, as if that declaration wasn't absolutely huge for her to hear. "And I won't let anyone treat you bad, Cora. Not even one of our own. You hear what I'm saying?"

She gasped. "Slider doesn't treat me badly." Cora hated that Dare might think that. Sure, Slider was often withdrawn, distant, and quiet as a heart attack—and not just toward her. She'd overheard enough chatter around the clubhouse to know that Slider had, for the most part, dropped off the face of the earth where the club was concerned, despite once being an active member. The guys seemed to understand that Kim's death had shattered Slider, but there was a little resentment and disappointment there, too. Still, that didn't mean he was ever out of line with her. Even with what he'd said this morning, he'd tried to backpedal away from how harshly it'd initially come out of his mouth. "He doesn't, Dare. Not ever."

He gave her another penetrating stare, then nodded. "Okay, good. Glad to hear it. But don't forget that there are people who have your back now. You're not out there anymore. You're here, with us."

Her gaze traced over the letters spelling out *PRESIDENT* on a patch on Dare's chest because it was suddenly too hard to meet his eyes. If she did, she was afraid she might tear up. "Got it," she managed.

"Good, then let's settle in," he said.

They did. All that afternoon, and well into the evening. Dare sat with Cora awaiting any news Slider might be able to share about Ben. Doc, Bunny, and Bear—Dare's grandfather, great-aunt, and great-uncle—joined for a while, as did Haven, Alexa, and Phoenix when they returned from their shopping expedition. And a variety of other Ravens dropped by one by one until they'd taken over nearly a whole corner of the waiting room.

The group alternated between small talk, long periods of silence imbued with a sense of togetherness, and bouts of talkative joking around. The guys told story after story—of Slider wiping his bike out and earning his club nickname in a round-robin fashion, each of them offering a new detail on what'd happened. Of how proud Slider was the first time he introduced his boys to the club. Of how he once brought infant Sam to one of the club's Church meetings because Kim was sick, and the baby burped so loudly after finishing a bottle of milk that the whole club erupted into laughter and someone immediately proposed making Sam an honorary member. Dinnertime came and went, and while some of the others went down to the cafeteria, Cora stayed right where she was. In case she was needed.

Around nine o'clock, Slider and Sam came out to give everyone an update.

"Uh, hey," Slider said, uneasily surveying the group as they rose to meet him. He appeared surprised to find so many people waiting for news. "So, uh, Ben's doing pretty good. Doc thinks he'll make a full recovery. His head scans looked clear. The elbow break was a clean one and, given his age, should heal up without any complications." It was possibly more words than she'd heard Slider say at one time since she'd known him. And judging by the expressions the others wore, they might've been thinking the same thing.

But that surprise didn't last long, because soon everyone celebrated the news with hugs and hand-shakes, laughter, and even a few prayers. And even though Slider still seemed a little uncomfortable with all the attention and interaction, Cora could've sworn she'd seen his mouth flirt with a smile. More than once. And that made her even happier that so many people had come out to show their support for him. She suspected he really needed to see that, whether he knew it or not.

"Mav's covering your shift tonight," Dare said, squeezing Slider's shoulder. "So don't worry about a thing."

"Shit. Really? I was just gonna call out, but that's . . . wow." He nodded and raked a hand over his hair. "Okay, well, I'm going to spend the night with Ben, so can someone stay the night with Sam?"

Even as a half-dozen people volunteered, Sam interrupted. "No, Dad, I want to stay at the hospital tonight. I'll just wait out here. It'll be fine."

"I thought two people could be in the room," Cora said, knowing Sam would hate to be parted from his brother.

Sam gave a little shrug. "They can, but Ben would really like to see you."

Cora's mouth dropped open and her heart kicked into double time. Because how cute was that little boy? "What? I mean, that's so sweet, but it should be you, Sam."

He shook his head. "I'll be right here. Ben's hurt and tired, and you know how he likes to be with you when he's not feeling good. He needs you, Cora. It's okay. Really."

"He's right," Slider said, those strange pale eyes peering into hers, asking her to be there. "Ben asked for you. Please come back with me."

Suddenly, Cora became very aware that everyone was watching their conversation unfold. Heat filtered into her cheeks. "Okay, sure. Of course," she said, even though the Evans men were kinda blowing her away with their sweetness.

And they really were. Every single one of them.

CHAPTER 4

*S*he brought *Blue Bear.*

In the hours after they'd arrived at the hospital, Slider kept coming back to that thought. Cora had brought Ben his favorite toy. The one he always had to have when he was scared or upset. The one he couldn't sleep without. The one that had become a lifeline of sorts in the months after Kim had died.

Slider had been concerned about getting to his son as fast as humanly possible. And Cora had been right there with him. But, still, she'd remembered Blue Bear.

And that little proof of her caring and thoughtfulness had put its hooks into him. Put them in, deep.

It made him feel like, for the first time in years, he

had someone as invested in his kids' well-being as he was. And to take care of his sons was to take care of him, too. Because they were the only things he valued anymore. Even more than himself.

So when Ben had asked for Cora to come back to his room while he fell asleep, Slider hadn't minded. Not one bit. And the fact that Sam hadn't, either, revealed a whole lot about how his sons viewed their babysitter.

Damn if that wasn't a wholly inadequate word for Cora Campbell. Not that Slider knew of a better one.

Back in Ben's room, Slider and Cora resumed the same positions as before—him on Ben's right, where his arm was now encased in a bright blue cast, and her on the boy's uninjured left side.

"Dude, that is, like, the coolest cast anybody ever had," Cora said, her expression like she was looking at the Holy Grail. Many times, Slider had tried not to notice things about Cora, but it was hard to avoid paying attention when someone made your kids feel special. Again and again. And she always did.

Ben gave a toothy grin, his voice sleepy as he spoke. "I almost picked purple."

She shook her head. "No way, blue is the awesomest. And tomorrow we'll find a marker and everyone can sign it."

His eyes went wide. "Really?"

"Oh, yeah," she said, leaning her elbows on the mattress so she could be closer. "You could get a bunch of the Ravens to sign it, and then when you go back to school, everyone will think you're the baddest dude on the block."

"Yeah!" he said, grinning wider.

Cora had such an easy way with Ben. With both of his kids, really. God, Slider admired that about her. Especially when nothing about him was easy, and hadn't been in years.

Ben yawned and peered up at Slider. "You're gonna stay with me, aren't you?"

"You better believe it, Benji. And remember what we talked about. Nurses are going to come in a couple of times throughout the night. Just to check on you. I'll be here the whole time," Slider said, leaning over the boy so he could look him in the eyes. There was nothing like the unconditional love and admiration of a kid. But that didn't mean Slider shouldn't have to earn it. And he hadn't done nearly enough these past few years, had he? He pressed a kiss to his son's cheek. "Now shut those peepers."

Ben giggled. "Your whiskers tickle, Dad." Slider ran his hand over the facial hair on his jaw. One more piece of evidence of the mess he'd become. But at least it made Ben laugh. The boy looked up at Cora next, his hand snaking into hers and tugging her closer. "You're staying too, right?"

"Wild horses couldn't tear me away," she said, squeezing his hand.

Ben made a face. "There are wild horses here?"

Cora chuckled and Slider shook his head. "Peepers. Closed. Now," he said.

The boy was asleep in an instant.

After not sleeping much today himself, Slider probably wasn't far behind him. Still, he nodded at the small sleeper sofa and quietly said to Cora, "You can take that. Nurse said there are pillows and blankets in the closet."

She shook her head. "No way. You haven't slept. And I'm kinda attached here," she said, glancing at where Ben still clutched her hand. "Seriously, Slider. Get some sleep while you can."

Frowning, he pulled out the sleeper, which was only a little wider than a twin-sized bed, found the bedding, and lowered the lights. "How 'bout this. We'll take shifts."

She smiled. "Sure."

On a bone-deep sigh, Slider sat on the bed's edge and kicked off his boots, and then he went horizontal still wearing his jeans and T-shirt. Cora laid her cheek against her arm, her face turned away from Slider toward Ben, her blond waves a soft cascade against the white hospital blankets.

And damnit all to hell, but it played with uncomfortable things inside his chest to see her like that. Things he didn't want played with. Not ever again.

So he closed his eyes. And woke up two and a half hours later when the nurse came into the room to check Ben's vitals. The kid hardly stirred, but Cora was still awake and making small talk with the woman about how her night was going.

"Your turn to get some sleep," Slider said when they were alone again.

"Don't worry about it. Go back to sleep."

"We had a deal," he said, his voice like gravel. Years of exhaustion did that to a man.

"Later," she said, her expression soft with sleepiness. He forced himself into a sitting position, his stiff movements making him feel ancient. "You need it more than I do."

He shook his head and pushed to his feet. "I'm not hogging the bed all night while you sit up in that hard chair."

"Don't be stubborn," she said. "Sleep."

He arched a brow. As much as he wanted to lie back down, he wasn't doing it at her expense. "It's your turn."

"Slider—"

"Cora—"

She sighed. "I'm trying to take care of you, too."

The words were like a sucker punch. Just nearly laid him flat out on the floor. And he had no idea how to reply. So he said the first thing that came to his mouth. "We could share the bed. To sleep." As if that clarification had been necessary. For. Fuck's. Sake.

"As opposed to?" Her brow lifted in a taunting little arch.

He scrubbed at his face. "As opposed to nothing. I just meant—"

"Don't have a coronary, Slider. I was just teasing." She eased her hand out of Ben's grip. "You sure?"

"Yeah. Of course." As she stepped into the little bathroom, he lay down again and made sure his body hugged the edge. And then he tried to remember the last time anyone had teased him. Definitely not since Kim's death. Man, once upon a time, he'd been teased relentlessly. It was how he'd received his nickname. *Slider.* He'd been on a ride up on the back roads of South Mountain with a bunch of other Ravens and taken a turn too fast. He'd wiped out, his bike just sliding out from underneath of him right off the road. And he'd walked away without a scratch, earning a new handle now sewn onto the name patch on his club cut.

For freaking ever, it'd seemed at the time, he hadn't lived that shit down. And, really, all he could do was take it and laugh. Not that he'd really minded.

But he'd lost all the easy rapport he'd once shared with his club brothers. Lost it to his grief and humiliation and shame. Lost it to caring for two brokenhearted, motherless boys—kids Slider wanted to make sure never learned the truth about their parents. Lost it when he'd withdrawn from the world around him rather than hear a million well-meaning but clueless people try to console him by saying how much Kim had loved him and how great a couple they'd been.

Damnit all to hell.

Finally, Cora emerged from the bathroom and toed off her sneakers. As she settled on her side facing him, she let out a little moan that stirred things that had no business stirring. "My back was getting tired, so thanks."

He tugged the covers up to his stomach. "Don't thank me when you're the one going above and beyond."

"I'm not doing anything more than anyone else would do for people they care about," she said, her voice trailing off into a yawn. "I'm just glad Ben's okay."

The words hung there between them for a long moment, and Slider's brain swam with possible responses as he stared at the ceiling. She *was* doing more than others would do. And in saying they were people she cared about, did she include him in that?

I'm trying to take care of you, too.

Her earlier words ping-ponged around in his brain, and he allowed himself to believe. On some level, Cora cared about him.

What the hell was he supposed to do with *that*? Or with the weird satisfaction it unleashed in his chest?

Finally, he manned up to meet her gaze, and turned his head to the side. "I'm glad you're in our lives, Cora," he said, his heart pounding from the unusual admission.

But he was too late. Her eyes were closed. Her

breathing was soft and even. Her pretty mouth was slack.

Probably just as well. No matter how true his statement had been, the sentiment still raised complications he was in absolutely no shape to handle.

CORA AWAKENED ON the nurse's next visit, but Slider didn't, and she was glad. The man had looked wrecked—dark circles under his eyes, hair a raked-through disaster, shoulders hunched from the stress of worrying about his kid. He needed the sleep.

But she was also glad because lying there in the tiny bed with him allowed her to really look at Slider in a way she didn't often otherwise take the liberty of doing. Her gaze ran over the longish lengths of his brown hair, and she couldn't help but wonder if it was as soft as it looked. Cora studied his face and tried to imagine what he'd look like clean shaven. She admired the sleeves of black-and-gray ink that ran up his arms, her gaze fixing for a long time on the intricate cursive *K* that filled the three inches on the back of his left wrist.

K for Kim. His dead wife.

How sweet was that? That he wore something permanently on his skin for the woman he'd loved and lost. What wouldn't she give for someone to feel so deeply about her? Just once.

The rest of his art included realistic depictions of flowers and a wolf's face, along with interlaced tribal markings and geometric designs that tied it all together. A burst of sun rays extended out from the round bulk of one of his shoulders.

Cora's gaze dropped lower. Slider was entirely covered, of course. Not just by his clothes, but by the thin hospital blanket, too. But none of that could keep her from replaying in her mind's eye what she'd seen that morning in the man's bedroom.

It was one thing to have witnessed him asleep in his bed, nude from the waist up, a huge tattoo across his back—the Raven Riders name and logo. His back and shoulders were all raw muscle, sinew, and bone. The guy didn't eat much, but he worked hard, and the result was a frame that was at once too lean and well-muscled.

And then . . .

And then he'd flown out of the bed naked as the day he was born, giving her an eyeful of his front before letting her look long and hard at his back as he'd dressed. And, wow, the Ravens tattoo had been even more impressive seeing him wear it and nothing else.

Of course, Cora felt like the world's biggest degenerate for having enjoyed even a single second of the view, given *why* he'd scrambled out of bed that way. But, damn, some things could *not* be unseen.

And Slider Evans completely naked was one of them.

Because every part of him had been more impressive than the last. He had the rangy, dangerous physique of a street fighter. A way-too-intriguing line of dark hair that ran from his chest to his groin. The hard-looking ass of a Renaissance sculpture. And a cock that, mostly soft, had hung surprisingly long against his thigh.

She squeezed her eyes shut. Not because the thought of his sex bothered her, but because it attracted her.

And that was confusing. To begin with, she was never sure what to make of this man who rarely said much and, when he did, it was often little more than a grunt or a handful of grumbled words. But more than that, the last time she'd had sex, she hadn't wanted it.

It wasn't sex, Cora, she reminded herself for the hundredth time. Right. Okay. Fine. It *wasn't*. It'd been . . . rape. But since the scumbag who'd done it could never do it again, there was no sense dwelling on it, was there? She was fine. She'd gotten away. She'd survived. Just like she always did.

She heaved a big breath and opened her eyes.

And found Slider watching her. That pale green stare locked on tight.

Cora couldn't look away. Didn't want to, even as her pulse kicked up and the sheer force of his gaze narrowed the room—*hell*, the world—to the eighteen inches that separated them. Her lips parted, a shiver raced over her skin, and her nipples hardened. Because Slider was suddenly looking at her like he was *starving*. And she might be the meal he'd been dreaming of all this time.

Or she was rocking some seriously desperate wishful thinking.

But she didn't think so. Not when he reached across that gap between them. Softly, slowly, his hand cupped the side of her face, his fingers slid into her hair, his thumb stroked her skin, just skimming over the corner of her mouth. Once, twice, three times.

Cora didn't move, didn't breathe, didn't look away. She feared the second she did, whatever spell was weaving between them would break. She didn't know what this was or what he was doing or what he even wanted, but she wanted the chance to find out. Plenty of men had looked at her with lust in their eyes during her almost twenty-four years, but no man had ever looked at her with such tormented longing.

He licked his lips, then gave a single shake of his head, like he was answering some question she hadn't heard anyone ask. "Cora," he whispered. Two more strokes of his thumb and he withdrew his hand. She was on the verge of protesting or pleading or launching herself at him when he said more, keeping her from doing a thing. "You should go back to sleep."

CHAPTER 5

I feel like I haven't seen you in forever," Haven said as they lay together on Cora's bed in her old hotel-like room in the Ravens' clubhouse. Her friend wasn't entirely wrong. It'd been four days since Ben had been discharged from the hospital, and Cora had been at Slider's house more hours than usual.

"I know," Cora said. "Ben has just been a bit of a handful and Slider's needed the extra help." While the poor kid had weathered the injury and the hospital stay like a trooper, once the pain meds had worn off, he'd been miserable—unable to sleep and too uncomfortable to make it through a whole day of school.

"They're really lucky to have you. I hope Slider

realizes that," Haven said. "Which reminds me, what was with you walking home the other day?"

Cora bit back a groan. She'd hoped Haven would've forgotten that. "It was just me making sure Slider realizes it," she fibbed with a dismissive wink she prayed would throw Haven off the scent. Lying to her bestie made her feel like crap, but the alternative was coming clean about why Cora had been equally desperate to run away from home . . . and that made her want to vomit. "Besides, I don't mind helping them out. It's not like I have anything better to do," she said. She'd meant for the comment to come off flippantly, but she'd failed, if the sympathetic expression on Haven's face was any indication.

"Whatever happened to your idea of checking out volunteer opportunities at the animal shelter?"

"Oh," she said, wishing she'd never voiced her pie-in-the-sky dream of one day becoming a veterinarian. Growing up, her parents had never let her own an animal, so she'd become the queen of the stray cats, once sneaking a little gray tiger-striped kitten into her bedroom for a whole weekend when she was about nine, and routinely leaving out bowls of milk or cans of tuna for a pair of orange tabbies when she was a little older. At first, they'd been too scared to approach if she moved at all, but eventually they'd gotten brave enough to sniff her hand. And the moment when they'd finally let her pet them remained one of her fondest memories. She'd wished she could do more for them, that she *knew how* to do more, because those cats, even with all their stand-offishness, had made her feel more loved than anyone who'd lived inside her house . . .

But what was the point of talking about her dream when it required, somehow, coming up with enough money to afford college, and then doing well enough there to get into a vet school? It remained as far out of reach now as it had when she first met those tabbies. She'd only shared it in the first place a few weeks ago in the hopes of getting Haven to admit and pursue her own much-more-realistic dream to open a bakery. The woman could be printing money with her cookies alone. "I have to save up for a car first," Cora said, "and probably also for an apartment, before I can think of doing anything like that. More importantly, what happened to your idea of—"

"Wait. Why do you need an apartment?" Haven asked.

"It's not like I can live in the Ravens' clubhouse for the rest of my life," Cora said. No one had said a word to her or Haven about moving on, and honestly, she didn't think they would. It also probably didn't hurt that the club's president was in love with Cora's best friend. But they were currently the only two permanent residents at the clubhouse, though members and the Ravens' other protective clients sometimes crashed here, and there was always someone around. And Cora wanted more for herself than being some biker groupie, even if she was still figuring out what exactly that was.

Really, it was the first time in her life she'd ever realistically had the chance to consider it. Her dad had made it clear there'd be no money for after she graduated high school, and he'd been true to his word, forcing her to get a series of part-time jobs to pay for food, clothes, the bus, and her phone. The only thing he'd done to help her was let her keep living in her bedroom. Some favor that'd turned out to be . . .

"And I'm no dummy. At some point, you're going to move in with Dare."

Haven's gorgeous face went immediately and cartoonishly red.

Cora flew into a sitting position and gaped. "No freaking way!"

Looking like she'd swallowed her tongue, Haven sat up more slowly, the pretty waves of her hair falling over her shoulders. "So, this was one of the reasons I've been dying to talk to you."

Cora bounced up onto her knees, her grin nearly making her cheeks hurt. "No freaking way, Haven. Are you serious? Details, woman. I need all the details! When did he ask you? What did he say?" She picked up a pillow and smacked her friend's shoulder with it. "Start spilling now!"

Haven laughed and yanked the pillow away. "It was Monday morning right after you called for a ride. We were at his place getting ready to come here and I was packing my bag from the weekend. And he said that he never minded me having things of my own to do, but that he absolutely hated that I didn't come home to his house every day after doing them. And that he wanted his house to be my house, too. To be *ours*." She reached into her jeans pocket and held up a set of keys on a little silver ring. "And then he asked me to move in."

"Oh, my God, you have keys to a house, Haven. And a man who loves you so much. Wow," Cora said, her heart overflowing for her friend. "I never doubted for one minute that Dare would be good at the sexin', but who knew he'd be so good at the romancing, too?"

Haven hugged the pillow to her chest as a little blush turned her smiling cheeks pink. "I know. It's really true."

"Wow," Cora said again, the reality that Haven was truly putting down roots here in Frederick— roots separate from Cora and the escape plan they'd hatched when they'd run from Georgia so many months before—really sinking in. "So when are you moving in? Why are you still sleeping here?" She sucked in a breath. "Please tell me it's not because—"

"I didn't want to leave you here alone," Haven said, finishing Cora's thought.

An uncomfortable whirl of emotion settled in Cora's belly—jealousy, irritation at herself for being jealous, panic over what she was going to do with her own life, uncertainty about where she belonged, and even a little feeling of abandonment, too, as unfair and ridiculous as that was when *truly* she was happy for Haven, too. So she masked that whole mess with sarcasm and humor, as she always did. Cora pointed her thumbs at herself and arched an eyebrow. "Big girl over here. A big girl who will hate you forever if you let her hold you back."

Haven grasped her hand. "You could never hold me back, Cora. Hell, if it wasn't for you, none of this would even be real. I'd still be stuck in Georgia, either trapped in my criminal father's house or married off to some equally criminal dirtbag in a marriage over which I had no say. You're my best friend. I wasn't making this decision without at least talking to you first."

"But now you're free from all that, Haven. And you deserve to be happy and have all the things you want. And that starts with Dare."

"I always thought we'd get an apartment together," she said, blue eyes so earnest.

Cora smiled and swallowed the selfish disappointment she felt, because she'd thought so, too. "Yeah, well, life is what happens when you're busy making other plans. Right? Besides, Dare lives ten minutes away. We'll still see each other here, and it'll be easy enough to visit. And when I finally get my own place, the door will always be open to you." Hesitation still colored Haven's expression, and Cora wasn't having that at all, so she pushed a little harder. "By this weekend, you'll move to Dare's, and then on Monday, you'll start laying out the plans for your own bakery. I've got it all planned out. Consider me your taskmaster."

Haven laughed. "Slow that down a little, won't you?"

"No way. You have a man willing to do anything for you, a safe place to live, a God-given talent you can't waste for one more day, *and* you've inherited enough money to get started with a business. Why go slow?" Cora asked, so badly wanting her friend to have all the things about which she'd dreamed. The only good thing Haven's dad had ever done for her was die and leave her that money to start a new life. At first, Haven had hesitated to accept it, because it was clear that at least some of it was ill-gotten gains from her dad's various illegal activities, but then she realized all the good she could do with it—and not just for herself. She'd donated some of it to the Ravens to assist in the protective duties the club undertook on behalf of people in bad situations with no other way out.

People like they'd once been.

"Well, for a couple of reasons," Haven said, putting her arms around her knees. "First of all, just being totally real here, I don't have any experience in running a business. I can bake the heck out of anything and make it pretty amazing, I'll admit, but I don't want to jump in without having the first idea what

I'm doing. So I've been thinking about applying to the culinary arts program at the community college, and maybe taking some business classes, too."

Cora nodded, a slow smile spreading on her face. "I'm liking this new take-charge Haven Randall. I think this is really smart." Cora meant every word. It was so gratifying to see her once timid and shy friend become so confident and brave.

"Yeah," she said, grinning. "It's too late to apply for the fall semester, but I think I can start in January." Her eyes went wide. "You could totally take some classes with me. How fun would that be?"

It was all Cora could do not to roll her eyes. "Haven, I can't afford coll—"

"I knew you were going to say that, which is why I would pay for the classes."

Cora dropped her face into her hands. "No."

"Why not?"

"No way."

"Yes way. Come on, look at me." Cora did, and Haven gave her the sternest glare she could manage. "Your dad worked for mine, which means he helped make some of the dirty money I inherited, which means some of it is rightfully yours, too." She arched a brow, her expression daring Cora to challenge her logic.

Instead, Cora changed the preposterous subject, because Haven's father had taken too much away from her for Cora to even contemplate taking any part of the one thing he'd given. "Okay, so what else? You said you had a couple of reasons to go slow with the bakery idea . . ."

Haven rolled her eyes. "We're not done talking about that yet." She stared until Cora finally nodded and waved her hand in a gesture to continue. "Well, for another reason, Dare is really twisted up over Jagger still being in jail, and worried about who Alexa's ex hired to set him and the Ravens up. I don't want to pile any more stress on him while that whole situation is still being resolved."

Cora shook her head. Jagger Locke managed the Ravens' main business operations at the racetrack they owned, and he'd been arrested over two months ago on several counts of illegal dumping of oil and tires, which carried surprisingly stiff penalties in Maryland. But the thing was, he didn't do it. The Ravens had already collected more than a little evidence that Alexa's now dead abusive ex-fiancé, a man who unfortunately had held a lot of influence as the town's biggest real estate developer, had hired someone to do the dumping to get back at the Ravens for helping Alexa. Cora didn't know Jagger well, but she knew that he'd been right there with the rest of the Ravens ready to help her and Haven out when they'd been in trouble. "What's happening to him is so unfair. Why the hell does it take so long to get a court date anyway?"

"I know, waiting is driving Dare insane. But it's

two weeks now. Hopefully they'll let him go on time served or just drop the charges altogether," Haven said on a sigh.

Just then, a knock sounded against the door. "Come in," Cora called.

"Hey," Bunny said. "Any chance you gals wanna help an old lady cook dinner for a bunch of miscreant bikers?"

They both laughed, because they'd fallen in love with Bunny McKeon in the time that they'd been with the Ravens. Bunny was the sister of the club's founder and owner, Doc Kenyon, wife of another founding member, Bear, and Maverick's mom, so she'd become something of a mother hen to all the younger guys. And she'd definitely become a mother figure to Cora and Haven, too. But with her wavy white hair, jeans, black T-shirt, and kick-ass black cowboy boots, she was the coolest sixty-something person Cora had ever met.

"You know we'd do anything for you," Haven said.

"And for those miscreants," Cora added.

Bunny grinned. "I was hoping you'd say that. Because word is that it's gonna be pretty busy in here tonight."

"WHY CAN'T CORA come over?" Ben asked Slider in what was possibly the twentieth rendition of the question since he'd gotten home from his only full day of school this week.

There'd also been: *Is Cora babysitting? Why isn't Cora babysitting? When is Cora babysitting again? Can we call Cora?* And too many others Slider couldn't remember, but all boiled down to this: his kid missed Cora Campbell. And maybe preferred her company to Slider's.

Not that Slider blamed him. Because he missed her, too. Her company, her positivity, her ability to distract Ben when he was cranky or bored or bickering with his brother. She'd been a lifesaver all week when Ben had been unable to make it through the school day and Slider had either been at work or sleeping after pulling an overnight shift. And when she wasn't around it was as if her absence sucked all the life right out of the house. The lights seemed dimmer. The rooms felt emptier. The quiet seemed lonelier. And the boys' smiles seemed fewer.

Actually, there was no *seeming* about that one. It was true.

"She's not working tonight, Benji. She can't always be with us," Slider said, patting the boy's feet, propped on Slider's lap while they sat on the couch together watching TV.

Footsteps padded down the hall, and Sam entered the family room only far enough to lean against the door, his arms crossed. "Why not?" he asked.

Slider frowned. "Why not what?"

Sam licked his lips and looked at Ben, and Slider caught some sort of silent exchange between them. "Why can't Cora always be with us?"

"Yeah," Ben said.

Talk about an ambush. How long had they been thinking about *this*? And what the hell was he supposed to say in response? After the night Slider and Cora spent together in that tiny bed in Ben's hospital room, no way was Slider allowing this question inside the weakened defenses of his imagination. Because when he'd awakened to find Cora's gaze sliding over his body like maybe she wanted to hold him down and ride him, he'd been tempted to invite her to do it. Right then and there. Nurses, doctors, and inappropriate time and place be damned.

And that lust-drunk, throw-caution-to-the-wind attitude where Cora was concerned was a problem he neither wanted nor needed. Starting with a father who left and a mother who didn't stay sober, the past had taught him too damn many times that people didn't stick around—at least for him—that they couldn't be trusted, and maybe even that he could never really know anyone else, even those he loved. Hell, maybe even especially those he loved.

Kim's betrayal and loss had left Slider wrecked enough. No way he was risking what was left of him. Because that belonged entirely to his boys. It *had* to. They already didn't get everything they deserved from him as it was.

The reality of that thought crept uncomfortably under Slider's skin. Ben was going to be fine, but for a few minutes the morning he'd been hurt, Slider didn't know what'd happened to him or how bad it was. Terror had flooded him at the possibility that he could lose Ben, just as he'd lost so much else. Given all that, shouldn't Slider be doing more with the time he had? Shouldn't he be doing more to pull himself the fuck together? If not for himself, then sure as hell for them.

"She just can't," Slider said lamely, moving Ben's feet off his lap so he could get up. The turn in his thoughts had him feeling like shit and craving a moment of solitude, so he made his way to the kitchen and got a drink of water. But the boys weren't having it, and there was no missing the fact that two pairs of eyes had followed him and were burning holes in his back.

"That's not an answer," Ben said. "*Why* can't she?"

Slider turned to find them standing shoulder to shoulder, a united front in their effort to demand this answer from him. Little carbon copies of him, the both of them, though they had pieces of Kim, too. Sam's brown eyes and darker brown hair. The shape of Ben's mouth and the freckles across his cheeks. Of course, the boys picked *now* to get along, and about something that made no fucking sense. "We can't just ask Cora to move in with us."

"Still not an answer," Sam said, brow arched.

"Okay, first off," Slider said, "she has her own place to live. Second, a babysitter is a part-time job, and we can't expect Cora to give up her whole life for it, and it would be weird to even ask. And finally," he said, his brain scrambling for more ammunition, "she's not family. The three of us, *we're* family."

A long moment passed, and then they were talking over each other as they fired off counterarguments. "Dad," Sam said, "Cora lives at the clubhouse. That's not really her own place. Do you even know how she came to be there?"

Slider blinked, because what the hell did his ten-year-old know about Cora's past? And why did he seem to know more about it than Slider?

"Yeah, but Cora was here a lot more than usual this week," Ben was saying in a tumble of words, "and I know she didn't mind because she told me she was happy to do it because she didn't have anywhere else she had to be."

Sam nodded and crossed his arms. "Besides, you're not related to anyone in the Raven Riders, yet you always call them *brothers*. So I think people you're not related to can be family if you want them to be."

Ben tried to mirror the tough-guy pose, but the cast on his elbow wouldn't quite allow him to pull it off. "I agree with Sam."

Jesus. He was totally outnumbered here, wasn't he? "You two practicing for your future careers as prosecutors, or what?"

"*Dad*," Sam said, his eyebrow arching.

"Sam—"

"Come on, you could use the help, and Cora could use a real house to live in. She could be, like . . . our *nanny.* It'd be win-win," the kid said. Ten going on thirty-five, apparently. Which made them the exact same age.

Sonofabitch. Cora, their nanny. It was crazy . . . but maybe not as crazy as Slider at first thought. And it wasn't as if he couldn't afford it. Kim's life insurance had given them a decent safety net that Slider only dipped into when he had to. He scrubbed at his face, all his unkempt whiskers suddenly irritating him in a way they hadn't before.

"At least think about it, Dad," Ben said, his tone a little defeated.

And even though he knew it was bad for his resolve, Slider looked his son in the face and found those way-too-persuasive puppy-dog eyes in full effect. "Fine," he said, really wanting to stop talking about the idea of Cora living with him. With them, he meant. "Now what do you want for dinner? I could make up some mac and cheese, or we have stuff for cold cuts."

"I want to go to the clubhouse for dinner," Ben said.

"Yeah!" Sam said. "Haven is such a good cook. Can we?"

"Maybe she'll make her peanut butter cookies. Can we, Dad?" the little one asked with those pleading eyes.

And of course Cora was over there, which they damn well knew. But, honestly, how often did they ask anything of him anymore? And given all they didn't have—a mother and a father who wasn't a wreck at the top of that list—they were hard to resist on those rare occasions when they did. "You two are killing me, you know that?"

Sam smirked. "I'll help you get your shoes on, Ben," he said, pushing his brother out of the room.

"Damnit," Slider bit out under his breath. Why did he feel like he'd just been played? And why did his gut tell him it wasn't over yet?

CHAPTER 6

With over half of the Ravens' almost forty active members present, dinner was a loud, raucous affair. Cora was positive she laughed at least as much as she managed to eat, and it was exactly what she needed to distract herself from the odd pit of sadness deep in her gut at the feeling that she was losing her best friend.

You're being so ridiculous, she thought for the millionth time. And she was. She *knew* she was. But it wasn't like she could talk herself out of how she felt.

And so, instead, she laughed. And joked. And teased Phoenix relentlessly. And got up half a dozen times to refill the platters of burgers, dogs, and corn on the cob.

It was on one of the trips from the kitchen that she returned to the most unexpected sight—Slider, in the big mess hall of what had once been an old mountain inn, standing in the doorway with the boys. From what Cora could tell, many of the Ravens were single guys without much in the way of family. A lot of them found their way here for meals throughout the week, particularly on weekend nights and mornings. That was when the two long rows of tables tended to be fullest. But never once in all her time around the clubhouse had Cora seen Slider Evans come to eat. His boys, sure. Early on, she'd watched them here on many occasions until Slider got off work and could pick them up.

But never Slider.

And Cora wasn't the only one who was surprised.

Because the room noticed him in a wave of sudden, surprised hush that was quickly followed by a chorus of welcome. Chairs moved to make space. The boys' hair got ruffled a million times. And Ben was grinning ear to ear from all the attention his cast was getting.

She came up behind where Sam and Ben had settled and placed a hand on each of their shoulders. Leaning in, she teased, "You two just can't get enough of me. Admit it. I'm the coolest ever."

"Hey, Cora," Sam said, smiling up at her.

"I missed you," Ben said, crawling onto his knees on his chair as he turned and wrapped his arms around her. It was awkward and clumsy with the cast, but it was so sweet that Cora's insides temporarily turned to goo. Across the table, she met Haven's gaze, and her friend's expression made it clear that the kid was turning her gooey, too.

But it was someone else's expression that most captured Cora's attention. When Ben slid back into his seat, she turned to find Slider staring at her, his gaze so blatant, unabashed, and tortured that for a second she could only stare back.

He frowned and looked away as someone passed him a platter of food. What the heck had that look been about, anyway?

Ever since they'd shared that hot but confusing moment in the little hospital bed—that moment when Slider had touched her face, her hair, her lips—he'd gone distant on her again. Not rude or mean or grumpy, but for a moment that night, she could've sworn that some sort of wall had come down between them. And it was back now. Higher than ever.

Or maybe it'd never really been down at all.

She peeked his way, happy at least to see him interacting with *someone*. He was nodding and talking to Doc, Bear, and Bunny, who used to watch the boys for him sometimes and asked Cora how they were doing all the time.

On a sigh, Cora slipped back into her chair between Phoenix and Haven. What did it matter how Slider looked at her or whether they'd made some kind of connection? It wasn't like they were friends. He was her boss. Her boss in a part-time babysitting job. Hardly the stuff of which forever was made.

Not that she thought forever was on the table here.

Dare was chuckling at something Haven was saying and double-fisting his own private, secret stash of her peanut butter cookies—with which her bestie might've paved her way to his heart. Well. Forever wasn't on the table for both of them, anyway. For Haven? Definitely.

And it was really freaking refreshing for good things to happen to such a good person.

Be a good girl and stop fighting.

The memory of the words nearly had Cora flying out of her chair, the adrenaline kick of the fight-or-flight response was suddenly so strong in her blood. She gripped the edge of her seat, trying to steady herself, trying to ground herself in the here and now.

Blinking away the sudden wetness in her eyes, she peered left and right under the curtain of her hair to see if anyone noticed her, because she was shaky and clammy and so damn exposed it felt like the whole world would know.

But no one was paying her any attention, and all she saw was Dare and Haven shamelessly flirting with each other next to her. "Next Friday night, then," Dare said, looking at Haven with so much affection and masculine satisfaction. "We're moving your stuff over to the house as soon as I wrap up here. Got it?"

Haven grinned. "Yeah. I can't wait."

"Hold up," Maverick said from across the table. "Haven's moving into the cabin?" Dare gave a nod, an arched eyebrow challenging anybody to say one teasing word about it. He had a protective streak a mile wide—which explained, in part, why the Ravens had a protective mission in the first place—but it was a hundred times stronger when it came to Haven. "That's fantastic news. Congrats."

Word spread around the room, and in the excited mayhem that followed, Cora finally felt like she could breathe again. Why did this keep happening to her, these out-of-the-blue memories that threatened to suck her back into that terrible moment? It had happened five months ago, and her father was now moldering in a grave. She should just get over it already.

She glanced up to find Slider staring at her again with that strange troubled expression from before still on his face. Except, as he looked at her, that expression changed to one of concern that seemed to ask if she was okay. Thankfully, a big mountain of a guy named Meat hit Slider on the arm and said something that made them both chuckle, and Cora turned away. She wasn't sure what was up with him tonight, but she couldn't take his weirdness when she was feeling so raw.

Taking a deep breath, she pasted on a smile and shook all of her own weirdness away, at least for now.

Leaning closer to Haven, Cora said, "I'm so happy for you. But why are you waiting till next weekend?"

"Because Dare's heading up a relocation trip for the woman and her daughter who've been living out in one of the guest cabins the past two weeks. There's no sense in me moving to his place when he's going to be gone for at least three nights."

Cora had been so busy at the Evanses lately that she hadn't had a chance to do more than see the Ravens' new protective client from a distance, but it wasn't unusual for them to sometimes offer a woman or a family in trouble a temporary place to live in the cabins near the clubhouse if the real-world authorities couldn't satisfactorily handle an abusive situation. The Ravens certainly had the room to do it, because their property had once been a mountain inn and resort based around the racetrack they now operated, all of which Doc had inherited decades ago. "I guess that's true," Cora said, "and a week will pass in no time at all."

Haven clutched her hand. "Are you sure this is okay?"

"It's so much more than okay. In fact, I think it's time we break out the chocolate cake and ice cream to celebrate."

Haven bit her lip, but even that couldn't hold back her smile. "I'll help."

"No way," Cora said, rising and needing a breather from the craziness of the mess hall. "You did most of the cooking. Besides, you should sit right there and enjoy this moment with your man."

"I like the sound of that," Dare said, hauling Haven's chair flush with his own, surprising a burst of laughter out of Haven. What would it be like to have that with a man? Confusingly, the question had Cora peering down the table, and it was as if her gaze drew Slider's, because he chose that exact moment to look her way. A shiver raced down her spine. She'd worked for him for months, but somehow something had changed between them lately, and it was almost like she was noticing him for the first time.

"I'm finished, so I'll help," Alexa said, pulling Cora from her thoughts. Together, the two of them grabbed a couple of the guys' dirty dishes on their way into the kitchen.

Long ago, apparently, Bunny had put her foot down and made sure the club didn't treat her or any of the other women as servants, expecting them to do all the work. So Phoenix, Maverick, Meat, and even Caine—the Ravens' quietly intimidating sergeant-at-arms—got up to clear the table, too. In the kitchen, the club's two prospects, Blake and Mike, pitched in scraping dirty plates, loading the dishwasher, and bagging up the trash.

Everyone pitched in, just like family. And that's really what the Raven Riders were all about.

Alexa gathered up dessert plates, and it was then that Cora noticed.

"Your ring!" Cora loudly whispered, gasping at how gorgeous the diamond was as she clutched gently at Alexa's scarred hand.

"I know. Isn't it amazing?" Alexa said, her hazel eyes sparkling with excitement. She peered furtively over at the guys working at the sink, making Cora wonder if the ring was a secret.

Which made Cora wonder . . . "Wait. Oh, my God. Does Haven know?" Grinning, Alexa shook her head. "Then hold that thought." Cora raced to the kitchen door, poked her head out, and waved. "Haven, we need you in here after all."

"What's up?" Haven asked, joining them.

Cora pantomimed at their friend with both hands, and Haven's blue eyes went wide when she finally saw it.

"You're engaged?" she cried, peeking closer at the emerald-cut diamond.

"Ssh," Alexa laugh-whispered.

"When? How?" Haven asked in a hushed voice.

"Yes, start from the beginning already," Cora joined in. "We're dying here."

Laughing, Alexa pressed her hands to her cheeks, happier than Cora had seen her in weeks.

"Maverick actually proposed the night of the fire," Alexa said, the three of them in a huddle, "in our hospital room, but we weren't ready to share the news that night. He hadn't planned to do it then, so he didn't yet have a ring. And he's been waiting ever since for the doc to give me the all-clear on wearing jewelry again anyway. Given all the recent craziness, we're not in a rush to do the ceremony, but he wanted to make it official, so he popped the question again today and gave me this."

"That's so sweet, Al," Haven said. "Maverick's one of the good ones."

"Yeah, he really is," Alexa said, tucking a long strand of her brown hair behind her ear. "The best."

So Haven was moving in with her boyfriend and Alexa was getting married. Cora was happy for her friends, she really was. But she couldn't help but feel stuck in the face of all the ways that their lives were moving on. This wasn't about her, though, was it? So she put on a smile and elbowed Alexa. "You're going to be an *Old Lady*!" Cora said, finding all the biker slang she'd learned kinda hilarious.

"Oh, my God," Al said, chuckling and pressing her hand to her forehead. "So crazy."

"Dude, so no one knows?" Cora asked. "We were just out there toasting Dare and Haven. We should've been toasting you guys, too!"

Haven gasped. "Tell me Dare does not know or I'll kick his ass for not telling me."

Alexa made a hesitant face. "Um, I'd seriously hate to be responsible for Dare getting his ass kicked . . ." When Haven's mouth dropped open, they all laughed. "Mav told him weeks ago, but asked him not to tell anyone else. So it's not his fault. And of course Mav told his mom." Bunny, she meant, which was how even Maverick referred to her.

"Well, you're wearing the ring now, so is he letting this secret out of the bag tonight?" Cora asked.

"I think so?" Alexa said in a giddy, questioning tone.

"We're making this happen now," Haven said, all fired up.

A few minutes later, the three of them had set the tables with dessert plates and the five big cake stands with the triple-layer chocolate cakes that Cora and Haven had spent the afternoon making. But no one moved to cut a piece yet, because Alexa and Haven had pulled Maverick and Dare aside, and just then, Maverick stood at the head of one of the tables, Alexa's hand in his.

"While so many of us are here together tonight, we wanted to share some news," Maverick said, the room going quiet as he smiled down at Al like she was the air he breathed. What Cora wouldn't give to have a man look at her that way. Just once. Mav's gaze swung back to the assembled crowd again, his stunning blue eyes scanning the group. "I asked Alexa to marry me and she said yes."

Everyone erupted in outright cheers that had Cora grinning and laughing and wanting to clap for her friend. For both of them, actually. And no way was she unraveling the thread that led to the tiny thought in the back of her head that she truly was the odd woman out in her little circle of friends—the only one without a man, and, more importantly, without a home and without even any obvious path for her future.

Nope. Not doing it. Not tonight, at least. Tonight was for reveling in the good. Cora hadn't had nearly enough of that in her own life, so for now, she could be content with living vicariously through the girls she cared most about in the world.

Soon, the Ravens' two newest couples stood together at the front of the room. "It's about time we had some good news to celebrate around here," Dare said. Nods and murmurs of agreement all around. "Maverick, for most of my life, you've been the closest thing to a brother that I have, and I couldn't be happier for you. And, Al, welcome to the family. We're not sure how Mav got so damn lucky to find someone like you, but we're thrilled that he did, for both of you."

Laughter and another toast went around the room.

"Now, we just gotta bring Jagger home, and all will be right in the Raven Riders' world," Maverick said.

"Damn straight," Dare said, an edge to his voice that everyone understood—and shared.

But they didn't linger on their problems. Instead, once dinner was over, the festivities moved into the big rec room, with its long, polished bar, pool tables, new air hockey table, and jukebox. It was the center of most of the Ravens' parties, and tonight was no exception.

"Wanna play air hockey, Cora?" Sam asked, Ben in tow. Slider was nowhere to be seen, and Cora hoped he was mingling somewhere and not hiding out by himself. These parties weren't his regular scene at all, but he had to miss hanging out with his brothers in the club. From the stories she'd heard of him, Slider had once been talkative and outgoing and fun to be around. It made her sad to think he'd changed so much.

"Only if you don't mind getting beaten by a girl," she said, eyebrow arched in challenge. Sam had a mile-wide competitive streak, and she kinda loved poking at it.

"You're going down," Sam said.

In the end, they tied, two matches each. The kid was ruthless.

"My turn!" Ben said, totally enjoying himself even though he had to play with his left hand.

In truth, Cora enjoyed herself, too. The whole time she'd played with the boys, she'd been in the moment, not once thinking about all the things she wanted but feared she'd never have.

Given Ben's disadvantage, she let him get away with a few cheap shots, and he threw up his hands with a wild little *whoop* when he won.

"Ready to go, alligators?" Slider asked, coming up to the table. "It's getting late." After a few grumbles, the boys agreed. "Thanks for hanging out with them," Slider said. "You didn't have to do that."

She smiled. "What, are you kidding? These guys always show me a good time."

For a moment, the boys and Slider waged some sort of weird, mostly silent little battle. Cora had no idea what was going on.

"*Dad!*" Ben whispered loudly as he not at all subtly moved his eyeballs toward her. She pretended not to notice even though curiosity was killing her. What the heck was going on?

Slider shook his head and made the universal parental expression for *knock it off.* The boys grumbled again, their hugs frustrated as they said good-bye to her. Then Slider was the one saying good-bye. Sorta. "Are you okay?" he asked.

Her? *He* was the one who'd looked at her again and again tonight like something was off. "Totally fine, why?"

"Forget it," he said, those pale eyes not quite willing to meet hers. "See ya tomorrow night. Regular time?"

"Yep," she said, bewildered. Apparently, *all* the Evans men were set to *weird* tonight.

After that, Cora hung out with Haven and Alexa as much as their guys could stand to be parted from them. The three of them chatted for hours and even enjoyed a round or two of Blow Jobs, much to the delight of the guys seated around them at the bar— and therefore to the chagrin of Dare and Maverick. When the two couples finally departed, Cora felt a bit at loose ends, but finally ended up shooting some pool with Phoenix.

What she really wanted to do was head to bed, but since her room was located over the bar, it wasn't going to be particularly peaceful up there until the party wound down. Which had her thinking about the peace and quiet of Slider's house . . . and wishing she had a home like that to go to . . .

CHAPTER 7

I t was all Slider could do to keep from banging his head against the nearest wall. Or at least his headboard. Because the boys' pleadings about asking Cora to become their nanny wouldn't stop poking at his brain. And because the idea was growing on him whether he wanted it to or not—they weren't wrong; with Slider's changing schedule and overnight shifts, he could use more regular help. Maybe even permanent help, especially if it benefited Cora.

But he'd fucking chickened out on asking her.

Beyond that, he wanted to bang his head against anything hard and immovable because something had been wrong with her at dinner. He would've put money on it. And he'd let her blow him off when he'd asked.

Now, he couldn't sleep for worrying about it.

And why the hell was he worrying about it again? Jesus.

Every time he closed his eyes, he saw one of two images that made sure they wouldn't stay closed: sharing a bed with Cora and catching her blatantly checking out his body, *and* the way her skin had gone ashen in the middle of dinner.

As appealing as that first memory was, it was the second one he couldn't stop replaying as he lay in the darkness of his room. Cora was many things. Funny. Sarcastic. A good caregiver. A straight talker. And not at all a pushover. That morning she'd walked out of his house, she hadn't hesitated to agree he'd been a dick or to tell him not to do it again. He respected the hell out of that, too.

But he'd never seen Cora scared and never once thought of her as fragile. And whatever had happened to her at dinner made her appear both. It hadn't lasted long, but he knew what he'd seen.

What the hell could have caused it?

And, as if all that wasn't enough to be pinging around in his brain at zero-dark-thirty, knowing that Haven's moving in with Dare would leave Cora to live alone at the clubhouse, with all its parties and the drinking and hooking up that often happened at them, was *not* sitting right in Slider's gut.

Question was: What was he going to do about it?

He was still asking himself that question twenty-four hours later when his shift ended in the wee hours of Sunday morning. His boss had let him cut out a little early because it'd been absolutely dead, and he'd arrived home a little after five, the house utterly quiet.

But it wasn't dark. Golden light spilled out from the family room, illuminating the hallway and just spilling into the darkness at the front of the house.

Why was Cora up at this hour?

He made his way to the family room. "Hey, Cora, I'm home early," he called out so he didn't scare her. But when he peeked into the room, he found her sound asleep. She lay facing the back of the couch, her knees drawn up, her body in a tight little ball. The blanket had slipped to the floor, leaving her arms and legs bare around the little white tank top and pale blue men's boxers she wore.

Damn, there was just no denying how pretty she was. Annnd now it was time to get out of there.

Quietly, he retrieved the blanket and bent to lower it over her again.

She jerked, her head turning to peer over her shoulder. A scream ripped out of her.

Heart hammering in his chest, Slider reared back so hard he nearly went ass over head over the coffee table. "Jesus, I'm sorry. It's just me, Cora. It's just me," he managed when he caught himself.

She scrambled into the corner of the couch, her eyes skittering back and forth, her whole body visibly shaking, as if she was terrified of her unfamiliar surroundings. A little cry of anguish spilled from her throat.

He held up his hands, his mind an absolute storm of confusion. "Hey. Cora. It's okay. I'm sorry. I didn't mean to scare you."

A tear spilled from one of her bright green eyes. Just a single, fat, slow-rolling tear. She fisted it away and unleashed a shaky breath. "Sorry. I didn't mean—" She shook her head and hugged the pillow tight, like maybe it was the only thing holding her together.

"Why are you apologizing?" he asked, something uncomfortable stirring in his gut. Because this seemed out of proportion for having been scared awake. "You did nothing wrong."

Still trembling, she gave an awkward little shrug as the fight drained out of her posture. "I . . . I don't kn-know." Her breathing hitched.

"Cora—"

Her bottom lip shook. Another fast head shake. "Please."

Still standing across the room, he frowned. "Please what?"

She peered up at him with those green eyes so glassy with unshed tears, and it nearly broke his long-dead heart.

"Cora, what's wrong?" Cautiously, he stepped around the opposite side of the coffee table and gestured. "Would it be okay if I sit?"

She managed an eye roll. "It's your couch."

He eased himself down like it was the sofa that was fragile, and then he looked at her again.

Little footsteps pattered down the hall. "Cora?" came Ben's sleepy voice from just outside the room.

Fast swipes at her eyes. "Aw, hi, Bean. You can come in."

"I heard a noise. Did you scream?" Feet scuffing the floor, Ben came in wearing a pair of Spider-Man pajamas, bear in his hand. "Oh, hi Dad." He sat between them, then peered back and forth like he was at a tennis match. "What happened?"

Cora gave a watery smile, but as Slider watched, she was already buttoning herself back up. "Nothing. Just a bad dream."

"Oh," Ben said, holding out his stuffed animal. "You should take Blue Bear, then. He'll make you feel better."

Cora took the bear and hugged it to her chest. And then she leaned against the kid. "You're the sweetest."

He sighed. "I know."

Slider watched the two of them together for a long moment, and damn if it didn't unleash an unexpected warmth inside his chest. Odd for a man who'd felt cold to his very core for so long. "It's still nighttime, Benji. Go get some more sleep," Slider said. "It's gonna take a lot of energy to eat all those pancakes in the morning."

"Okay," he said, his ready willingness proof that

he was still tired. He gave them both hugs and kisses and then was gone again, leaving a stilted awkwardness in his wake.

"I'm sorry I freaked out," Cora finally said, looking down at Blue Bear like it was suddenly fascinating.

Slider drew one leg up on the couch, turning toward her and coming a little closer. "Look at me," he said, his gaze running over her pretty blond waves. Out of nowhere, the urge hit him—hit him *hard*—to slide his fingers into her hair, haul her close, maybe even into his lap, and . . . Jesus, the universe of things he wanted after that was suddenly, surprisingly, and dizzyingly infinite. But he held himself still, because where the hell had that come from? And because, just then, his needs weren't what was important. Finally, Cora looked up. "You'd knocked the blanket off, and I was afraid you'd be cold, but I scared you awake. Nothing to apologize for, Cora. Okay?"

"Okay," she whispered.

"You believing me or just telling me what you think I want to hear?" He arched a brow.

She gave a little smirk that probably wasn't supposed to come off as sexy but did. "Hello, Talkative Slider, nice to meet you."

Now he was the one smirking. "Hello, Humor as a Diversionary Tactic Cora. Pleasure's all mine."

She sighed. "Well, damn. I believe you, okay?"

He gave a single nod. "Are you sure you're all right?"

"It was just a nightmare. I'm fine. Just feeling like a giant idiot," she said, the self-deprecation another of the defense tactics he'd noted in all the time they'd spent together.

He wasn't buying the nightmare line, not at all. And he wanted to push. Like, *really* fucking wanted to push. Because his gut demanded there was way more to it. But Slider didn't know this woman that well, and their relationship had almost never veered into the personal. He'd been convinced he didn't want it to, either.

But now, God help him, now he was thinking maybe he did want it to.

He wanted to know what Sam knew about her past. He wanted to return some of the amazing care this woman had shown his boys—and him—all these months. And if his protective hackles hadn't been up over her living alone at the clubhouse, they were fucking up *now* over the gut-deep belief that there was a reason his waking her had scared her so bad.

Women who'd had an easy go at life didn't end up in the Ravens' protective custody, after all.

All of which had Slider deciding that Sam and Ben's idea wasn't so crazy, even though that meant he was taking parenting advice from his ten- and six-year-olds. Honestly, he didn't think they could do much worse than he'd done these past couple years, and though there was humor in that somewhere, it also left him feeling like it was well past time to fucking step it up.

So he silenced his head and boxed up his bruised heart and let his gut lead this. "I'd like to ask you something, although I'm aware that five o'clock in the morning isn't really the best time."

There was a bit of wariness in her gaze, not that he blamed her, but still she nodded. "What is it?"

Slider took a deep breath, then let all kinds of words he'd been stuffing down just fly. "Cora, it's quite possible you're the best thing that's happened to my family in a long time. And since, to be frank, I'm not the father I once was, I could use your help. Even more of your help, I guess. Because you're amazing with the boys. A natural. And they love having you here." He looked at her.

Green eyes wide, her mouth dropped open in surprise. "Okay. Wow," she whispered. "That's really kind of you to say. But . . . what does that mean, exactly?"

Jesus. He was an idiot. "Right." He chuckled. "I guess it would help if I actually asked the question. Would you consider moving in here and working for us as a full-time nanny?"

MAYBE IT WAS because it was still the middle of the night. Or maybe it was because the remnants of a flashback-induced panic attack were still circulating through her blood. Or maybe it was because Slider had opened up to her in a way he never had before. But Cora could barely believe what she'd just heard.

"Excuse me?" she managed, her pulse tripping into a sprint.

"Oh, hell. You hate the idea." Slider raked at his hair. "Damnit. Forget I said anything. We'll just keep things how they are, which is fine. No, it's great. Really." He rose in a rush.

"Wait," she said, standing, too, Blue Bear still in her hand. "I just . . . I'm not sure I . . . did you really just ask me to live here as your nanny?"

His gaze narrowed. "Uh, yeah?"

Cora blinked. Wow. *Wow.* "That's . . ." *Wow!* "Oh, my God. I would *love* that," she said. Hadn't she just been thinking how much she would love a home like this? An actual real house to live in? The Ravens had been amazing letting her stay rent-free at the clubhouse all this time, but that wasn't a viable long-term solution for her life, especially now that Haven was moving out. She'd never thought of being a nanny before, and maybe it wasn't a permanent plan, either, but at least it was a job.

At least it was a start.

And now she had fun news of her own to share the next time she talked to Haven. So Cora didn't need to think about it. "I'd be happy to accept, Slider."

A slow smile crept up his face, and holy wow, it was the first actual smile she'd ever seen on him. Even with the beard, it made him look younger, it made those odd, pale eyes look livelier. "Yeah?"

She nodded when what she really wanted to do was break into a victory dance. "Yeah." What would it be like to live with Slider? The man with the surprising smile. The man whose naked image lived in her head, whether she wanted it to or not. The man with whom she'd shared some sort of a moment in that hospital bed.

"Well, okay. Great. That's . . ." He nodded. "The boys are going to be thrilled."

Grinning, Cora hugged herself, then belatedly realized she was hugging a stuffed bear. They both chuckled. "I'm glad, because I'm definitely thrilled, too," she said. And she really was. She'd always appreciated and enjoyed babysitting for them, but now it felt like a real opportunity.

"Good. Seems to me," he said, peering down at the rumpled blanket on the couch, "first thing I need to do is make you an actual place to live around this place. A couch in the family room isn't going to cut it. I'll get on that right away."

"Okay, that sounds great." How ridiculous was it that the idea was so exciting? But having her own space to decorate and call home seemed like a little life victory, even if it was *little*. Still, she'd take it.

"So, would six hundred dollars a week plus room and board seem fair?" he asked. "And there'd be time off, of course. Paid vacation. I think the club is paying for your cell, and I'd take that over since you'd need it for the job. I looked into it a bit so I'd know all the rules people usually follow."

Cora's mouth dropped open and her belly went all jiggly, like she was on a roller coaster and had just crested the highest hill. With that kind of money, plus what she'd been saving with all the babysitting, she could afford some sort of car. And maybe, just maybe, even to take a class at the community college, too. Which made her realize there was something else she needed to ask about, if she was going to take on a full-time job. "So, before this, I'd been wanting to look into volunteering at the animal shelter. Would you be okay with me doing something like that as long as I was available for Sam and Ben's care and took care of my other duties?"

Slider nodded. "Animals, huh?"

She gave a little shrug. "Unlike people, their love is unconditional, so yeah."

He tilted his head, and nailed her with a stare that suddenly felt like he might be able to see into the very heart of her. "I don't see why that would be a problem, Cora."

Yesyesyes! "Then your offer sounds fair to me," she said, all cool-like, even though on the inside, she was jumping up and down like a schoolgirl. When was the last time she was this excited about something? When was the last time something this good had happened to her?

And it was all because of Slider and his beautiful boys.

Slider held out his hand.

Slowly, Cora slid her hand into his. Nothing so cliché as a spark happened, but that didn't stop a few butterflies from taking flight inside her stomach at the heat of his skin, the rough caress of his working-man's calluses, or the firmness of his grip. It reminded her of the way he'd touched her face that night at the hospital, and suddenly longing roared through her—to feel those big, rough hands on her even more. Maybe even to feel those big, rough hands on her everywhere.

But, *dude*, this man was her boss. Her boss whom she lived with. Her boss who was also the dad to two young kids whom she was also going to live with. Her boss who'd admitted to being a wreck over the loss of his beloved wife just a few years before.

So. Well, damn. Given all that, there could be no boss's big, rough hands involved. But, fine. Whatever. That didn't diminish her excitement about this new chance one bit.

"Thanks, Slider," she said, an idiotic grin finally breaking through, but she was too happy to resist.

He gave her a single nod, his suddenly intense gaze locked onto hers. "No, thank you, Cora. Welcome to the family."

CHAPTER 8

Slider opened a door he hadn't walked through in almost two years—the door to the master bedroom. The room he'd shared with Kim through twelve years of marriage. The room in which she'd spent the last days of her life.

Dust motes swirled in the sunlight pouring through the windows. Slider flicked on the ceiling light over the room, mostly empty except for a few dressers and nightstands. Their bed was long since gone, the frame of which he'd stored in the attic, having been replaced by a hospital-type bed during the final months of her illness. But the medical device store had taken that away, too, leaving the room with a forgotten, neglected feeling.

One he was here, at long last, to rectify. For Cora, but also for himself.

"Can we help?"

Slider turned to find Sam and Ben in the hallway, warily looking at him. They hadn't entered this room in the past two years either, not that Slider had ever forbidden it. "You guys sure you're okay with this?" he asked, sensitive to their feelings since this was where they'd spent time with their mom at the end.

"Yeah, Dad. Cora needs a place to stay, and it's just sitting empty," Sam said. The boys had been ecstatic when, over Sunday-morning pancakes, Slider and Cora had announced that she'd be moving in. So ecstatic that, when it was time to take her home, they'd argued that she shouldn't go. But she'd asked if she could officially start her new gig with them the following week so that Haven wouldn't be living alone at the clubhouse while Dare was away. And that worked just fine for Slider, since he needed time for this.

Ben nodded. "It's just a room, Dad." He'd been only four when Kim died, and Slider suspected his memories of the months before were murky at best. But that wariness was still present in Sam's eyes, which meant the kid was, at least on some level, putting on a brave front.

"Okay, then. I'd appreciate your help."

Three hours later, they'd dusted everything, washed the windows and mopped the hardwood floor, and retrieved the queen-sized bed frame from storage. They'd also cleaned out and scoured the adjoining bathroom, perfect for Cora to have a little privacy. Finally, they'd bagged up the clothes from the closet and drawers. Slider had been worried about doing the last in front of them, but the boys had been all business about it. All business about everything except the more personal things on top of Kim's dresser.

"We should save those Disney figurines," Sam said quietly. "Mom collected them."

"Okay," Slider said. "Let's box them up and figure out where to put them." Nodding, Sam grabbed a box and wrapped each figurine like it was priceless.

"I . . . I know it's girls' stuff, but could I . . . can I keep Mom's jewelry box?" Ben asked, tracing the flying blackbirds carved into the top.

Slider crouched down and looked his son in the eye. "You can have absolutely anything you want."

"Okay, Dad," he whispered, peering back at him with suddenly glassy eyes. Then his little face absolutely crumpled.

"Aw, B, come here," he said, hauling Ben into his chest. The kid burst into tears, tears like he hadn't cried since the long-ago conversation when he'd finally understood that Kim was never coming home again. If Slider thought he was a wreck now, it was nothing compared to how trashed he'd been back then—from the rawness of her death, from the pain of watching her deteriorate, from the bitter poison of having to keep her infidelity secret, from the acidic curiosity of never having learned the name of the man she'd cheated with. In the midst of all that, had he been there enough for his boys in their grief?

Damnit, he wasn't sure he wanted the answer to that question.

But maybe it wasn't too late to be there now.

"Just let it out, Benji. It's okay to be sad that Mom's gone. It's okay to miss her. And it's okay to talk about her and want her things nearby," he managed around the lump in his throat. He peered up at Sam, but his older son was too studiously ignoring them as he picked up Cinderella and wrapped her in paper.

Finally, Ben pulled away, and Slider had to help him dry his face because the cast prevented him from reaching both eyes. "Your whiskers are scratchy," he said.

Slider gave the kid a smile and tugged at his beard. "Not a fan, are you?"

He shook his head. "You look like one of those *Duck Dynasty* men."

Sam snorted. "Oh, my God, he's right."

Slider peered up at his older son. "Now you're just ganging up on me."

"Deal with it, old man," Sam said with a smirk. And just then, Sam reminded him of Cora. Trying to squirm out of his questions with humor. Except Sam's defense wasn't humor, it was sarcasm and feigned apathy.

Still, Slider barked out a laugh at the comment. And, damn, it felt good. Just joking around with them the way he used to. A million years ago . . . "Why don't we break for lunch. And then we can run to the store and buy a new mattress set for the bed in here."

Sam fingered a scratch on the pale yellow wall near the light switch. "Maybe we should paint, too."

"Yeah!" Ben said, struggling to carry the jewelry box under one arm. "Wonder what Cora's favorite color is? Maybe it's blue. 'Member she thought that was the coolest color for my case?"

Standing in the doorway, Slider peered back into the clean room, now empty of its ghosts. Or, at least, most of them. "I don't know," he said, "but that's a good idea."

Over a lunch of cold-cuts sandwiches, chips, and some of Haven's cookies that Cora had brought over for them, the boys were abuzz with ideas of things they should do for Cora's room. They didn't just want fresh paint, they wanted to raid Target for every pretty, girly thing they could find.

"Maybe we should get throw pillows for her bed, too. Don't girls like that stuff?" Sam asked.

"I think she needs a pink beanbag chair," Ben said.

"*You're* the one who wants a beanbag chair, doofus," Sam said. "Besides, what if she doesn't like pink?"

"What if she doesn't like throw pillows?" Ben shot back.

"Okay," Slider said, chuckling. "We'll pick up some

new stuff at Target. But maybe we should let Cora do the actual decorating. It's her room, after all." That seemed to satisfy them. But there was still the question of what color this theoretical new stuff should be.

Debating, he pulled out his phone and texted Dare. Can you ask Haven what Cora's favorite color is?

He might as well have typed, Hey Dare, I know I barely talk to you anymore, but can you do me a solid and play go-between with your girlfriend to answer a completely ridiculous question for me?

Three little dots appeared, evidence that Dare was replying. And then they disappeared. Reappeared, then disappeared again. His cell rang.

"That complicated, huh?" Slider said by way of answering.

"Slider, it's Haven," she said, amusement plain in her voice. "And, yes, it's a little complicated, which is why I'm calling."

"Tell him I wasn't typing all that shit out," Dare called out in the background loud enough for Slider to hear.

"Sorry, ignore him," she said, chuckling. "Can I ask what it's for? Because if you're talking clothes, she really likes blacks and grays and dark blues, but if you're talking flowers, she adores pink and yellow. Roses, carnations, gerbera daisies, you can't go wrong with those colors. Just not the typical red."

Flowers? Why the hell did Haven think he'd want to know about flowers?

"Uh, what if I wanted to paint a room for her," he said, feeling way too damn exposed.

"Oh!" She laughed. "I'm so excited that she's going to be your nanny, Slider. She's so good at taking care of other people, and she adores your boys."

"Yeah," he said, clearing his throat. "So, what do you think?"

"Man, this is a lot of pressure. I'd say definitely *not* pink or purple, because that would be too like her old room at home. I think she'd like blue, though. I think she'd like it a lot."

"Blue. Okay, sure. Thanks, Haven."

"Blue! See, I knew it!" Ben said. Slider gave him a thumbs-up.

"No problem," Haven was saying. "Hold on, here's Dare."

"You're painting a room for Cora?" he asked. Slider could almost imagine the look in his eyes, observing all kinds of things you didn't really want anyone else seeing, but Dare always saw anyway.

"Yeah. Just freshening things up for her," he said matter-of-factly.

"Want help?" he asked.

That wasn't what Slider expected at all. He had a kneejerk *no* on the tip of his tongue, but if he was going to start doing a better job with the people in his life, that had to include his brothers, too, didn't it? And there was no better time to start than now . . .

So . . .

"If you don't mind, that would be great. But I'm

doing this today. I know that might be too last minute—"

"Count us in."

Which was how, three hours later, a painting party got under way in Cora's bedroom and bathroom, with Dare, Haven, him, and his boys all working on different parts of the walls, ceiling, and trim. They'd pushed all the furniture to the center of the room, and the new bed was covered in bags of what Ben called *their loot* from Target.

Music playing from Dare's cell phone, the open windows welcoming in the fall afternoon breeze, and the sound of everyone's chatter and laughter made the house feel alive in a way it hadn't in so long, as if asking Cora to move in was rousing the old farmhouse from a long slumber.

Maybe it was waking Slider up, too.

When they were done, the men cleaned up the tape, plastic, and paint supplies, while Haven and Ben unpacked the Target bags and took a load of new bedding down to the washing machine.

"Hey, Sam," Dare said, "would you mind grabbing me a cold soda from the fridge?"

"No problem," Sam said.

"Wash your hands before you touch anything," Slider said.

"You mean, like this?" On a laugh, Sam lunged at him and managed to grasp the bottom of Slider's beard, leaving a swipe of blue in his wake.

"What the hell—heck—ya little monster," Slider

said with a disbelieving laugh. He pulled the kid into a playful headlock. It wasn't a hug. But it was one of the first times in Slider's recent memory that the two of them had touched.

Sam laughed. "Now will you finally get rid of that thing?"

"No way, I'm leaving it blue and scruffy and walking you into your classroom tomorrow morning," Slider said, grinning as Sam groaned and got away. And then he disappeared to get Dare's drink.

Leaving Slider alone with Dare, who was looking at him like he had three heads in addition to a blue beard.

"What?" Slider asked.

Dare shook his head, the expression on his face like he was debating, and then he held out a hand. "Welcome back, brother."

The words lodged an immediate knot in Slider's throat. Slider grasped his friend's hand, and it felt a whole lot like a lifeline. "I'm not sure if I'm all the way back yet. Or if I'll ever be."

Nodding, Dare didn't let go. "I get that. But you'll never get anywhere if you don't try. And the man I'm looking at is trying, and it's damn good to see."

Sam came flying back into the room. "Here you go."

"Thanks, buddy," Dare said, dropping Slider's hand and taking the can. And then their focus was back on home improvement, as if Dare hadn't just made two years of Slider's bullshit okay with a single handshake.

That night, the boys refused to go to bed until Cora's room was all put back together again. The blue walls were still drying, but that didn't keep them from rearranging the furniture, making up the bed, putting down the new area rug, and stacking fresh towels in the linen closet.

"Think Cora's gonna like it?" Slider asked, really hoping she would.

"Yeah," Sam said.

"Me too," Ben agreed. "Today was fun, Dad. I liked painting and having Dare and Haven visit."

Slider had, too. And that surprised him, this apparently new ability to pull his head out of his ass. "It was fun, wasn't it?"

Both boys nodded.

"I think . . . I think we're going to try to have more fun around here. What do you say?"

"Yeah!" Ben said with a jump that proved his cast held him back not at all.

Sam was more reserved, giving a *whatever* nod and shrug that Slider didn't buy at all. He cared, he just didn't think he should show it. What was it going to take to get through to him? Slider wasn't sure, but today felt like a beginning.

And that was more than he thought he'd ever have again.

CORA HOPPED INTO Slider's pickup truck where it had waited outside the clubhouse for her a hundred times, but this time felt different. In less than a week, he wouldn't be picking her up here anymore because she'd be living with him.

"Hey," she said, unable to suppress her excitement.

Sitting behind the steering wheel, he turned toward her. "Hey."

Which was when Cora did a full-on, walk-into-a-sign, gobsmacked kind of double take. "Your beard. Your hair."

His face—which she could actually see—slid into a slow smile.

And, baby Jesus in the manger, Slider with a fresh haircut and a clean shave was not just handsome . . . he was panty-droppingly hot. Like, she was half tempted to reach down and make sure her panties were still on, despite the jeans she wore. His hair was shorter on the sides and longer on the top, long enough that she could tell he'd raked at it with his fingers, which totally made her fingers jealous. He had cheekbones for *days*, and a dimple. A freaking dimple. Just one. But that smile showed it off enough that she couldn't help but stare. "You have a dimple."

He chuffed out a laugh. "I know. I'd almost forgotten."

"Did you just laugh?" She reached for the handle. "I'm sorry, I think I'm in the wrong truck. I'm waiting for Slider . . ."

He rolled his eyes. "Giving me a hard time is *not* part of the job."

She couldn't help but laugh. "Have you met me before?"

Shaking his head, he put the truck in drive. But Cora couldn't stop staring.

"Look that bad?" he finally asked.

"No. No, not at all," she said, her face going hot at being called out. "It looks good. I didn't mean to stare, but I—"

"You never have to apologize for looking at me, Cora."

She blinked. Blinked again. What the hell was she supposed to say to that? *Well, good. Better get used to it, Slider. Because you're about a gabillion times hotter than I ever imagined. Can I lick you now?*

Oh, my God. It was everything Cora could do to not bury her face in her hands at how far south her thoughts had just turned. And she was about to move in with this man.

The man who was her boss, with the kids, with the broken heart.

"Um, what did the boys think?" she finally asked.

"Liked it," he said. "Said I looked younger. Apparently, they felt I'd gone *Duck Dynasty* on them."

Chuckling, she nodded, drinking in her fill of him again since he'd given her permission. His face in profile now was killer. Not just because of the high cheekbones, but because of his angular jaw, too. And the kids weren't wrong—getting rid of the beard had taken at least ten years off his face. Although maybe it was the smile that was doing that. Either way, something seemed different about Slider, and it wasn't just the makeover.

Back at the Evans house, Cora had barely walked into the living room before the boys each grabbed a hand and pulled her up the steps.

"What's going on?" she asked with a laugh.

But Slider just shook his head and followed them up, something close to a smile playing around his lips. Full lips. Lips that had a little scar on the bottom right that distracted her to the point of wanting to taste it.

God, what was wrong with her?

But she didn't have a chance to answer that, because just then, the boys tugged her to a closed door at the end of the hall and told her to open it.

Whatever it was, she'd never been in this room before, so she opened it like a clown might jump out at her.

Sam reached in and flicked on the light switch. And all Cora could do was gasp. The smell of fresh paint hung lightly on the air, which meant . . . they'd done this for her.

"Go in!" Ben said, giving her a little push.

Cora walked in like it was a museum. Quietly. Reverently. Not touching a thing. Her gaze went from the big bed, covered in a beautiful and fun blue and white comforter with a kind of bohemian medallion-and-floral design, to the lamps with their pretty crystal bases, to the soft-looking, cream-white area rug with a light blue design all through it. A bay window looked out onto the side yard and a cornfield beyond, and another window offered a view of the front yard, together making the room bright and cheerful.

"There's a bathroom over here, too," Ben said, skipping through the room and turning on the light inside.

"Really?" she asked, crossing to peer into the adjoining room. Larger than the hall bathroom the three of them shared, it had a separate shower and tub, a big linen closet, and double sinks. "This is all for me?"

She turned to find all three Evans men nodding, and each looking prouder than the last.

Slider gave a nervous shrug as he glanced around the space. And, man, all his raw masculinity was ten times more potent when you could see his handsomely rugged face. "If you don't like the color, or anything, we can—"

"I love it. I just can't believe you did all this. It's beautiful. It's the most beautiful bedroom I've ever had," she said, blinking away threatening tears. It was just that no one had ever done something like this for her before. She'd left their house midmorning yesterday, which meant they'd spent all day yesterday creating a place for her, just like Slider said he would. It really touched her.

Ben scrambled awkwardly up onto the bed. "You

gotta try the mattress. It's new." He bounced as much as he could with one arm in a cast.

"New?" she said, sliding up next to Ben. "I'm going to have to pay you all back for—"

"No way," Slider said. "This is the least we can do. You're our guest, and we want you to be happy here."

He nailed her with a stare that stole her breath. Because she believed him, and it made her feel hopeful and valued. Cared for. Wanted, for the first time in so very long. Maybe ever.

"Well . . ." She flopped back onto the bed, and a giggling Ben flopped back next to her. "I think I'm going to be so happy here you guys just might never be able to get rid of me."

CHAPTER 9

We brought a bottle of champagne, strawberries, and dipping chocolate," Haven said when she and Cora walked through the front door of Maverick and Alexa's house, "because we have things to celebrate." Maverick was gone on the same club business Dare was, so Alexa had proposed a girls' night in on Tuesday since Cora didn't have to babysit. They'd readily agreed.

"That sounds fantastic," Alexa said, welcoming them into the lakeside cottage out on the edge of the Raven Riders' property. Not many of them lived on club lands, but this house had once been Bunny's, the founder's sister, and now belonged to Maverick. "I also made a seven-layer dip, salsa, and a big pot of chili. So I hope you're hungry."

When they'd served everything up, they settled around the table in front of a window that looked out at the lake. From the cat climber a few feet away, Alexa's sweater-wearing Sphinx cat Lucy watched them.

"Okay, what are we toasting first?" Cora asked. "Definitely Alexa's engagement." That got the first enthusiastic round of toasts. The bubbles in the champagne tickled Cora's nose.

"Are you setting a date?" Haven asked as she scooped some dip.

Alexa shook her head. "Not yet. But maybe next spring. I'm holding out hope that my mom could still get better, and I'd like all the stuff with Grant to be entirely behind us." She shuddered a little when she mentioned her ex's name.

"How about a toast to the fact that the people who hurt us will never be able to do it again," Haven said, raising her glass.

"Hell, yes," Alexa said. They all clinked glasses, and Cora joined in the toast, even though she felt a little guilty that they didn't know all the ways she'd been hurt. No one did.

"You okay, Cora?" Haven asked.

"Oh, yeah. Sorry. Just daydreaming." She forced a smile. "I understand I have you to thank for my pretty new blue bedroom."

"No, no," Haven said. "That was all Slider. I just helped with a few ideas. Seriously, it was so cute, Cora. He really wanted everything perfect for you."

Cora couldn't quite bite back her grin. "He and the boys are being really sweet about it. And with what he's paying me, I might be able to join you in a class in the spring."

Eyes wide, Haven gasped. "Really? That would be great. I think that's toast-worthy, too."

Cora didn't disagree, so they raised their glasses one more time.

"We better keep eating with all these toasts," Alexa said.

Laughing, Haven nodded. "Especially because I kinda got a job today."

Pandemonium erupted around the little table.

"It's just part-time. But, do you remember Dutch, the man who owns that little diner downtown? Well, I sent him a basket of my baked goods after his hip replacement surgery, and he liked them so much he wants to hire me to do all his pastries, cakes, and cookies for the shop. Apparently, he wants to try opening for longer hours, so he needs the extra help."

"Haven, you got a job as a baker. A real, honest-to-goodness baker," Cora said, just beside herself for her friend.

"I did," Haven said. "Can you believe it?"

"Yes," Cora said, just as Alexa said, "Absolutely! When do you start?"

"Soon, but we're still figuring it out," Haven said. "We're going to go over his current menu, and then I'm going to suggest a new one and he'll order all the supplies and inventory in time for my first shift."

"Wow, this is so awesome. What did Dare say?" Cora asked.

Haven's smile was immediate. "That he wanted to be my very first paying customer."

It was all news that necessitated another round of toasts.

"Look how far we've come," Alexa said. "We should be proud of ourselves."

Cora laughed, but it was true. They'd all walked through their own paths of fire, and come out the other side. Maybe not unscathed. Maybe with some scars. But they'd made it through. And that counted for something. No, it counted for a *lot*.

And it made her feel bad for not coming clean with them about everything she'd been through, when they'd been so open about everything that'd happened to them. But tonight was about triumphs, not trials.

At least, that was how Cora justified it to herself.

Between dinner and the movie that followed, they ended up polishing off the bottle of champagne, and a bottle of wine besides, so they decided a sleepover was in order.

Except Cora didn't anticipate Alexa suggesting that they all sleep on the couches in the living room together, the three of them and Alexa's weird little cat, too. And that put Cora in the position of having to ask something she'd rather not. "If we're going to sleep out here, can we leave a light on? I always have to get up to pee and I don't want to wake you guys up stumbling around."

"No problem," Alexa said. "I'll grab us blankets and pillows."

"I thought you hated sleeping with the lights on," Haven said, laughing. *Of course* she would remember that, given how many sleepovers they'd had growing up.

"Yeah, well, I guess it doesn't bother me as much as it used to." Not after months of getting used to it, it didn't. And, usually, it helped keep the nightmares away, because her dad had come after her in the dark. First, where she'd fallen asleep on the living room couch, and then where he'd chased her into her dark bedroom.

Problem was, Cora was so nervous that she'd have a nightmare in front of Haven and Alexa that she never fell asleep. She'd had this problem before, back when she and Haven were on the run, but then she'd brushed off her sleeplessness as keeping a lookout and being cautious.

When morning came, she was absolutely wrecked.

"Did you sleep at all?" Haven asked.

"A little," Cora hedged. "Just insomnia, I guess."

"Probably all the excitement of moving," Alexa said.

"Yeah, probably," Cora said.

That poor night of sleep no doubt explained why she fell so dead asleep when they got back to the clubhouse—and was still sleeping when Slider arrived to pick her up on Wednesday afternoon.

A knock at her door jolted her awake. "Yeah?" she called, still half asleep.

Slider stepped in, his expression immediately transforming into a frown. "Are you okay?"

"Oh, God, what time is it?" she said, shifting out of bed.

He caught her by the arm, and sank down on the bed next to her. "Seriously, it's okay. There's time."

She dropped her face into her hands. "I'm sorry," she said. "I slept terrible last night, so I laid down for a nap, but I didn't mean to sleep so long."

"If you're not up for working tonight, I'll figure something else out," he said, concern etched onto his face. He wore a thin layer of scruff on his jaw, and somehow it was even sexier than the clean shave had been.

"No, I'm sorry, I'll be fine."

But by the next day, it was clear, she wasn't fine. She was getting sick. But she refused to give in to it, not when Dare and Maverick had returned from their relocation, which meant they could both move a day earlier than planned. This was supposed to be a good day for her. So she pushed on, popped some ibuprofen, packed up all her meager belongings, and arrived at Slider's via her final clubhouse pickup.

"Welcome home," he said, smiling at her across

the bench seat of his pickup. And oh man, there was that dimple.

"Thank you," she said. Good thing she was tired, or she'd have a hard time restraining herself from climbing over there and straddling Slider so she could examine that little mark of softness a little closer. "That sounds really nice."

But later that night as Cora helped Ben take a bath without soaking his cast, she was shivering with fever. "You don't look so good, Cora," Ben said, his face too like his father's with concern shaping his little features.

"I'm okay, Ben."

But apparently not. Because when she rose to help Ben climb out of the tub, she must've gotten up way too fast. The whole world went topsy-turvy.

Cora fell, just catching herself against the toilet, before going down to the floor again.

"Cora!" Ben yelled, scrambling out after her. "Sam, it's Cora!"

Dazed, Cora blinked and tried to right herself, but she couldn't seem to make herself move.

The door burst open, and Sam was there above her. "What happened?"

"I don't know," Ben said. "I think she's sick. Look how red her face is."

Crouching over her, Sam put his hand to her head. "Jesus."

"That's a bad word," Ben said, his voice wobbly.

Sam rose, opened the medicine cabinet, and returned to her again.

"I'm okay," she said, her teeth chattering. Why was she so cold? "Just help me up."

"Did you hit your head?" Sam asked. "I took a first aid class in school, and I think you're supposed to ask that when someone falls."

"No," she managed. The boys helped her sit up until her back was against the tub.

"I think you should take this," Sam said, holding out a thermometer.

"I'm supposed to be taking care of you," she said, but she did as he directed.

Kneeling in front of her, both boys watched her like she might fall again at any second. When the thermometer beeped, they both leaned in.

Ugh. 103.7. Not good.

"That's bad, isn't it?" Ben asked.

"That's real bad," Sam said, brow cranked down. "Should we call an ambulance, Cora?"

"No," she said. She didn't have insurance, so no way did she want to go that route. "Let's just try to get it down."

So while she gave orders, the boys fetched her what she asked for—ibuprofen, a couple of wet, cold washcloths, her cell phone. Just in case.

But she was kind of stuck on the bathroom floor, because every time she tried to get up, the world spun on her again. "I'm just gonna rest here," she said, curling over on the little rug in front of the tub.

"Okay, Cora. I'll be right back," Sam said, adjusting the cold cloth on her forehead again. "Stay here, Ben."

She wanted to reassure them, to take away their worries, but them talking over her was the last thing she knew.

"DAD, CORA'S SICK. Real sick."

Sam's panicked voice echoed in Slider's ears the whole way home. He didn't care that he was midshift. Or that he hadn't been able to find a replacement. He'd bailed and gone immediately home.

Because Cora and his boys needed him.

"Sam?" he called the minute he walked in the door.

"Up here, Dad."

Damnit, he hated the fear he heard in the kid's voice, and as he skidded into the hall bathroom, he saw why.

Cora lay in a ball on the bathroom floor, face splotchy red, body shivering.

"She has a real bad fever, Dad," Ben said, his eyes wide, his little forehead furrowed.

Slider's gut went on a Tilt-A-Whirl. He'd been here before. Taking care of someone he lo—well, someone he cared about. "Let me in there, guys." He crouched beside her. "Cora, can you hear me?"

Her eyes eked open. "Aw, no. You're home. I'm sorry."

Slider put his hand on her forehead. "Jesus." He grabbed the thermometer. "Can you take this for me?"

She managed something like a smile. "You remind me of Sam."

103.2.

"It's gone down a little," Sam said.

"But not enough. Sam, turn on the tub. Make the water cool, but not cold." It was a good plan with one major problem: getting her jeans off, because they'd be hell to remove once they were wet. "Okay, boys, why don't you give Cora a little privacy here, because I'm going to put her in the tub and let the cool water help her." Neither wanted to go, that much was clear. Slider grabbed each of their hands. "Hey, she's gonna be fine. It's just a fever." He hoped.

When the door closed behind them, Slider brushed Cora's hair back from her face. "I'm going to sit you up on the toilet and take off your jeans, okay?"

"Okay," she whispered. "Sweet talker."

Why did he suspect that her humor here was more for his benefit than an attempt to play down the situation? Sliding his arms under her shoulders and knees, he lifted her up to the toilet seat, where he undid the button and zipper on her pants. "Now put your arms around my neck. I'm going to stand you up and push your jeans down."

With eyebrows raised, she gave a smile that looked like she really wanted to offer some more smart-ass commentary, but she was too sick to do it. And damn, that slayed him, it really did. "Okay, then."

"Here we go," he said, supporting her back with one hand as he worked the denim down over her hips. He returned her to the toilet seat and tugged the jeans the rest of the way off.

"Shirt, too?" she asked.

"Yeah, probably," he said, gently pulling it over her head until she sat there in a white bra and a pair of white silk panties. He tried to keep his focus all on the business of helping her, he really did. He felt the water. "Okay, I think this is ready." And, man, as hot as she was, it was going to suck for her. Lifting her once more, he stepped to the tub, but it was almost hard to let her go when she laid her head against his chest.

She hit the water with a shriek, eyes wide, hands flailing. "It's freezing."

"I know. You don't have to stay in long."

"Slider," she whined.

"Ssh, I know. Scoot down as much as you can."

She did as he asked, peering up at him with bloodshot eyes as the water crested her shoulders. He found one of the washcloths she'd been using and soaked it again before bringing it to her face. Rinse and wipe, rinse and wipe, until he had her hair mostly wet. She hugged herself so tight and held herself so rigidly that the bones of her clavicle protruded.

"Just a few more minutes," he reassured her.

"You know," she said, licking the water off her lips. "I suspected a really hot guy hid under all that facial hair, but I never expected just how sweet a man hid under all the gruffness."

The comment hit him about a dozen different ways.

Pleasure. Surprise. Embarrassment. More. Plus, she thought he was hot?

No, no. He was *not* starting down that train of thought while she lay there mostly naked and sick. "I think the fever is going to your head."

"No, just using the cover of the fever to say something I might not otherwise. Guess I blew that cover, though, huh?"

He managed a chuckle, because this playfulness was evidence that she was doing a little better. "Let's see where your fever is," he said, handing her the thermometer again.

102.1.

Better. Improved enough that relief flooded through him. "I'd be happier if we got this down into the 101 range before getting you out," he said. "Think you can make it?"

Teeth clattering, she nodded. "Yeah, I can feel it working. Thank you. I'm sorry you had to come home."

"I'm not," he said. And he wasn't. Admittedly, it raised some memories he'd rather not revisit to be taking care of another woman in this house, but that was where the similarities with Kim ended. Cora wasn't terminally ill. She didn't have cancer. And she was a cooperative patient, which Kim had never been. Maybe that was because Kim knew, as he did, that if she hadn't gotten sick, she'd have still been with the other guy, whoever he was. And she knew, too, that that other guy hadn't stuck around when she'd told him about her cancer. But Slider had.

Because that was what family should do, even when that family had fucked things up. Big time.

Still, he sometimes wondered whether the other man or he was the bigger asshole. Because that douchebag had abandoned her when she was ill, but Slider had taken care of her knowing she wanted to leave him. Sonofabitch.

"Slider, I can't take it anymore," Cora said.

He reached in and pulled the plug, and then he turned and grabbed a towel. "You did good, Cora. Real good."

This time, the thermometer read 101.5.

"I think I can stand," she said.

"Let me help at least." He offered his hands, and together, they pulled her to her feet.

"If you'll hold up the towel, I'll slip out of these wet things."

He gave a nod, looking away as he held up the towel to give her some semblance of privacy. Wet clothing slapped against the tub, once, twice. And he tried like hell *not* to think about the fact that she was utterly, totally naked two feet away from him. An arm's reach away. Because he was finding it damn hard not to want to take her into his arms.

She wrapped the towel around herself.

And then she listed to the side.

Slider caught her in his arms after all, and then he lifted her into a carry against his chest. "I'm putting you in my bed tonight so I can keep an eye on you."

"Okay," she said.

After that, he put her in one of his shirts and a pair of his boxers and tried like hell not to like the look of her in his clothes as much as he did. And then his bed became the center of activity for the rest of the night. Ben brought Cora drinks and Popsicles on a tray, and she invited them to stay and play a game of cards to keep her company. And Slider had the weirdest, most unexpected thought.

Family.

They felt like a family.

He liked Cora. He did. Obviously, he couldn't deny that anymore.

But he should *not* be thinking of her as family.

She was his employee, an employee who now lived in his house. That was boundary-pushing enough. And he was still a man with significant faith, trust, and abandonment issues when it came to relationships with anyone but his kids. And, Jesus, his kids loved Cora far too much for Slider to risk doing anything that might mess up their relationship with her.

So he and Cora could be friends, sure.

But family, that was something he was better off defining by those who shared his blood.

Maybe that was no guarantee, either. Because his parents sure as shit hadn't done right by him. But Slider knew how he felt about his boys—and always would. So blood ties were the best chance he had to create something true, real, and lasting.

Just once.

CHAPTER 10

By the time the boys were in bed, Cora was slipping in and out of consciousness. She seemed so tired that she couldn't keep her eyes open and when she spoke, it came out in a slur. But her temperature was down to 100.9 as of the last time they'd taken it, so at least they had this thing moving in the right direction.

Which meant he could get ready to hit the hay, too, especially since he'd finally found someone to cover the rest of his shift. Usually, Slider slept naked, but tonight he pulled on an undershirt and a pair of sweatpants.

"Leave a light on, please?" she mumbled against her pillow.

"Yeah. Okay," he said. "Need anything else?"

She didn't answer, which left Slider standing at the edge of his bed and debating. Sleeping with her seemed all kinds of problematic, given how much she got to him. And she did, he had to admit that much. But he didn't think she should be alone. Maybe he should just sleep on the floor . . .

"You getting in?" she asked, trying to peer over her shoulder but not quite strong enough to do it.

He sighed. It was fine. They'd slept in the same bed together before. They could do it again. He crawled into the empty side.

Cora made a little whining sound that immediately had him propping himself up on an elbow. "No, not behind me. Can't take you behind me." She dragged herself to turn over, finally coming to lie on her side facing him.

"What?" he said, his gut churning at her words. He hadn't given her request to leave the lights on a second thought. But hell if it didn't look different with her saying she couldn't tolerate him at her back. And, oh, Jesus, the way she'd freaked out that night in the family room . . .

"That's better," she whispered.

"I'm worried about you, Cora," he said, not meaning just the fever she'd come down with tonight. That was only his most immediate concern. "I think we have to take you to urgent care if you're not better in the morning."

"Just need to sleep . . ."

And then she was out. But Slider was wide awake, again, worrying about Cora Campbell. And wondering exactly what she'd been through before she'd arrived in Maryland. Whatever it was, Slider's gut told him it wasn't good.

A suspicion that escalated the protectiveness he already felt toward her by a factor of about a thousand. At least.

At some point, he finally dropped off to sleep, and eventually he found himself in the middle of the most fucking amazing dream. Cora, sliding into his bed in the middle of the night. Climbing on top of him, covering him with her feminine curves. Grinding against him and making him moan.

Coming with his name on her lips.

"Slider," she moaned.

His eyes blinked open, and he found his dream coming true. Except then his brain came back online enough for him to realize that he was a goddamn pervert and Cora was pressing up against him not in an effort to seduce him, but to try to get warm. She shivered against him. Her fever had spiked again.

"Wake up, Cora," he said, reaching for the medicine he'd left on the nightstand. "I need you to take some more of this to bring the fever down."

"Cold," she whispered, bleary, green eyes blazing.

"I know." He dropped two pills onto her tongue. "Drink."

"Sorry I woke you. Didn't realize . . ." She pushed herself away.

Slider hauled her right back against him. "Whatever you need, sweetheart, okay? Just want you to feel better."

She was back to sleep in an instant. And, oddly, so was he.

And that was the way they woke up. Right away, Slider knew something was off. The house felt oddly empty, but the light coming through his blinds made it feel late. He turned to the nightstand and found a note propped up against the lamp in his ten-year-old's hand.

You guys were out cold so I got us ready for school. No worries.

—Sam

Damn. Aw, *damn*. At some point, Sam, and maybe Ben too, had come in here . . . and found Slider and Cora totally entwined. As they still were.

Cora lay with her head on Slider's shoulder, her arm across his chest, her thigh across his. And his arm was around her shoulders, holding her to him, his face pressed to her forehead. Sure, the blankets had covered most of that, but no doubt his kids had seen enough to raise an eyebrow of curiosity.

But at least Cora's fever didn't seem as bad this morning. No more than a hundred, if Slider had to guess. But he wasn't waking her up to find out, and holding her like this wasn't something he was going to be able to do again. So he let himself enjoy the feel of her while he could, relaxed against the pillow again, and drifted off with her in his arms.

CORA DIDN'T WANT to wake up. She was warm and comfortable, and that seemed miraculous after being freezing and achy all night long. But finally, her eyelids blinked open against her will, and then she *really* didn't want to move.

Because she was lying on Slider, touching him from face to toes, in his bed. And he was holding her, too.

In that moment, Cora wished more than anything that they were like this because they were together, rather than just because he'd taken pity on her for being sick. She'd always had some fondness for Slider, even in his most withdrawn version, but the past couple weeks, she'd felt like she was finally getting to know him. She'd seen more of his sweetness toward his sons. She'd witnessed his vulnerable side when Ben got hurt and when he'd admitted he needed her help. And she'd certainly found him to be thoughtful in preparing such a wonderful welcome for her coming to live at his house.

He'd given her a few glimpses of his sense of humor—and proved he could sling some highly effective sarcasm. She still couldn't decide whether to chuckle or groan at his calling her out for using humor as a defense mechanism. It had been as annoyingly observant as it had been accurate. And she kinda wanted to get T-shirts made that read *Talkative Slider* and *Humor as a Diversionary Tactic Cora*. Or maybe dolls. Perhaps she'd add to the line, *Tall, Dark, and Scary Dare*; *Can Do Anything To and On a Bike Maverick*; and *Cute but Seriously Annoying Phoenix*. She could make a million. Annnd this train of thought proved she still probably had a fever . . .

Cora sighed. If all that wasn't enough, that wasn't even taking into consideration the way Slider had taken care of her last night. Or the way he was holding her now.

And that was when she realized she liked Slider Evans. *Liked* liked him. And she had no idea what the hell she was going to do about that.

"Hey, Cora," he said, his gravelly morning voice so damn sexy.

"Hey," she said, tilting her head back to look him in the eye. She wondered if she should get off him, but didn't really want to.

Not making any move to get up, Slider just looked down at her. "How you feeling?"

"A lot better," she said, hyperaware that her hand was lying on his chest. His heartbeat faintly registered against her palm. "Still achy and a little off, but better."

"Good. You should probably take it easy today,

though. Whatever that was isn't likely out of your system yet."

She nodded. "I will."

Talking like this, their faces so close, felt so damn intimate that Cora could almost imagine that nothing existed outside of Slider's bed. She almost didn't want it to. Especially when his arm squeezed a little tighter around her shoulders and brought them just a little closer. Cora shifted into his embrace, pressing her chest totally flush against his side, and sliding her thigh up until—

Oh, hell. Until she felt the part of him she'd accidentally seen. And it was hard.

He sucked in a breath, and his hand clamped around her thigh. "Shit, I'm sorry. I didn't mean—"

She placed her fingers loosely over his mouth. She didn't want him to apologize. Or explain it away. Or push her away.

Cora knew she shouldn't want the things she did, but that didn't make her desires go away. It felt *good* to want Slider, it made her feel normal, even if she was a little nervous. After what her father had done, that seemed like a victory she didn't want to relinquish.

And, oh, now that she was touching his face, she really didn't want to stop. His lips were full and soft under her fingers, his stubble was more ticklish than prickly, and his cheekbones were prominent under his skin.

He licked his lips, and her gaze latched on to the movement.

"Cora," he rasped, his cock getting even harder against her thigh.

His arousal fueled her own, her hips tilting with the need for friction. The movement had her grinding herself against the firm muscle of his thigh and made both of them suck in a breath. His grip tightened on her everywhere. His arm holding her tighter yet to him, his hand pulling her thigh wider across him.

Her fingers returned to his mouth again, and traced across his lower lip. His tongue flicked out and swiped at her pointer finger, and Cora was instantly wet, her body slowly but surely forgetting her aches. Trembling with need and adrenaline and the fear that at any second, he would cut this off, Cora shifted ever so slowly, ever so slightly, bringing her face closer to his. He watched her like she was a tigress about to strike, but just as her mouth almost reached his, he flipped them and pinned her to the bed.

And Cora realized she had it all wrong. He'd been the feral animal about to attack all along.

"I wasn't going to do this, Cora. I wasn't going to start this between us. I know that's not why you're here," he said, his voice full of grit.

"I wasn't going to start it, either," she said, her heart pounding in her chest—from his closeness, from the way he was holding her, from what might be happening, and from the honesty she was about to let loose from her lips, "but I can't help that I want it. Want you."

"Jesus." He was almost shaking with restraint. "I'm worried about you not feeling good," he said.

"With you looking at me like that, I feel better than I've felt in a really long time."

"Cora—"

"Slider, just this once," she whispered, desperate for his touch, desperate for a connection, desperate for *him*.

It was as if her words snapped something inside him, because suddenly he was kissing her like she was the water and he was a man who'd been lost in the desert. For a fragment of a second, she worried about her breath, but he didn't give her time to think on it, because his hands clutched her hair, his tongue plundered her mouth, and his body settled atop hers with the most delicious weight and friction. Cora moaned and sucked hard on his tongue as she wrapped her legs around his lean hips and grasped at his shoulders, his back, his ass.

"Christ, sweetheart," he said, coming up for air, but not for long, because his mouth was at her jaw, her ear, her throat, and moving south. And, *oh, God*, that term of endearment had her holding him to her, holding him tight. Her shirt went, then his, and then he was at her hips with his mouth and his hands, his fingers playing with the band to his boxers that she'd slept in.

"This can be enough. Just getting to kiss you is a fucking privilege."

But Cora wanted more, especially when he said things like that. Because it felt good to be able to choose this. Because she wanted this man. And because she feared once they got out of this bed, their senses might return, and she might not get another chance to have him. "I want you Slider. I want all of you."

"You're sure?"

The care he was taking to be certain she really wanted this made the decision easy. "Yes, Slider. So sure."

He removed the cotton shorts, a groan ripping out of him at remembering she wore no underwear beneath. Sitting back on his knees, he stared down at her like a starving man at a buffet deciding where to start first. He didn't take long.

Slider parted her thighs, pushed her up the bed, and settled himself in between. He peered up her body with those pale green eyes, like ice on fire, and watched her as he put his open mouth flush against her pussy. He licked and sucked mercilessly, until the room was filled with the wet sounds of his mouth and the gasping moans from hers.

Only one other man had ever done this to Cora, and that might as well have never happened, because it so paled in comparison to what Slider was doing to her that she nearly lost her mind. She slapped her hands down against the bed and clawed at the sheets, trying to gain some purchase against the storm he was unleashing inside her body. Then Slider's hands slid under her thighs and held her wrists down.

A ribbon of fear curled through her belly, but his actions refused to let her concentrate on it. She wasn't sure if it was the restraint or the possessiveness or the shift in angle, but she was immediately right at the edge, until she was thrusting into his mouth and rocking her head against the bed. Everything inside her strained and strained until finally she was coming, shattering, screaming into the stillness of Slider's room, her whole body jerking in a series of spasms that just wouldn't stop. And she never wanted them to.

Slider reared back off the bed, grabbed a condom from a new box in the nightstand drawer, and shed his sweatpants. Another whole-body shudder wracked through Cora's body. Because if she'd thought Slider was impressive when he wasn't hard, he was freaking stunning when he was. She'd had sex with four guys in her life, so she was by no means an expert, but without question, Slider's cock was the longest she'd ever seen. Eight inches, easy. Maybe more, because it appeared big enough that she bet she could easily wrap both hands around his length, one stacked atop the other.

"You look at me like that and I don't want to go slow," he said, his voice low, his eyebrow arched.

"Then don't go slow," she said, watching him roll on a condom.

A niggle of unease rolled through her. Because this was really happening. She was really going to have sex with Slider. And the last time . . . wasn't sex.

But this also wasn't the last time. Cora forced herself to latch on to everything that was different. The lights were on. It was morning, not night. She was on her back, not facedown. And most importantly, she'd chosen this man and this moment.

"I want this," she said for herself and for him. "Just like this." Her thighs fell open.

He braced himself above her, his eyes searching hers. And then he kissed her, took himself in hand, and found her center. His cock sank deep inch by sanity-stealing inch.

"Fuck, Cora. You feel so damn good."

Her fingers clutched at his ass, but all she could do was moan in response. At the fullness, at the goodness, at the sensation of triumph she felt for being able to even do this.

"God*damnit*," he bit out as he buried himself deep. Gripping the edge of the bed with one hand, he curled his other into her hair as he began to move.

And, holy wow, the way he moved. Fast and frantic, with his hips tipping forward on each downward thrust in the most infuriatingly delicious way. The movement ground against her clit every time, until she was meeting him stroke for stroke, fucking him even as he was fucking her.

His forehead fell against hers, and his eyes absolutely blazed as he took her. And Cora didn't want this to end. She *never* wanted it to end. That look. This feeling. This stolen moment.

"Too good," he rasped.

She nodded. "So good you're already making me want more, Slider."

"Yeah," he said, hammering her harder. "Tell me."

A strangled cry spilled out of her, because he was moving faster now, harder, chasing the end. "I want to ride you. And I want you to pin me up against a wall. And I want—"

"Christ, the mouth you have on you," he said, claiming it in a rough, demanding kiss. Finally, he pulled away. "Know what I want?"

"What?"

"I want you to come again. I want to feel it while I'm buried in you. I want you to give me that, Cora." He fell atop her, his arms clutching her tight, and fucked her in a series of fast, grinding strokes that hit her clit every time.

She hadn't thought she would get there again, but suddenly she was close, closer. "Don't stop," she gasped, curling her arms around his neck and holding on. She closed her eyes and arched her spine and used her feet on the backs of his thighs for leverage, and then she was coming and shaking and shouting, and so was Slider.

"Cora," he groaned, his hips slowing but still moving, his cock jerking inside her, his breath rasping in her ear. Still, he fucked her in long, lazy strokes as he lifted his head to look at her. Satisfaction made his eyes softer than she'd ever seen them before, but there was still interest there, too. "Jesus, Cora, I'm still hard."

A moment of uncertainty rolled through her. To cut this off with the incredible sex they'd already shared, or to push for more? More won out, because who knew if this was a line they'd ever cross again after today? "That's because we're not done."

"WE'RE NOT?" SLIDER asked, his head, heart, and cock at war.

He knew what he wanted, because nothing had made him feel this good in a long, long time. But he posed it as a question anyway because he didn't want to be taking advantage any more than he was. Things were way muddied now. What was right here? And if this was wrong, why did it feel so right? But while he was still inside her, only one part of him could emerge as the winner, even if it was probably the wrong damn part.

"You wanna ride me, Cora? That what you want?" He imagined it, imagined what she'd look like taking him inside her body, holding him down, using him in a way that made them both feel so good. And, God, he wanted what he imagined, though he fucking shouldn't. Not if he was smart.

"Yes," she said, biting her lip.

Aw, that fucking lip bite. He felt it in his cock. And

he surrendered to what he wanted—just one more memory with her, like this. Because after today, memories were all he was going to let himself have.

For both of their sakes.

Withdrawing, Slider turned on his back and hauled her on top of him, and then he kissed her until neither of them could breathe but didn't care. "Get another condom, and then I want you to show me just what you've been thinking about."

A series of fast movements had her quickly straddling him, centering herself over him, and sinking down tight. She braced herself against his chest and lifted and lowered herself, her gaze going to where they were connected.

He couldn't help but look too, because *fuck*, they looked so good together, with his cock disappearing inside her little body. "I find everything about you so damn beautiful," he said, letting words fly that maybe he should've held back. Cora's gaze snapped to his, the soft surprise on her face endearing and honest and vulnerable. Her guileless pleasure made him glad for giving voice to how he felt. His whole life had been about holding back for too long, and he just didn't want to do it anymore. Not in that moment. Not while they were so bared to each other. Not while they were so deep into each other.

And not when he hadn't been with a woman who looked at him that way in so damn long. Maybe even his whole life.

"Slider," she moaned, "you're so good."

The words hit him in ways that were both healing and uncomfortable as fuck, so he turned them, twisted them, made them about the sex. "Use me to feel good, Cora. That's what I want." He clutched at her hips, lifting her, moving her faster, grinding her down again. She leaned back and braced against his thighs, her hips shifting forward, her breasts and the soft waves of her hair swaying, her mouth dropping open. She rocked her hips forward and back, and Slider helped her move even as her strokes had him groaning and straining to go deeper.

He palmed her lower belly and rubbed her clit with his thumb.

Cora nearly screamed at the contact, and it only made Slider want to torment her more. She clutched at his wrist, not pulling him away, but holding his hand there, and then she rode him until she was coming again. Shaking and cursing. Her wetness spilling out over his groin, his balls.

"Now it's my fucking turn," he said, banding her upper body down against his. Drawing his knees up, he braced his heels against the mattress, and then he let his hips fly in a fast rhythm that had him drilling up into her. Their skin smacked and their breaths sawed and their fingers dug into one another. And it was the best that Slider had felt in years. Jesus, maybe even in more years than he wanted to admit, more than he'd ever let himself think about before.

"God, I want to feel you come again," she breathed against his ear. "Want to know I made you come."

It was her words that did it. One, two, three strokes more and his orgasm nailed him in the back of the spine and had him hammering her with a series of punctuated thrusts as her pussy squeezed him dry.

He couldn't breathe, couldn't move, couldn't think about why this should never happen again when his instincts screamed to know when it would be happening next.

Finally, their bodies calmed and stilled, and Slider was forced to withdraw from her whether he wanted to or not. And then they lay together for a long time, Cora again positioned in the nook along the side of his body, both of them occasionally drifting off to sleep, and neither of them talking because they both knew what they had to say.

It didn't surprise him that, when one of them finally spoke, it was Cora. She was brave and honest like that, and she'd never struck him as someone to play games. "So, earlier," she whispered. "I said, 'Just this once.'"

"Yeah," Slider said, regret slinking around in his gut.

"I'm open to not being held to that," she said, that same regret slinking around in her voice, "but I also understand if you feel like we need to."

Slider sighed and tipped her jaw so that they were looking eye to eye. "I don't regret this Cora, not one fucking bit. But I'm your boss. I don't want you to feel taken advantage of. I wasn't lying when I told you I'm kind of a wreck, and I also don't want to confuse the boys." The boys, who had already seen them in bed together. So Slider was already screwing that one up.

"Yeah," she said. "I know. And I'm still trying to figure my life out, so . . ."

So. Fuck.

"So then, this can't happen again," he said, knowing the words coming out of his mouth were the right call, but hating them all the same.

CHAPTER 11

"Slider, would you be willing to help me buy a car?" Cora asked after the boys left for school on Wednesday morning. She'd recovered from her illness, started to set up her routine as the Evanses' nanny, and accomplished all the legwork she could online and by phone about getting a car, volunteering at the animal shelter, and applying for spring enrollment at the community college. Now all she needed was the wheels.

He turned from the bowl of cereal he was pouring for himself, which in and of itself was an interesting development. Because making pancakes was some sort of big family tradition, he often ate a few with the boys on Sunday mornings. But when was the last time she'd seen him eat breakfast during the week? "Uh, what did you have in mind?"

"I know it's a lot to ask, but I've never bought my own car before, and you know a lot about them. So I was hoping you might have time to come along, ask all the right questions, and help me negotiate a good deal."

Leaning against the counter, he crossed his arms. "Actually, I've been thinking about this. And I have an alternate idea." As he spoke, she tried not to notice how crossing his arms made the muscles of his biceps pop out, or just how sexy his old worn jeans were hanging on his lean hips. But after she'd clutched at those muscles and felt those hips between her legs, it was incredibly difficult *not* to notice such things.

Or want them again . . .

"Which is?"

"Well, a lot of people who employ nannies apparently provide vehicles. So I was thinking maybe you could have my truck to use."

She frowned. "What about you?"

He ducked his chin, his gaze dropping to the floor between them. And then he gave a little shrug. "I have my bike."

It was only because he wasn't looking at her that she didn't rein in the surprise that must've hit her expression. Because Slider had never once ridden his motorcycle the whole time she'd known him. Not even in the procession at the funeral of the prospect who'd died a few months back during an attack on the clubhouse. Hell, he didn't even wear his Ravens' cutoff jacket like all the other brothers did. And Cora had heard more than a little commentary around the clubhouse that Slider hadn't ridden or participated much in club business in years. It was like when Kim died, she'd somehow taken all the other parts of Slider's life with her. All except the boys.

"Your bike," she managed.

Another little shrug. "Yeah. I mean, I'm sure it needs a tune-up, but I've been thinking . . ."

She held her breath and prayed for him to finish that thought, because she really wanted to know what was going on in this man's head. But he offered no more.

"Anyway, you could have the truck and then you wouldn't need to put out money on a car." He lifted that pale gaze to her again.

For a moment, Cora wasn't sure what to say. On the one hand, she really wanted him to get back into riding again. Because it was something for *him*. And it was something that would pull him back into the club he'd once loved. And Slider couldn't go on forever isolating himself from everything about which he used to care.

On the other hand . . . "That's really generous, Slider. And I'm definitely tempted. The thing is, as much as I'd love to save the money, I'm also eager to do this for myself. To feel like I've achieved a major life event. Not that buying a car is that major, I guess, it's just—"

"No, I get it. And it is. It's something to be proud of. So, sure, yeah, count me in. I'd be happy to help."

Cora could've squealed, but instead she just grinned like an idiot.

He arched a brow. "And when did you want to do this?"

"Today?" she squeaked, knowing he had the day and night off. "Or, you know, not today . . ."

He stared at her, and finally shook his head. "You're as bad as Ben. Both of you make it impossible to say no."

A fleeting wisecrack jumped to the tip of her tongue about how he'd been able to say no to more sex, but she was too excited about possibly buying a car today to give it voice. Besides, she'd agreed to the *no more sex* rule, too, hadn't she? "Is that a yes to today?"

Four hours later, they were browsing their second car lot. Slider had talked her out of one car for being expensive to repair and convinced her that another wasn't a good value given its mileage.

"Ooh, this one's pretty," Cora said, coming up to a red sedan. She peered in at the tan leather seats as Slider went to the sticker on the window.

"Cops love to tag speeding red cars. How heavy is your foot?" he asked.

She chuckled. "I mean, I'm no grandma, but I don't approach the highway like it's a racetrack, either."

He smirked at her, bringing his dimple out to play, and it was a look that drew her right back into his bed. "Never in a million years would I take you for a grandma."

She cleared her throat. "Right. So. Actually, now that I think of it, Bunny could be a grandma and she could probably kick my ass, so maybe I shouldn't use grandmas as my reference point," she said in a flustered rush. "Anyway, what do you think?" The amount looked reasonable, and with just under forty thousand miles, the mileage looked good, too.

"Camrys are very reliable. I've seen more than a few of them hit two hundred thousand miles before nickel and diming their owners. You should take it for a spin."

Cora grinned, a grin that only got bigger when she was behind the wheel and driving the car up Interstate 70. It rode like a dream. And it had a great sound system. And a moon roof. She was in love, but she knew she was supposed to be playing it cool.

"Push it going up the mountain," Slider said from the passenger's seat. "I want to see what its pickup is like."

"Okay," she said, hitting the gas and moving into the passing lane. From the backseat, the car salesman started extolling the virtues of the car's V6 engine, but all Cora could focus on was Slider's big body filling her car—because it already felt like her car—his posture relaxed, his thighs spread. Her brain very unhelpfully imagined all the ways they could break her car in, none of which fell into the *no more sex* category. Stupid brain.

The car took the mountain without any resistance at all.

She grinned at Slider and tried to telegraph her thoughts: *I love it so much!* His expression was amused as he shook his head, and it made the skin crinkle around his eyes. And, damn, humor on his face made him even more good-looking. He'd taken to wearing a bit of scruff on his jaw, and Cora couldn't look at it without remembering the way it had felt against her face and breasts and thighs.

She hadn't minded the bite of that scruff, not one freaking bit.

Finally, they returned to the car lot, and the salesman turned to Slider. "So, what do you think?"

Slider's gaze narrowed. "Ask the lady, she's your customer."

"Oh, of course." The older man turned to her with a smile. "And what do you think, little lady?"

Seriously? Now her eyes were the ones narrowing. Thankfully, Slider had given her advice on negotiating on price and all the games car salesmen played, so she had some idea what to say and do. "I like it, but it *is* older than I was hoping for. And I'm worried about the color being so flashy. I've heard the police go after red cars that speed more than other colors." She twisted her lips as if she were truly debating.

The man dove in with his counterarguments, but Cora started walking down the line of cars again as if she weren't wedded to her beautiful red baby.

She sighed and glanced at Slider. "Maybe we should go see that other car again, don't you think, honey?" She couldn't look at his face as she called him that, not because she thought he'd be angry, but because if he wore any surprise on his face, it would make her laugh.

Hands in his pockets, he nodded. "Yeah, babe. This one could use new tires, too, to be honest. So that's another expense."

Inside, her reactions warred between *Babe!* and *Oh, no, did it really need new tires?* She gave Slider a look and caught both the suppressed humor and the minute shake of his head. She almost really did laugh, then. They were totally teaming up on this poor salesman. Not that she really felt bad for him.

"How about this," the man said. Herb. That was actually his name. "Why don't we go inside and let me talk to my manager about what else we might be able to do on the price."

"Will it take long?" Cora asked. "Because I really think I need to see this other car I was looking at."

"Oh, no, ma'am," he said, escorting them inside. So she'd risen in stature from *little lady* to *ma'am*. Interesting.

When Slider and Cora were alone in Herb's office, she whispered, "I want this car so bad I might die."

"I know, little lady. I know." Slider winked at her. "Just keep playing it disinterested."

Oh, man, Playful Slider was even more appealing than Talkative Slider. Gah.

Finally, Herb returned with a deal sheet that took eight hundred off the price of the car.

Cora stood up, and Slider rose with her. "Oh, I'm sorry, Herb. I thought you were interested in my business. Given that the car needs tires, that price needs to come down at least another twelve hundred before I'll think you're serious. If that's not possible, please tell me now so I can head back to that other dealer."

"Oh, no, no. Please sit, I'm sure we can work something out." Herb gestured to their chairs. With a little back-and-forth, he came down another seven hundred, which had been Cora's goal all along. She was completely flipping out on the inside. "I'll write it up," he said, shaking her hand.

"Write it up with new floor mats, Herb. Won't you?" Slider asked, eyebrows arched, hands crossed over his flat belly, legs extended, and ankles crossed. The picture of ease. The picture of sex on a stick, too.

Cora wanted to hug him. Or kiss him. Or straddle him in that chair.

Herb sighed. "I'll see what I can do."

Forty-five minutes later, Cora was the proud owner of her very first car, newly washed, to boot. And a set of new floor mats. "It's mine!" she said, gripping her key fob, awe and excitement flowing through her in equal measure. "It's really mine."

Standing next to her driver's door, Slider chuckled. "Sure is. You did a great job in there."

"*We* did a great job," she said with a grin she couldn't hold back. And she was so grateful to Slider for helping to make it happen that she couldn't hold it in. "Thank you." She threw her arms around his shoulders.

His arms came around her more slowly, but when they did, they held her tight. And they didn't let go.

AFTER THAT, CORA hadn't thought her week could get any better. She'd started a new job. Received a beautiful new bedroom. And had incredible sex, even if they'd decided it could happen only that one time. And on top of it all, she bought a new car, which also just happened to be the single nicest thing she'd ever owned.

But then the animal shelter had enthusiastically asked her to come on as a volunteer. Not only that, they'd been so busy lately that they asked her how soon she could start. They'd agreed on Monday.

And if the boys thought she'd been cool before, it was nothing compared to them knowing she now officially worked with animals, even if it wasn't paid.

"Can we come visit you sometime?" Sam asked.

"Ooh, can we adopt a dog of our own? Can we, Dad?" Ben said, flinging spaghetti off his fork in excitement.

Cora threw Slider an apologetic look. They were having an early dinner so he could join them before his overnight shift began, and it was nice, the four of them eating together, talking and sharing things about their days.

She'd never had that, even growing up. Her parents had divorced when she was eleven, and her mother had always been too involved with trying to please new boyfriends to pay Cora any mind. Apparently, having a preteen daughter about had done bad things to her mom's self-esteem, which was how Cora wound up living with her dad. So Cora intended to enjoy this, to revel in it, even, every single time it happened. She winked at Ben and said, "Maybe we should get used to me living here before we bring another mongrel into the house." Ben chuckled.

"So what exactly will you get to do there?" Sam asked.

"I'm not sure yet," Cora said. "Starting out, I think I'll mostly get to walk the dogs and help at feeding time, clean out cages, and work at the reception desk. But what I'm really hoping to be able to do is assist in the exam rooms." She took a deep breath, and chanced sharing her probably silly dream. "Someday, after a *whole* lot of classes, I might like to work as a veterinarian, and I thought this would be a way to see if I'd really like it."

"That's *so cool*, Cora," Ben said, slurping up a noodle.

"I think so, too," Sam said more quietly. From across the table, Slider gave her an appraising look.

Her cheeks heating, she chuckled. "I think so, three. And the lady I met with said my timing was really good, because there have apparently been a lot of dogs getting dropped off and abandoned around the area lately. Dogs in bad shape. So I guess things at the shelter have been busier than normal." Seeing injured and abused dogs was going to be the hardest part of it, Cora knew. How could anybody hurt a defenseless creature? Then again, she'd seen enough of the underbelly of human nature that she shouldn't even be asking such a naïve question. Some people just got off on hurting those weaker or more vulnerable than themselves.

Cora and Haven wouldn't even live in Maryland if that weren't true.

"Why would someone just abandon a dog?" Sam said, scowling.

"What kinds of dogs are they?" Slider asked, clearing his plate. "Did the lady tell you?"

"No," Cora said, shaking her head. "But certain breeds get dumped more than others. Pretty much any shelter you look at online has more pit bull mixes for adoption than almost any other kind. It's sad." But hopefully, in helping to take care of the animals and maybe even helping them to find homes, Cora could make a difference. After all, she knew what it felt like not to be wanted, too. "I guess I'll learn more once I'm there. For now, it looks like I'm going to volunteer on Mondays and Thursdays, if that's okay.

And maybe an occasional night, because the shelter has an emergency after-hours clinic. Does that sound okay?"

Slider nodded. "I think it's important that you do this, so I'm sure it'll be fine."

Cora ducked her chin and kinda lit up inside at how supportive they were all being.

After dinner, Slider cleared the table as she stowed the leftovers in containers. There was an odd intimacy to working with him in his kitchen this way, and it made Cora feel a little tingly inside.

"I gotta go," Slider said, settling the last of the dishes in the sink. His hand fell on her arm.

"Okay?" she said, surprised at his touch. Save for the impromptu hug she'd given him in thanks for helping her buy a car—a hug he'd let her out of none too quickly—he hadn't initiated touching her since she'd risen from his bed *that morning*.

"I just wanted to say that you doing this volunteering and talking about taking classes, I think you're a good role model for my kids, Cora."

Cora's mouth dropped open. Her eyes pricked. Her breath caught in her throat. "That's the nicest thing anyone has ever said to me, Slider."

He tucked a blond curl behind her ear. "It's just the truth."

Then he was gone. And Cora wasn't sure how she ever got so lucky as the day she was invited to be a part of this family, even if it was just temporary.

CHAPTER 12

Slider had promised himself all week that he'd finally do it, so when he woke up from sleeping on Saturday afternoon, he got dressed, grabbed a sandwich, and headed out back to his garage.

In the center of the space sat his motorcycle, covered by a tarp.

He pulled off the dusty drop cloth to reveal a 2009 Harley Softail Cross Bones. Man, he'd always loved this bike. And seeing Cora's excitement at buying her first car reminded him of how fucking thrilled he'd been the day he'd bought this Harley.

His Cross Bones was one badass-looking ride, combining some vintage styling with the look of a stripped-down custom bobber. Gloss black finishes made it gleam, even in the dark, as did the bright chrome exhaust and mufflers. It had a rough-and-tumble attitude that had been a good match for his own personality, at least once upon a time. And it had a crossbones-and-skull graphic on the oil tank and the Raven Riders' raven/dagger/skull logo on the gas tank.

It was a fucking piece of rolling art and some kick-ass engineering.

And it needed a ton of TLC.

Just one more thing Slider had neglected.

So he got to work making his baby roadworthy once again. He gave everything a once-over inspection—brakes, chain, fuel system, valves, air filter, fluid levels. Then he tuned her up until she sang and shined her up until she blazed.

"Looking good," came a voice from the open doorway.

Talk about blazing.

Cora stood in the sunlight, her hair like a halo, her smile like the sun itself had been pulled from the sky. And it was all directed at him. He shouldn't like that as much as he did. Nor should he like the way she looked with a pair of form-fitting jeans tucked into tall brown boots. But that shit was sexy as hell.

"Yeah?" he said, wiping his greasy hands on a rag. He didn't mind the dirt, not when it was evidence that he worked hard on something he loved. And that hadn't happened in a long damn time.

Tentatively, she stepped into his space and came around the other side of the bike. "I don't know anything about motorcycles."

"Ever ridden one?" he asked.

She shook her head, her expression full of admiration as she looked over his bike. "Never. Bet it's awesome, though." Her interest hit him nearly the same way her studying his body had. Heat stirred in his blood.

Slider debated, but the words sneaked out of his mouth before he'd fully thought them through. "Wanna ride with me?"

Her eyes went wide. "Now?"

"Scared?" he asked, making sure there was a playfulness to his tone—despite the fact that he really wanted her to say yes.

Cora crossed her arms and jutted out a hip. "No."

He came round to where she was standing, got close, close enough to tower over her. "Then ride with me."

He wasn't sure why he was pushing her—scratch that. He knew *exactly* why the hell he was pushing Cora. Because he liked her. And staying away from her was hard as fuck. Harder than he expected, especially with her living in his house.

He saw her fresh from bed and sleepy at night. He heard her shower water running and couldn't help but imagine what he'd once touched. He talked to her and listened to her and watched her make his boys fall in love with her a little more every day. And he liked her. At least this way she'd be all over him, without it leading to them getting naked and sweaty. Theoretically, at least.

"Okay. But what about the boys?" she asked.

Five words that threatened to reach right inside his chest, because she always thought of them. Always. "We won't go for long."

"Then just show me what to do."

Atta girl, he thought, loving that she was game for this.

He ran inside and washed up at the kitchen sink, but on the way to the stairs, something made him stop dead in his tracks. The coat closet by the front door. He opened it. Pulled out his Raven Riders cut. Denim and leather, with the Ravens' colors on the back and other patches here and there. He walked to the mirror by the door, looked himself straight in the eye, and slid it on.

Damn. *Damn. Where have you been all this time, Slider?*

It was his own thought, but he heard his brothers' voices asking it. Dare and Maverick and Jagger and Phoenix and Doc and all the rest. He didn't have a good answer for them, because the past was dead and buried. But he had now. And he had tomorrow. And those he could do something about.

A stair creaked behind him.

Slider turned, and found Sam standing at the banister.

Wasn't it a bitch that he was suddenly self-conscious? That was how much he'd lost himself. "So, uh . . ." He held out his hands. "What do you think?"

Sam nodded, his face solemn. Too solemn, Slider thought, for a boy of ten. "I think it's good."

"Yeah," Slider said. "Would you be okay if I take Cora for a spin? Twenty minutes. Thirty, tops."

Sam's eyebrows went up. In truth, his whole face lit up. Cora Campbell seemed to have that effect on his boys. Hell, on all the Evans men, if he was being honest. "Cora's gonna ride?"

Slider couldn't help but quirk a little smile. "First-timer, even."

His son nodded. "It's cool, Dad. No worries. I'll watch Ben."

With that, Slider was out the door and crossing the yard. He found Cora sitting on an overturned bucket in the sun, her back against the garage wall, her eyes closed, and she was singing along to the radio.

He just stood and watched her. Because he couldn't do anything else.

Her eyes fluttered open, the green even brighter in the sunshine. "Oh!" she said, breaking into a chuckle. "What are you, a ghost? I didn't even hear . . . you . . ." She rose, and her mouth dropped open as she took in what he wore. "Wow." She walked all the way around him, and her fingers fell against his back. He knew the Ravens' colors well enough that he knew exactly what she was touching. She traced the raven to where it perched on the handle of a dagger, and then followed the blade as it went through the eye socket of a skull.

Then she stood in front of him again.

He arched a brow and borrowed from her book of defense mechanisms. "I make this shit look good."

She barked out a laugh that was as sweet as it was sexy. "Someone's full of himself today," she said.

Oh, hell, what he wouldn't give for *someone* to be full of him today, but he kept his mouth shut. Still, she seemed to realize the innuendo that could be weaved by her words because her cheeks went pink and she rolled her eyes. "Seems like something's put me in a better mood lately, that's all."

And then those cheeks went pinker.

Damn if Slider didn't enjoy making Cora squirm. In *all* sorts of ways he had no business thinking about at all. Or wanting to repeat.

"Ready to ride?" he asked. Because he sure as hell was ready to feel her holding him, her body molded to him, her thighs wrapped around his ass. Some bikers were more particular about who they invited into their saddle than they were about who they invited into their beds, and though Slider had never been that hard-core about it, on a certain level, he got it.

"Let's do it," she said, arching a brow of her own.

He suited her up in a lightweight jacket and a helmet, and then he pulled on a brain bucket of his own and a pair of shades. Sitting astride his bike was like coming home, and then he helped Cora on behind him. She had to sit close and tight, because he had only a slim two-seater, which he'd customized from the original solo seat so that Kim could ride, too. Though she'd enjoyed riding when they'd first been together—hell, they'd met at one of the Ravens' race nights at their racetrack, so she'd known he was a biker from the very start—her interest in it had declined after the kids were born until she no longer wanted to ride at all.

"This is so freaking awesome," Cora said, chasing away his thoughts. Because she clearly wanted to ride, and that rushed a deep satisfaction through him. "I hope I don't fall off."

Slider chuckled and peered over his shoulder. "Well then, sweetheart, I suggest you put your arms around me and hold on tight."

GLADLY, CORA THOUGHT as Slider revved the engine. She'd no more scooted flush against him and gripped his chest then he'd pulled out of the driveway and onto the road in front of his house.

And then they were off.

The rush was almost enough to make her forget that he'd called her sweetheart again. The endearment threatened to pull her right back into his bed, his sleep-roughened voice saying it for the very first time. Did he even realize he'd said it again?

Cora let it go, because it felt like they were flying, even though she suspected they weren't going that fast. But it was absolutely exhilarating, freeing, and so much damn fun. The thrill of it made her laugh and laugh, as if she were a kid riding a roller coaster that she never wanted to get off.

Every once in a while, Slider grinned back at her, and if the genuine pleasure in that smile hadn't been devastating enough, the total package of him right now was an absolute killer. The shades and matte black helmet over the five-o'clock scruff. The badass Ravens' cut layered over a long-sleeved black T-shirt. The chunky black motorcycle boots. And, damn, the bike.

It was like sex on wheels. That had been her first thought when she'd walked into Slider's garage. It was sleek and aggressive, sexy and cool, utterly masculine, and looked fast as hell, too. Seeing him stand behind the machine, it totally fit—this man and this bike. And it was as if a new piece of the puzzle that was Slider Evans clicked into place.

And he wanted to share it with her.

"Okay?" he called.

"Can we go faster?"

He laughed. He actually laughed. And then did exactly as she asked.

Before long, they'd skirted around the Ravens' big tract of land, and then Cora recognized where they were. The twisting rural road that Dare lived on. Sure enough, that was his destination. The bike tilted as he pulled into the driveway next to a two-story, log-cabin-style home, and they found Dare on his knees working on his bike.

"I just need five with Dare. You mind?" he asked.

"Not at all. Gives me the chance to see how Haven is settling in," she said as he helped her off the bike. When she removed the helmet, her hair was a wind-blown mess, but she just shook it out and laughed. No sense worrying about it when they still had the ride home yet to do.

Wiping his hands on a rag, Dare got to his feet. "Hey," he called in that super serious way he had. Cora couldn't decide if it was funny or really freaking endearing that Haven had ended up with such a gruff and frankly intimidating man when she'd once been so shy it was almost painful, but it just went to show how far her bestie had come.

"Hey," Slider said. The two men clasped hands, and Dare's gaze was all over Slider's cut, the bike, her.

That expression seemed like Cora's signal to give them some privacy. "Haven inside?" she asked. When Dare nodded, she made herself scarce. "Knock, knock," she called, as she knocked and opened the front door at the same time.

"Cora?" Haven called from upstairs.

"Yep. I can't stay long though. Where are you?" she asked, making her way up the steps.

Haven stepped out into the hallway. "Hey. I was

just unpack—" She blinked. "What are you wearing? Is that a motorcycle jacket?"

Cora grinned. "Slider took me for a ride."

Haven's eyes went wide. "Slider's on his bike?" She rushed for one of the front windows. "Wow. Wow, Cora. What is going on?"

"He's . . . I don't know, he seems like he's doing better. Not sure what he and Dare are talking about though, but Dare looked pretty surprised to see Slider wearing his vest." The two of them had their faces pressed to the glass like little kids.

Haven turned toward her. "No, I mean, what is going on with you and Slider?"

Cora could've smacked herself in the head, because she'd walked right into that one. "Weelll . . ."

On a gasp, Haven smacked her arm. "Shut up!"

That made Cora laugh. "I didn't even say anything."

"You didn't have to. But now you totally have to," Haven said, grabbing her hand and dragging her back into the room she'd originally stepped out of— Dare's bedroom, by the masculine look of it. Though Haven's things were all over it now, too. And actually *seeing* Haven at home in such a nice place—a place that was hers, now—was almost enough to make Cora a little misty. "Turnabout is fair play, missy. You made me spill all my secrets about Dare when we first got together, and now it's your turn."

They plopped down on the corner of the bed. "It's complicated."

"Story of our lives," Haven said with an eye roll.

Wasn't that the truth. "Okay, well . . . I like him, and I think he likes me. And *wesortahadsex* but we can't do it again because I work for him and neither of us are really in the best place for a relationship."

Haven's eyebrows were up at her hairline. "You had sex with Slider?"

"Twice. Well, twice in one morning." Downstairs, the front door opened, and voices and footsteps filtered in.

"I can't believe you had sex with Slider!" Haven said excitedly.

"Ssh!" Cora said, and then she dropped her face into her hands. "It was so good, Haven. Like, so so good. I can't freaking stop thinking about it. And he sleeps across the hall from me now. It's so distracting."

"How good was it?" Haven whispered, sending them both into a fit of giggles.

"So good. Like, super good. Extra amazingly good."

Haven put her arm around Cora's shoulders. "He invited you on his bike and took you for a ride. And he's doing better since you moved into his house. I mean, hell, Cora, from what Dare said, Slider hadn't touched his bike since *before* Kim died. All that with what you told me, I'd say just give it time and let whatever is going to happen between you happen naturally."

Cora blew out a breath. "How'd you get so good at giving advice?"

She bumped their shoulders. "I learned from the best."

"Speaking of the best, my extraordinary baker friend, any more word on when you'll start at Dutch's?"

"I met with him yesterday and showed him my new menu. He thinks he can have everything ready for the changeover in two weeks, three tops."

"Oh, Haven, that's so awesome. I can't wait to come sit at the counter and order up all your goodies."

Haven laughed. "You don't have to do that, silly. You can get them any old time."

"Ready when you are, Cora," Slider called.

They went downstairs and exchanged some small talk, along with a promise to get together for dinner that put that surprised expression on Dare's face again, and then they were back on Slider's bike and heading home.

Only this time, Slider kept his hand pressed against hers over his heart.

The gesture made Cora feel like her heart might just beat right out of her chest. Because this *like* she felt for Slider Evans was getting stronger every day.

CHAPTER 13

It was the first time that Cora got to handle one of the dogs that her new job at the animal shelter became real. Well, not *job* job, but even though it wasn't paid, it still felt important to her. Because it was a step toward figuring out her future, and at almost twenty-four, that wasn't something she'd had the chance to do nearly enough.

Her first furry friend at the shelter was an eight-year-old basset hound named Bosco, a beautiful red-coated old man who'd been left behind by his family when they moved across the country. "How could someone do that to you?" she asked as she stroked his long, silky ears. "You're so handsome and so sweet."

He leaned into her pets with a satisfied grunt.

Bosco was the first of the dog walks she got to go on, and it was no hardship at all walking dogs outside in the early October sunshine, a breeze blowing through her hair, and a grateful companion at her side. She enjoyed herself so much that she already worried how she'd wait till Thursday to return. And her five-hour shift was nearing its end way too soon.

"Good first day?" the shelter's director of operations, Maria Colter, asked when Cora came back inside. In her mid-fifties, Maria had shoulder-length salt-and-pepper hair and a smile that had immediately put Cora at ease during her volunteer interview.

"It really was," Cora said. "How do you avoid falling in love with them all?"

Maria winked. "You don't. At least, I don't."

"I don't think I will, either," Cora said.

"Probably means you're in the right place. I'm glad you've joined us, Cora. Many of our volunteers are retired ladies looking for something to do once a month or high school kids needing a few community service hours, and both are very welcomed, of course. We need every single pair of hands. But it's exciting having someone here because they're exploring working with animals as their career."

The online application had required a statement of interest, and Cora had shared her goal of one day becoming trained to do this work for real. Hearing Maria take her dream so seriously gave Cora an incredible boost of confidence in it that she really appreciated. "Well, I'm a long way off—"

Suddenly, the door to the veterinary clinic pushed open. "Maria, we've got another one," Dr. Josh said, his dark face set in a scowl. Dr. Joshua Pierce was the shelter's director of veterinary medicine, a young guy in his thirties with a nerdy-but-cute look and the biggest smile Cora had ever seen. Well, normally.

"Damnit. Every Monday . . ." Maria's tone was part worried, part angry.

"Is everything okay?" Cora asked.

Frowning, Maria hesitated. "This might be a lot for your first day . . ."

"I have time, if you need help," Cora offered. A glance at the clock told her she had seventy-five minutes until the boys' bus reached their house. Whatever this was, she really wanted to assist and learn.

Maria gave her a nod. "I suppose you'll have to see it at some point. For today, just observe. This is the rough part, Cora, so if you're not sure . . ."

"I am." Inside the clinic's exam room, Cora found out exactly what Maria meant, and realized she wasn't as prepared as she thought. Then again, how could anyone prepare for *this*? "Oh, God," she whispered, hands going to her mouth.

"Dear Lord," Maria said.

"I've got him sedated," Dr. Josh said, frustration rolling off him as he pushed glasses up on his nose. One of the vet techs coolly cleaned and bandaged numerous wounds covering a tan-and-white pit bull's body. "But I've said it before and I'll say it again. This is the face of dogfighting right here. When is this going to end?"

Dogfighting? Someone had made one dog do this to another? For . . . for *fun*? "How can he breathe?" Cora asked, tears squeezing her throat. Because it appeared that the dog's nose had largely been torn off, along with part of his cheek. Even sedated, he made a labored, wet, rasping sound with each breath. Those injuries were the worst, but not the only ones. Cuts and bites covered his muscled body.

Dr. Josh frowned. "He's struggling. I've called in Dr. Lisa to help with an emergency surgery."

Maria shook her head. "Can he be saved?"

"Time will tell," the doc said. "But I think this is a case for Noah's Arks. See if they're up for a transport if he makes it."

"I'll call them right away," Maria said. "And the police, too. At some point, they have to start giving this more of a priority."

"Who is Noah's Arks?" Cora asked as Maria nodded.

She gave Cora a sad look. "A rescue down south that specializes in caring for and rehabilitating abused and neglected animals. This guy's bad enough off that he needs them."

Cora had to leave just as the docs were taking their newest patient into the operating room, and she felt like she was leaving her heart behind at the shelter the whole way home. Not even driving her new red baby gave her any pleasure. She was a watery, wobbly mess all night, and finally had to retreat to her room after dinner.

Sitting on her bed, she hugged a pillow to her chest. And burst into tears. Sadness rolled through her until she sagged sideways onto the bed, her knees drawn up, her tears rolling over the bridge of her nose and wetting her comforter. Maybe it was ridiculous to feel this bad, and maybe it was a stretch to identify with an animal, but it just hurt to see another living thing used, discarded, and in so much pain.

Cora knew too well what that was like.

Voices reached her from the hallway, but she couldn't do anything to rein herself in. And then her door was opening and Slider was there, his face a storm of concern. He closed himself in and went to his knees beside the bed, lining up his ruggedly handsome face with hers. "What's wrong, Cora? What happened?"

She shook her head, unable to talk even as she tried to make her tears stop.

"Jesus, sweetheart, you're scaring me."

"S-sorry," she managed. "Just . . . this dog . . ." Trying to explain made her cry harder again.

Slider wrapped himself around her, his forehead against hers, his arm around her shoulder. She pulled him closer, needing his touch, needing his comfort, needing *him*.

Eyes still flooding, Cora heaved a deep breath,

then another, until her breaths were shuddering but becoming more even. But her eyes wouldn't stop leaking. Damnit.

"Come here," Slider said, his voice full of grit. He pulled her off the bed and into his lap there on the floor of her bedroom.

Cora wrapped her arms around his neck. "Just being stupid," she said.

"No way," he said. "Big hearts are bound to get bruised, Cora, and yours is the biggest I've ever seen."

Annnd now she was crying again. She laid her head on his shoulder, her face pressed to his neck, and cried herself out until she was limp and exhausted. He rubbed her back and stroked her hair the whole time, just holding her and being there for her. And, man, that would've been enough. But it was the little kiss against her hair that had her too-big heart feeling entirely too full for her chest.

For being wrecked, broken, and more than a little lost, Slider Evans had a well of sweetness so deep that Cora wasn't sure how she'd ever find her way out. Or if she even wanted to.

On another deep breath, Cora finally lifted her face and met Slider's blazing light green eyes. He cupped her face in one big hand and swiped at her tears with his thumb, but it wasn't enough, so he lifted the edge of his shirt and used that instead.

Cora managed a chuckle, even as she messed him up to put herself back together. "Sorry."

"Don't be," he said, his voice full of gravel. "Aren't we a pair?" He swallowed hard. "You feel so much, and I can't feel enough."

The words were so revealing that they nearly made her gasp. "Oh, Slider," she said. "I think you feel more than you let on." She hadn't meant about *her*, but the flare of those strange eyes told her he took it that way. And it made her want to backpedal. Fast. "I mean—"

He kissed her. Hand in her hair, his lips came down on hers in a soft press of skin on skin. It wasn't the frenzy of their first kisses in his bed, but there was an intimacy in the softness, in the sweetness that hit her just as hard.

When he pulled away, his expression was intense and thoughtful, like he wanted to say something and needed to figure out exactly what it was. And then he nailed her with a stare and said, "Cora, you—"

Knock, knock. "Dad?" Sam called from outside Cora's door.

They jolted apart, and Cora scrambled into a standing position and scrubbed at her face, her heart pumping hard. She knew Slider didn't want the boys confused about what was going on with them, and since nothing *was* going on, there was no sense in giving them any other impression. Besides, Cora really didn't want Slider to think of her with the slightest hint of regret.

Hands braced on his thighs, he dropped his head

in what looked like a posture of defeat. Or, after all, regret . . . "Yeah, Sam?"

The boy poked his head in the doorway, his gaze ping-ponging between them.

"What did you need, son?" Slider asked, pushing himself off the floor.

Worry was plain on the kid's face, so Cora didn't make him voice it. "I was just upset," she said. "Over something I saw at the shelter today. They found another dog that had been . . . really badly injured. And they think it was from dogfighting. It was . . . pretty terrible." She hugged herself and tried to block out the images, images she had no intention of describing more graphically for Sam, whose expression already looked like she felt.

Slider frowned. "Dogfighting? Is that where this uptick in dumped-off dogs is coming from? Have they all been like this?"

Cora shrugged, but then something Maria said came back to her. "I don't know, but Maria mentioned that this seemed to happen pretty regularly on Mondays. God, is there dogfighting nearby on the weekends?" The thought was truly horrifying.

"I don't know," Slider said. "But I can ask around."

"I'm sure the authorities are looking into it," Cora said. "From what I understand, animal control is bringing them in when they find them."

"That really sucks, Cora. I'm sorry," Sam said. "Did the dog . . . did he live?"

Cora wished she knew. "He was in surgery when I had to come home, so I don't know what happened." And she spent all night wondering.

The next morning, she couldn't take another minute of not knowing, and she called as soon as the shelter opened. He'd survived the surgery and the night, and that was all Maria could say for now.

It was something.

But the uncertainty was kinda driving Cora crazy, so she threw herself into housework. If she was going to be a full-time nanny, she figured that meant she should take on more around the house than just what the boys needed in the moment. And though Slider kept the house neat-ish, it really needed the same TLC that they'd given to Cora's room.

Not that Cora believed redecorating fell under her purview. So instead, she threw herself into a deep clean, starting with the kitchen and moving into the living room. The floors. The fridge. Scrubbing every surface. She took down the curtains in both rooms and threw them in the washer.

In the living room, she found a box of figurines sitting on the floor next to a corner display cabinet. Kneeling, she unwrapped them one by one. Collectibles of the Disney princesses, villains, and a few dogs. It was Pluto that really got her. She stroked his funny little head and wished it was the hurt dog that she could be petting.

Were these sitting here waiting to be displayed?

Cora took everything out of the cabinet and wiped it down, then dusted the shelves and rearranged to make space for the figurines all on one shelf. She removed the kids' old school artwork, much of which had bent and faded from sitting propped up on the shelves for so long, and stacked all of it inside the cabinet, thinking she'd look for a keepsake box or scrapbook album to keep the art safe.

God, there was nothing like throwing herself into the mindless productivity of cleaning to make her feel better. At the very least, she felt like she'd accomplished something today.

Kneeling in front of the corner cabinet, she peered around the room and looked to see if she could tell the difference. The rooms were brighter. Surfaces gleamed. The air smelled lemony fresh. Yeah, she'd definitely made a difference.

The door opened behind her. "What are you doing?"

She turned to find Slider coming in, two pizza boxes in hand. He'd been out running errands most of the day, but she hadn't expected the nice surprise of him bringing home dinner. Thank God he did, because she'd lost track of time.

"Oh, cleaning. And that smells good. Thanks for grabbing it."

His brows cranked down. "You don't have to do that."

Cora got onto her feet and pushed stray waves from her messy bun behind her ears. "Of course I do. Nannies don't just take care of kids." She gestured at the room. "They take care of the house, too."

He peered around like he was uncertain, or like a snake might jump out from under the couch, but finally nodded. "Well, it's the nicest this old place has looked in a long damn time." He did a double take, and Cora followed his gaze to the corner cabinet, and then that frown was back on his face.

"Oh, I found those figurines in a box beside the cabinet. I thought maybe they were there to be put out . . ." But now, seeing his reaction, Cora wanted to smack herself in the head. *Of course* they must have belonged to his wife. And she'd had absolutely no business touching them.

"It's fine." He took the pizza into the kitchen.

"Slider, I can put them away—"

"I said it's *fine*," he said, a gruffness to his voice that she hadn't heard in so long. He huffed out a breath that came close to a growl, and agitated displeasure rolled off him in nearly physical waves.

Frozen in place, Cora didn't know what to do. She just knew that somehow, she'd messed up. Big time. So much so that Slider wouldn't look at her. After what they'd shared—even if they'd agreed it shouldn't happen again—it left her feeling . . . adrift and unwanted. Burdensome, even. Feelings with deep roots in her past that could too easily reach out to the present.

The sound of the school bus pulling up saved her.

Slider's shoulders fell. "Cora—"

"Boys are home," she said, turning and making for the front door. Outside, she breathed in the fall spice on the air and waved as the kids ran off the bus and straight to her.

Like she belonged there.

But she didn't, did she? Not really. God, she didn't belong anywhere.

Back inside, the boys beelined for the pizza, and Cora headed for the steps.

"Aren't you going to eat, Cora?" Ben called.

"I need to wash up," she said. It wasn't a lie. A day's cleaning left her feeling grimy and sweaty. But she also wasn't sure she wanted to sit across from Slider and see anger or distance on his face. Either would be too much for her to handle right now. Besides, quarter after four in the afternoon was a little early for her to eat.

So she indulged in a long shower, and the hot water revived her. Afterward, she towel-dried her hair, threw on some yoga pants and a long-sleeved shirt, and lingered around her room until hunger necessitated that she go downstairs. She couldn't hide out forever, particularly as the sound of the TV playing in the family room indicated that someone remained downstairs.

Remembering that the curtains needed to go in the dryer, she headed to the laundry room and shifted the load over. And then she heard her name.

"Cora?"

Closing her eyes, she heaved a deep breath. And then she followed Slider's voice until she found him sitting alone on the couch, but he didn't look at all like he'd been relaxing. Instead, he sat forward, elbows braced on his knees, fingers laced together, head hanging low.

"Yeah?" she asked, her belly roiling with dread.

"Shut the door, please."

Oh, God. Why in the world did he need her to close the door? What could be so bad that he'd want privacy to say it? She closed them in. Whatever this was seemed like it was not going to be good.

Finally, he lifted his gaze to hers. But what she saw there wasn't anger. Cora couldn't tell what it was exactly. He just looked . . . shredded. "Thank you for making the house so nice."

"Sure," she said.

"The boys saw what you did with their mother's figurines and loved it, so thank you for that, too." She hugged herself and waited for the other shoe to drop. "But thanks isn't all I owe you. I owe you an apology, too."

Cora blinked. That wasn't what she was expecting at all. "I was the one who touched something I shouldn't."

He waved a hand. "Bullshit. This is your house now. There's nothing off limits to you, Cora. Understand?" Slider peered up at her, those pale eyes so intense.

If she'd been feeling more sarcastic, more sassy,

she might've asked if that included him. But she wasn't feeling playful just then. "Okay."

He placed his hand against the cushion beside him. A silent invitation. "Would you sit with me?"

She sat like he was a wild animal that she couldn't help wanting to get close to, even though she knew there was a chance it would take off her head.

"I wasn't upset with you for putting out the figures," he said, his voice sounding so defeated that it was hurting her heart. "They were there because we wanted to find a place for them and just hadn't done it yet. What upset me is that they belonged to Kim—"

"I should've realized that right away, Slider. It was so stupid of me. I can only imagine how much she meant to you, so I—"

"No, you can't. You really fucking can't." Cora's feelings were well on their way to getting hurt again, when he continued. "Nobody can. Because nobody knows that it was . . . that it was all a lie."

Cora's head whipped up, her eyes on him, her mind trying to process if she'd really heard what she thought she heard. The room was silent, utterly still.

Slider heaved a breath that sounded like the weight of the world sat on his shoulders. And his words made her think that maybe it really did. "Nobody knows."

"Knows what?" she whispered. Goose bumps ran over her skin, because she'd been holding on to something no one knew, either.

He shook his head, and she thought he wasn't going

to answer, but then he did. "Kim . . . cheated on me. Was going to leave. And then she got the cancer and the sonofabitch wanted nothing to do with her. So I took her back."

Cora could barely breathe. After being betrayed and abandoned, he'd spent months taking care of the terminally ill person who'd wronged him. "And you kept it quiet for the boys," she ventured. She didn't need him to answer or even to nod, because the minute the words were out of her mouth, she knew she was right. And that was everything she needed to know about what kind of a man Slider Evans was. Loyal, even when that loyalty hadn't been returned. Honorable. Compassionate. Selfless.

Nothing like any man she'd ever known.

But Slider *did* answer. "For the boys." He gave a single shake. "But for me, too. I never want the boys to think bad of their mother, and I certainly don't want them to know that she was leaving them, too. Because I damn well know firsthand how being abandoned can mark you in ways from which you can never recover." His swallow sounded thick, tortured. "But I also didn't want people to look down on me."

The revelations were making her head spin, and so was the fact that he was opening up to share them. With her. But, for now, she focused on what she thought he most needed to hear. "No one would look down on you. What you did . . . it was *heroic*, Slider."

He chuffed out a humorless laugh. "I'm no fucking hero, Cora. Don't forget that for a second."

"You are . . . you are to me." Her belly did a flip-flop on the admission, but she didn't want to take it back. She'd never thought of Slider in those terms before, but *hero* definitely fit. He lived his life to take care of his kids. He'd devoted his life to taking care of his dying wife, even though some might say she didn't deserve his devotion. He'd kept her secret to preserve their children's happy memories and their self-esteem.

And that was a lot. A lot more than some people did. A lot more than what her parents had done, even before her father's terrible violation.

His eyes absolutely burned as they looked at her. "I'm sorry for snapping at you."

"You don't have to apologize," she said, stunned by everything she'd learned, heartened that he wanted her to understand, and so damn angry on his behalf. Why did some people search their whole lives for love and never find it, while others found love and threw it away?

He cleared his throat. "The boys and I talked over pizza. They loved the way you rearranged the cabinet. They think you should do whatever you want to freshen up the house. Redecorate. Give it some new life. And I agree."

"Slider, I couldn't do that on my own. This is your hou—"

"It's yours now, too," he said, simply. "Strip it all away, Cora. All but those figures that the boys love. Get rid of as many of the reminders as you can. Make me forget."

He might as well have reached into her chest and squeezed her heart with his bare hand. That's what it felt like his words did. But forgetting was a charade. The past never went away. And it never could. "How about instead of trying to forget, we make new memories that are brighter and louder and bigger than the old ones?" She didn't want to guess at what she saw in his eyes, but it sure as hell looked a lot like affection.

Finally, he said, "Does that work for you?"

For a long moment, his question hung in the space between them. A challenge. Maybe even a plea. For her to tell her secrets, too. She wasn't oblivious— she knew she'd given more of herself away than she would've liked on a few occasions. But she just couldn't. Cora feared that telling her secret would make it real in a way that hiding it didn't. She feared that people would look at her and think *rape victim*. She feared that people would think she deserved it, or asked for it, or didn't fight back.

Damnit, she just . . . feared.

So Cora hedged. "It's a work in progress."

"I guess that's all any of us are," Slider said, and she couldn't tell if she imagined the disappointment in his voice or if it was truly there.

That night, they passed each other in the hallway before bed. She was coming out of Ben's room after he'd had a nightmare, and Slider was going in. Wearing a pair of sweatpants and nothing else. Well, nothing else except for that glorious tattoo and those beautiful sleeves of ink.

She wanted to take his hand or hug him or offer him some other way to begin making those new memories, but that wasn't what they were. So instead she tried not to ogle him. "Good night, Slider."

His gaze scanned over her bare shoulders and dragged down over the tank top and boxers she wore. Her body lit up in the wake of his perusal. "Night," he said.

She watched him disappear into the dimness of his son's room. And wished that when he was done, he'd join her in bed. Or, at the very least, that he wanted to.

Because he hadn't lost a loving wife after all. Or even a faithful one. And that made Cora wonder exactly how long it'd been since somebody had truly, deeply, and unconditionally loved Slider Evans.

The way that she was suddenly, irrevocably, and completely sure that she did.

CHAPTER 14

Just got out of court. News isn't good. Emergency meeting of Church tonight, 8PM.

Slider had received Dare's text before lunchtime, and it'd been eating at his gut ever since. *News isn't good.* That could only mean that Jagger hadn't been set free.

Sonofabitch.

From what Slider understood, the guys on the Ravens' board—Dare, Maverick, Phoenix, and Caine— had been all over investigating Jagger's situation ever since he'd been arrested. Though the club had one close friend in the local sheriff's department, it also had at least one staunch enemy, so the Ravens weren't leaving it to the cops to be a force for justice when it came to the freedom of one of their brothers.

It just didn't make sense that Jagger hadn't been released. Their club's friend, Sheriff Henry Martin, knew as well as they did that the Ravens hadn't dumped the oil and tires that'd landed Jagger, as manager of the racetrack, in jail. Not only was Jagger legit brilliant and devoted to the Ravens' main business venture, the guy had been preparing for the track's annual licensing inspection, so no way would he have jeopardized that by illegally dumping where the inspector would see.

If that wasn't proof enough, Alexa's ex, Grant Slater had told her that he'd do whatever it took to force her to come back to him, even though he knew she was with Maverick. Before his death, Slater had been Frederick's biggest real estate developer, and he'd had the mayor and at least one of the sheriffs so far up his ass it was almost laughable. Add to that Slater's years-old grudge against the club, both because Alexa had dated Maverick years before and because Slater wanted the club's land, and two plus two equaled fucking four.

Jagger was innocent. And justice wasn't being served.

Which was why Slider was attending Church for the first time in a long damn time. And why, even though he was midshift and therefore driving the tow truck, he was doing it wearing his cut.

It was time he stood with his brothers again.

At the clubhouse, he parked the truck at the end of a row of Harleys, proof that a number of guys had beat him there. He'd been a member of the Ravens for sixteen years, so walking up the steps and crossing the wide front porch of the old two-story inn should've felt like coming home. But since he'd been lost for so fucking long, he was still figuring out what, where, and who home exactly was.

Which, of course, had him thinking about Cora.

The only person who now knew the secret he'd kept for so damn long.

He hadn't been able to hold it in for one more second. Not after nearly taking her head off for doing something he'd planned to do anyway, and not when the bleak look of hurt on her beautiful face had nearly gutted him. It was just that seeing Kim's things on display in the living room had been a sucker punch. He hadn't been ready for it. And it'd hurt like hell. So Slider had lashed out.

But Cora hadn't deserved it. Not one bit.

Coming clean had seemed like the only way to truly set things right, even though a part of him worried that she'd think less of him. He already had a hard time believing that she thought all that highly of him to begin with.

Then again, she'd called him a hero . . .

He didn't believe it. Not for one fucking second.

Inside the clubhouse, Slider stepped into the main lobby. The old inn's long reception desk remained, but otherwise, the room now resembled a giant lounge with big brown leather couches. Framed pictures of club members dominated one wall, and the Ravens' motto was carved into the woodwork above the desk: *Ride. Fight. Defend.*

Exactly what Jagger needed from them now.

To the right sat the big mess hall and to the left, their bar and rec room, but both of those rooms were quiet. Voices filtered from the back of the clubhouse, though, from the direction of the big room they used for Church—the club's official business meetings, open only to fully patched members of the Raven Riders.

Slider tried to ignore the way those voices died down when he walked into the room, where about twenty guys were already congregated. And then the surprise ratcheted up even more when he chose a seat at the table instead of one of those against the wall at the back of the room.

"Anyone sitting here?" he asked, grabbing a chair.

"Just you, my brother. Just you," Meat said, clasping his hand.

Feeling a little bit like a science experiment gone wrong, Slider sat his ass down.

And then his brothers included him in run-of-the-mill conversation that made the weirdness go away.

"Anything new at the shop?" Meat asked. Feeling like he was testing the waters of their reaction to him, Slider detailed the same-shit, different-day problems around Frederick Auto Body and Repair.

"How are the boys doing? Ben making out okay with his cast?" Bear asked, when Slider had answered Meat.

"You'd never know he had a broken bone," Slider said. "He's doing great. Both of them are."

Doc chuckled, his deep laugh part of the reason that he made a perfect Santa at Christmastime. Well, that and the white beard and mustache. "If we could bottle up the way kids bounce back from things— and their energy—our old asses would be A-OK." Nods and laughter all around.

More brothers filtered in until there were nearly thirty men taking up every seat in the joint. Proof of just how well respected Jagger was.

"Cora still liking her new ride?" Phoenix wanted to know as the newcomers got settled.

Slider did a bit of a double take at that one. When had Phoenix seen the Camry? "Yeah, she calls it her baby."

Phoenix grinned, which he'd always done easily and readily, even in the worst of times. Slider admired that about the guy. "She looked good behind the wheel."

Slider wasn't able to restrain an arched eyebrow or the *come again?* glare.

"I mean, you know, she looked happy," Phoenix said, apparently catching the vibe Slider was throwing off even though he had no damn right to be throwing it. For fuck's sake.

Thankfully, that was the moment Dare banged the gavel and called the meeting to order. "Thanks for coming," Dare said, his gaze snagging on Slider long enough to be an acknowledgment. "Got some news I wanted to share, and I wanted to do it in person."

Tension hung thick in the air, because Slider wasn't the only man who'd deduced enough about Jagger's fate to be unhappy.

"Jagger's hearing was today, and he was sentenced to four months. He's been credited with time served, but that still means he has almost six weeks to go." Dare's expression was a storm cloud of discontent, and his voice was tight with righteous anger.

The room erupted with echoes of that same anger.

Dare held up a hand. "Phoenix has agreed to keep running things at the track until Jagger's home again, so that's one problem solved."

"He's been doing a damn fine job, too," Maverick said. "Attendance is up since the carnival we held back in June, and it's thanks to Phoenix's efforts."

Even as the men nodded in agreement, Phoenix shook off the praise. "It's what we do here. We step up for our brothers and for the club. I need no special thanks for that." Of course, the comment had Slider feeling shitty for the attitude he'd given the man before the meeting started. Because he was right. Being a Raven meant stepping up when the chips were down, and Slider hadn't done nearly enough of that these past two years.

But that was changing. Or, at least, it would right now.

Slider cleared his throat. "It doesn't need to be said that I haven't been around." He forced himself to look around the table and meet his brothers' eyes, even though it was about as comfortable as eating crushed glass. "But if there's anything I can do— either at the track or in general—consider me available. And interested."

Another round of approving murmurs circled the room.

Phoenix nailed him with a surprised stare. "Actually, the grader, water truck, and roller could all really use some maintenance. With doing double duty, I haven't been able to give the track equipment the TLC it deserves. Any chance you could come by before Friday's race to take care of it? Jagger's gonna kick my ass if he gets out and sees I haven't taken care of his babies."

Slider didn't even have to think about it. Because it was a brother asking. Because maintaining the equipment they used to prepare the dirt surface of the track that was the club's financial lifeblood was right in his wheelhouse. And because it felt damn good to be useful. "Consider it done."

Dare nodded, approval and appreciation clear in his dark eyes. "Okay, next. Grant Slater's death has made tracking down the people responsible for the dumping hard as fuck. All signs point to him having hired a crew to do it, and the PI we hired finally thinks he's got a lead. Get this, he got it by tailing Curt Davis."

The name of the sheriff who they all knew had been on Slater's payroll elicited groans from everyone there.

Maverick sat forward. "Davis was the one who responded to the so-called anonymous tip about the dumping." Coincidentally, Slider had been present the day of Jagger's arrest because he'd been dropping the boys off at the clubhouse for Cora to watch. It still boiled his blood to think about that asshole Davis being the one to arrest Jagger—and Dare, too, though he'd been released. Some of his brothers had a higher tolerance for club business that crossed any lines, but Jagger was one of the most law-abiding of all of them because he wanted to keep his nose clean for the track. "So Davis was in on this from the beginning. Looks like he might still be getting some kind of a cut from the estate, too, because he's been in and out of the company headquarters these past weeks."

"Which is what led our guy to start tailing him. The PI was in Slater Enterprises posing as a photocopier repairman when he overheard Davis and some suit arguing about covering Slater's tracks."

"Well, that sounds ominous as hell," Slider said.

"Fucking A it does," Mav said. "Who the hell knows all the dirty pots he had his hands in."

"Is someone following the suit, too?" Caine asked, his ice-blue gaze slicing across the table. Their sergeant-at-arms was the club's enforcer and some-one Slider had never managed to get to know, be-cause the younger man said little and socialized even less.

"Our man's doing what he can, but this investiga-tion has tentacles for days precisely because Slater was so dirty. He's stretched thin," Dare said.

With jet-black hair and gauges in his ears, Caine put off an intimidating air on a good day. But then his eyes narrowed, and his look was downright lethal. "I'm on it."

Dare nodded and surveyed the room. "We all need to expect some shit when we get to the bottom of this. This is your heads-up."

Slider's gut tightened. He was one of the few men here who had kids, and so he'd always kept some distance from club business that might turn violent because he never wanted to abandon the boys—by choice or by circumstance. But when an enemy came at you with the clear intent to do you harm, you had to assume he wasn't going to stop until one of you was in the ground. That was just the hard reality. And, clearly, if Slater hired the dumping out to some associates, he wasn't their only enemy.

After that, Dare moved through a few other topics. He and Maverick briefed them on the relocation they'd just undertaken for one of their protective clients, and Phoenix shared a few new clients they were considering taking on. Slider's father had ghosted on the family before Slider turned ten—Sam's age, it killed him to realize—and his mom had been a drunk and a recreational drug user ever after. Even with all their failures, his parents had never taken a hand to him. But Slider had still been drawn to the club's protective mission from the very start. It felt good to create a little hope in the midst of devastation.

Annnd he was thinking of Cora again. Wasn't she doing that for him and his boys? Damn. *Damn*. His chest went tight at the thought.

Slider tuned back in from his thoughts just as Dare called a vote to make one of their two prospects, a young guy named Blake Green, a fully patched member. After his best friend, Jeb, had died defending the clubhouse a few months before, Blake had thrown himself into club business like a man on a mission—or, more likely, like a man trying to outrun his grief. Slider recognized that shit from a mile away, because pot, meet kettle. Either way, it was time for the club to reward Blake's loyalty and commitment. And they did with a unanimous vote of support.

"Anything else?" Dare asked.

Slider sat forward. "Not club business, but I've got a question. Cora's volunteering at the county animal shelter, and they've been having a problem with abused dogs being dumped off in the area. These animals are in bad shape, and the vet thinks the injuries are evidence of dogfighting."

"Fuck," Caine bit out. "If it's who I think it is, she needs to steer clear."

Slider's gut did a slow plummet, because a warning like that from Caine's mouth was like a siren in the night. "Who do you think it is?"

A few looks got traded around the table, and then Caine nailed him with a stare. "The 301 Crew."

"Aw, hell. Fucking miscreant lowlifes," Dare said.

Ice snaked down Slider's spine. The 301 Crew operated forty minutes away in the far northeast of the county, a homegrown gang with white supremacist leanings that got its start decades ago as muscle for one of the East Coast's most notorious crime syndicates, now largely out of business after a series of federal stings and arrests. Years ago, they'd proposed a business partnership with the Ravens around race betting and Doc had said hell no. Not just because the club ran its own under-the-table betting, but because the Crew was the lowest of the low, referring to themselves as *Dead Men* because the number of kills each member had determined their status and rank in the organization.

Given that they were into a little bit of everything, dogfighting sure wasn't any stretch. "You got definitive intel that it's them?" Slider asked, his gut a stew of dread. "Because I've never heard of them being into this before." Frankly, it seemed almost too tame for the Crew.

"There's been some rumbling the past few months," Caine said. "Want me to dig?"

Slider nodded, and his voice was much more even-handed than he felt. "I'd appreciate it." He needed Cora safe, and he wanted the peace of mind that she was.

Church broke up not long after that. Slider didn't know what to think of this Crew bullshit, but his brothers helped chase some of his worry away by coming up to him one by one, some of them just saying hello, some wanting him to know they were glad he was back, some offering condolences for all he'd been through that were still hard to hear.

Dare hung back and waited until they were alone. "You being here tonight—really being here—was just about the only good thing in my whole fucking day."

The two of them clasped hands. "I'm here. And I'm sorry as hell about Jagger," Slider said. As the club's president, Dare carried the responsibility for every single member like a weight on his shoulders, and the guilt and grief he felt for Jagger was apparent in the dark circles under the man's eyes. "How did he seem? Did you get a chance to talk to him?"

"He's tough," Dare said. "Was more worried about how his sister was doing and how things were going at the track than about himself."

"That's Jagger for ya," Slider said.

"Truer words." Dare let out a troubled sigh. "You hanging around for a while?"

"I wish." Slider said the words almost reflexively, but there was some truth behind them, and that surprised him. It'd been a long time since he'd wanted company or craved friendship. He almost didn't know what to do with those feelings. "But I'm in the middle of a shift."

Dare nodded, though the look he gave him was suddenly challenging. "When you gonna do more than run that emergency towing service? Jeff Allen's been ready to retire and sell that shop for about a million years. It should be yours by now."

Well, hell. Slider hadn't been expecting *that*, had he? He managed a chuckle. "Why don't you tell me how you really feel?"

Smirking, Dare shook his head. "Just calling it how I see it. I get that you've gone through some shit, but don't forget that I've known you for close to twenty fucking years. I know who you are and what you're capable of. And you, Sam Evans, were never one to coast through life. Hell, most of us aren't married and aren't fathers, but you wanted those things and you went after them. *That's* who you are."

Slider swallowed hard, his friend's words poking at things that Slider had almost forgotten. "What if that was the Sam I was, and not the man I am?"

"Bullshit," Dare said, crossing his arms, that fierce face challenging Slider to disagree.

Slider thought about it—*really* thought about it. His gut felt the truth in Dare's analysis of him and the situation, but his heart had been so trashed that it was still hard to believe in almost anything.

"I'll think about it," he said.

"Don't think too long," Dare said, nodding. "Because none of us has forever."

CHAPTER 15

"How's the dog?" Cora asked Maria first thing after she arrived at the shelter on Thursday.

Maria smiled. "Dr. Josh named him Otto. And he was stable enough to be transported to Noah's Arks last night. So he's got a fighting chance."

Cora sagged into the chair in front of Maria's desk. "Oh, thank God. I've been beside myself all week."

"Me too." The smile slid off her face. "If only his case was the last one we'd see . . ."

"Has there been another already?" Cora asked.

Shaking her head, Maria sighed. "No, but Otto was the eleventh dog picked up around Frederick in the past three months that we suspect had been used in dogfights. And we're not the only ones finding them.

Shelters in Washington and Carroll counties reported it, too."

Eleven! "This is so terrible, Maria. Do the police know? Is anyone doing *anything* to find these guys?"

"There's an investigation, but crimes against animals don't rate the same kind of attention as crimes against people. Or even property, sometimes." Her shoulders fell in a gesture of defeat. "Dogfighting is usually an underground activity, and not widely advertised. Hard to hear about it without the wrong kind of connections. The police are doing the best they can, I guess."

Cora was torn between relief and cautious hope for Otto, and anger about the likelihood that he wouldn't be the last. So she was really grateful to be asked to walk the dogs again, because that meant she could spend some time loving on—and being loved by—the dog-shaped potato sack known as Bosco the Lovable Basset. "Who's a handsome man?" she asked, scrunching his saggy face and rubbing his floppy ears.

He peered up at her with droopy eyes Cora couldn't help but think were filled with satisfaction and affection. If she owned a dog that looked at her like that, she could never ever give it away. Never in a million years.

The thought made her feel like she'd walked into a wall, because it lodged a seemingly obvious but also impossible idea into her head.

She could adopt Bosco.

Except, she totally could *not* adopt Bosco. She didn't own her own place. And she couldn't possibly ask Slider if she could bring a dog to his house, especially a dog that, given Bosco's age, probably wouldn't be around for that many years. Would it be fair to the kids if, somehow, Slider agreed and then Bosco lived only long enough to make them all fall in love?

She attached his leash, took him outside, and walked him for a long time, until his stubby legs gave out and he flopped contentedly onto the grass in the sun.

There was another way to look at this, wasn't there? Would it really be fair to Bosco *not* to love him just because he might not have that much time left? For all Cora knew, neither did she. Neither did *anyone*.

That last question stuck with her all day and into the night. At dinner, she found herself posing a question. A *hypothetical* question, of course. "So, I'm curious." All three Evans men looked up from the burgers and Tater Tots she'd made for dinner. "Would you adopt an awesome but older dog if you knew that he might not live that many years longer?"

"That would be hard," Sam said thoughtfully. "You'd know you'd lose him."

"I'd want a puppy," Ben said, looking back and forth between Cora and Slider. She felt a little guilty because Ben had been dropping not-at-all-subtle dog hints ever since Cora first talked about working at the shelter.

Slider put down his burger and licked some ketchup off his thumb. Cora tried not to pay attention to his mouth, and his tongue, and the enjoyment he seemed to be taking in her cooking lately, but it was hard when literally everything the man did drove her to distraction. Plus, he was wearing his cut after a day over at the track, and he looked so freaking hot in it—tough, edgy, maybe even a little dangerous. "Don't a lot of older dogs end up at shelters?"

"Yeah," she said. "It's crazy how people can have a dog its whole life and abandon them toward the end. I can't imagine ever doing that. They'd be like family." Hell, they'd be *better* than any family she'd ever had.

"I bet they don't get adopted much, either," Slider said, and Cora shook her head.

"Why not?" Ben asked.

She gave him an understanding smile, not wanting him to feel bad. But then Sam smirked and said, "Because people want puppies."

"Oh." He popped a Tater Tot into his mouth and swung his legs so that his feet kicked the rails of his chair. "What happens to dogs that don't get adopted?"

Cora met Slider's gaze across the table and silently asked if he wanted to handle this or if he wanted her to.

Slider braced his arms on the table. "Well, buddy, if it's a no-kill shelter, the animal lives its life out in the shelter. And I guess there are some rescues that take in abandoned animals. But not all shelters are no-kill . . ."

"They *kill* them?" Ben's eyes went wide. "That's not fair!"

Cora rubbed the boy's shoulder, hoping she hadn't done the wrong thing by bringing all this up. "Where I work is a no-kill shelter, Ben. But you're right . . ."

After dinner, Cora and Slider cleaned up the kitchen while the boys took turns getting showers. And even though Slider seemed totally relaxed—actually, way more relaxed than usual, at least for Slider—Cora felt like she should apologize. "I'm sorry about where that conversation went," Cora said, leaning back against the sink. "I should've guessed it might lead to talking about shelters that put dogs to sleep."

Hand towel thrown over his shoulder, Slider stood in front of her. "Death is a part of life, Cora. My boys are more acquainted with that fact than most kids their age. No sense hiding it. It's not something we can hide from, not any of us."

Dropping her chin, she nodded. The reminder of the loss they'd suffered seemed more of a reason against than for.

Slider grasped her chin and forced her to meet his eyes. "Tell me about this awesome but older dog."

Her mouth fell open, from the touch and from the too perceptive question. "Oh, no. I didn't . . . I mean, I wasn't . . ."

His lips quirked just the littlest bit. "Uh-huh. What's his name? Or her name?"

Chagrined, Cora gave a small smile and cringed at the same time. "Bosco the Lovable Basset." She blinked.

He arched a brow. "Bosco the Lovable Basset."

"Well, officially, Bosco. I added the Lovable Basset part." She gave him the most innocent expression ever, or at least hoped it came off that way.

His eyebrow was still arched. Over that incredibly sexy, scruffy, masculine face. "How old do lovable bassets tend to get?"

Cora's belly squeezed. She'd looked this up. Damnit. And the news wasn't great. "About twelve years."

He shifted a half step closer, close enough that she could easily reach out, fist both hands in his shirt, and haul him to her. *God*, how she wanted to. "And how old is Bosco?"

"Bosco the Lovable Basset," she quickly corrected. That eyebrow went higher, and her shoulders sank. Humor wasn't getting her out of this, apparently. "Eight."

He nodded, then stared at her for a long moment. Long enough that Cora had time to get distracted by the soulful cast of Slider's eyes and the shape of his mouth and the little scar on his lip. "You want him," he said.

She'd been so deep into the man in front of her that she nearly forgot they were talking about the dog.

Shrugging with one shoulder, she peered up at him. "We can't always have everything we want."

Slider braced one hand against the sink behind her, and then the other, boxing her in tight against the counter. He swallowed hard, and tension filled the spare inches between them. "But maybe we can have *some* things we want."

Oh, holy hell. What did that even mean? "Like?" she whispered. Suddenly, she remembered the last time they'd been this close. In her room on Monday night, while he'd comforted her about Otto. Slider had been about to say something, but they'd been interrupted . . .

Those light green eyes burned. "Christ, Cora."

She placed her hand flat on his chest. Just the one hand and nothing more, but still his muscles went rigid underneath. "*Like?*"

"I don't know," he said, his tone gruff, but his gaze vulnerable. "Like honesty. Like certainty. Like forever."

Cora's heart beat harder. After thinking about Bosco all day, she'd been contemplating two of those herself. But honesty . . . honesty had her thinking about—and considering for the first time—the possibility of finally, *finally* sharing more of herself. Sharing *all* of herself. Including those parts she'd been trying so damn hard to hide. Given what Kim had done, it didn't surprise Cora that Slider would value the truth, and that meant she owed him hers.

At least, she did if he was someone she wanted in her life . . .

And, God, she did.

She swallowed hard. "There's no such thing as certainty, Slider. But forever definitely exists for every single one of us. Love doesn't end because someone dies. It stays with us in memories and stories and smells and sounds that are connected to other times and places. Just because those things are painful doesn't mean forever doesn't exist."

Under her hand, his heart beat harder. He leaned closer, and now she could feel the heat of him. "And honesty?"

Cora's fight-or-flight response threatened to engage. The room spun a little and her chest went tight. No matter how much she wanted to give him what he wanted—*her* honesty—it was still hard to let go of a secret she'd never told another soul. One she knew Slider wanted to know. And now he was asking. She didn't have any advice for him on wanting honesty, but maybe . . . maybe she could show it to him. "My hair was longer when Haven and I first ran away from Georgia. Down to the middle of my back."

He frowned, and his gaze flicked to her shoulder-length waves. "Didn't know that."

"Our third night on the road, I borrowed a pair of scissors from a girl at the cash register at a truck stop and went into the bathroom and chopped it off to my shoulders." The words spilled out in a rush, because adrenaline was making her jumpy, nervous, restless.

She glanced at the open doorway, but the boys were holed up in their rooms.

"Go on," he said, as if he understood something important was happening.

"You see . . ." Forcing out the words was drawing her back there, back into that dark room. "That . . . that was how . . ."

"Cora—"

She fisted her hand in the cotton of his black T-shirt. "Don't. I'm giving you this." She met his tortured gaze. "I need to."

A single nod. "Tell me."

"My long hair . . . that was how he grabbed me."

For being so pale, Slider's eyes were absolutely on fire. Questions swam in his gaze. His muscles braced with the need to act. His jaw was tight with restraint.

And, God, she appreciated that. She appreciated it so much. Cora could tell he was holding back from reacting, from talking, from trying to make it better so she could get this out.

Now that she was talking, she couldn't stop the words, and they spilled free almost mechanically, faster and faster. "I got away from him when he woke me up on the couch. Then he chased me and backed me into my room, but when I turned to run through to my bathroom, he caught me by the ponytail. Pushed me facedown onto my bed. Got on top of me and pulled down my pajamas. His breath sm-smelled of b-beer . . ."

A tear she hadn't even been aware of spilled over

onto her cheek, then another. She was trembling. And hot. Sweat trickled down her back. The scent of beer was suffocating in her nose. The memory of it smelled as real as if a bottle was in her hand.

"After, I came up with a plan for both me and Haven, and we ran away in the middle of the night three days later."

"Who, Cora?" Slider asked, his voice like it had been scoured with sandpaper.

She lifted her gaze to his. "M-my f-father."

It was his eyes going glassy that made her crack. Just cracked her wide open. Long-suppressed agony ripped out of her.

"Can I hold you now?" he asked, even as she curled against him. "Please, sweetheart, can I hold you?"

All she could do was nod, and then his arms were around her so damn tightly that he was all that held her together. He swept her into his arms and cradled her against his chest as he carried her . . . somewhere. He kicked a door shut with one foot, and then he was sinking down and holding her to him even though she was a sobbing wreck.

And though memories threatened to pull her down like weights in dark waters, Cora Campbell felt safer than she'd ever felt in her whole damn life.

Right there in Slider's arms.

FUCKING HELL. JESUS fucking hell.

Slider couldn't help the tenor of the refrain running through his head. Given what little he'd known, suspected, and deduced, it was what he expected. And also a million times worse than his worst imagining.

Her father. *Her fucking father.*

It made him want to retch. And rage. And tear the motherfucking world apart with his bare hands.

But his hands were full of her. And Slider realized that was the only place that mattered.

Because Cora mattered. Because, *goddamnit*, he was falling in love with her. Despite his rules and his fears and his insecurities. He was falling in love with Cora Campbell.

But that didn't matter just then, either. The only thing that did was her and how she was feeling.

So Slider held her until she cried herself dry, and then he held her some more. He stroked the damp waves of her hair off her face. And kissed her forehead. And silently whispered, *I'm sorry*, and *It wasn't your fault*, and *You never deserved that*, and *I'll never let anything hurt you like that again*.

He said it again, just to be sure she heard him. "I swear it. I'll never let anything hurt you like that again." Slider wasn't sure of the entire universe of what he was promising just then, but that didn't keep him from promising *this*.

Finally, her tears quieted, and her muscles went limp, and he wondered if she was asleep but didn't want to ask and chance waking her. So he let himself relax against the soft back of the overstuffed family room couch, and he drifted off, too.

It was her voice that woke him some hours later.

The clock read after midnight, which explained the stillness of the house around them.

"Slider?"

"Yeah, sweetheart. I'm here."

Her fingers traced along the edge of his cut. "I wonder if I did enough, fought hard enough, said no loud enough. You know? Part of me wants to analyze the whole night bit by bit, but the bigger part of me is too terrified to do so and maybe find that it was partly my fault—"

"It wasn't, Cora," he said, his voice cracking from sleep. And emotion. "It wasn't your fault at all. He was your father, the single person on the whole fucking planet whose number one job was protecting and providing for you. Not one thing about what happened to you was your fault." He leaned over until he could make eye contact. And, aw hell, the tears had made her eyes as bright as emeralds. "Do you hear me?"

She nodded. "Still . . . do you think less of me?"

"Look at this face. Look into these eyes. And never, *ever* doubt that you're looking at your biggest fan, your staunchest defender, and the man who will always hold you up and have your back."

She swallowed, hard, her eyes searching his. So he let her see it. The emotion. The confusion. *Him*. He let her see it all.

"I don't know how I'm going to do this."

"Do what?" Of course, healing from this was going

to take some time. And he'd help her with that however he could. And forgiving herself, well, even when there was nothing to forgive, it was possible to beat yourself up till the end of time. Slider knew that too damn well, didn't he? As for getting justice—or revenge— the Ravens had already taken care of that when they'd killed her degenerate drunk of a father at their race-track the night Haven's father attacked the club.

But none of that was what she meant. Instead, she surprised the hell out of him—not with what she revealed, exactly, because he had an inkling. But instead she surprised him with her courage. "Pretend that I don't have feelings for you," she said.

If she hadn't owned him already, she did as of that very moment. Emotion thick in his throat, he tried to tell her. "I've been such a fucking wreck, Cora."

"I know. I didn't admit that to try to make you say anything back."

He cupped her face in his hand, because he sure as shit was going to respond to that. "I'm a wreck, and I'd convinced myself that I always would be. But lately, I've been trying. I've been better. Hopeful, for the first time in years." Admitting that should've been freeing, and it was. But, maybe ridiculously, it was also scary as fuck. Because when you'd become wed to a certain narrative of your life, letting go of it threatened to crumble the ground beneath your feet, leaving you with no idea where you'd be left standing when the dust settled.

Her expression went so, so soft. For him. "I'm really glad of that, Slider. So glad you feel better."

"It's you, Cora. It's me, too, some. But you worked your way into my heart and my head and my house and my whole life until I could see again that I *had* a life. One I'd been neglecting. One I hadn't been appreciating. So I don't know how I'm going to pretend, either. And frankly, I don't want to, not anymore. Because I care about you, too. And not just as a friend."

"You . . . really?" she asked, her eyes so wide and her face so damn pretty.

God, she didn't get it, did she? Just how much she'd done to change his life . . . But he was going to make sure she did from here on out. "Really. I don't know where we go or what we call it or how public we go with it, but there's something here. And I want it. I want *you*."

CHAPTER 16

Cora could hardly believe what she was hearing. She'd been so scared of what he'd think once he knew her horrible secret, and here, revealing the truth had brought her this . . . this *chance*.

"Except for that one terrible moment when I wished for it, I've been invisible my whole life. A father who didn't want to be bothered with me. A mother who resented me and didn't want me around. Teachers that didn't believe I'd amount to anything because of where I was from."

Slider shook his head. "I won't let you feel that now. *I* see you, Cora. And I don't want to stop seeing you."

"Then don't, Slider. Don't stop."

Urgent and deep, their kiss felt like a promise, an oath, a beginning. Cora climbed Slider until she straddled him, her body rising up over him, forcing him to recline against the back of the couch. Clutching his face, his scruff rough under her palms, she sucked his tongue into her mouth and ground her body against his. His fingers dug into her hips and his grip urged her to rub her core against the bulge of his cock. And God help her, she did. Shamelessly and frantically and breathlessly until she was gasping into his mouth and shaking.

"Fuck, Cora. I want inside you," Slider rasped around the edge of a kiss. "Before you come, take my cock inside you."

She fumbled with her jeans, giving a frustrated groan when she had to separate from him to take them off. Watching her strip from the waist down, he shoved his jeans to his knees. They both needed it too much to do more, and then she was climbing astride again, her heat to his hardness.

He didn't ask her if she was sure, and she fell in love with him a little bit more.

She knew her mind and her heart and her body. What her father did took none of that away.

So Cora took Slider's cock in her hand and centered herself over his long length. Looking him in the eye, she impaled herself on him, inch by maddening inch.

"Christ. Oh, Christ," he said, fisting his hands

at his sides like he didn't want to demand what he needed. Or take it.

But she wasn't having it. "Don't hold back on me, Slider. Touch me and hold me and take me, but don't hold back on me."

Her words unleashed something in him, because his hands were on her ass again, strong fingertips digging into her soft flesh, and guiding her down until she'd taken everything he had to offer.

And then they were a frenzy of movement and emotion. Her riding him with abandon, him using his muscled thighs to hammer up into her. The slaps of their skin and their breaths and their strained curses were loud in the midnight room. She clutched at his shoulders, his chest, the edge of his club cut he still wore over his shirt, and the picture of her hand fisted around his cut shot a jolt of lust through his blood.

"Fucking me so good," he growled, tearing her shirt off to kiss the mounds of her breasts.

He slid down on the couch, flattening himself under her. With one hand on her ass and the other firm on her belly, he forced her to rock back and forth on his cock, her clit grinding against his pubic bone on every thrust. And it shoved her right back to the edge again.

And then straight over it. "Slider," she cried before the orgasm stole her breath, her thoughts, her very sanity. Her whole body shook with the force of it, until all she could do was brace against his chest and ride it out.

Slider didn't let up one bit. He fucked her the whole way through it, drawing out her release and making the whole world spin. "That's it, Cora," he said. "That's fucking it."

Just at the moment her body started to calm, Slider flipped them over, her legs folded up between them, both of her ankles crossed near one shoulder. He was so deep inside her she didn't think he would ever be able to find his way out, and she didn't want him to. She could only moan at the overwhelming fullness and the devastating goodness of it.

His pace changed, his strokes shifting to hard, punctuated thrusts that rocked the couch and shoved Cora inch by inch toward the corner. She grasped at him and the cushions and pushed against the armrest. And once she was braced there, he combined those punctuated thrusts with rolling curls of his hips that made his cock hit places inside her she didn't know she had. "Oh, my God, Slider. Oh, my *God*."

He tore off his cut, and then his shirt, gifting her with the most mouthwatering view of his ink and his muscles. And then he lowered himself atop her, his weight pressing down her legs and opening her to him even more. Leveraging his arms around her head and her shoulder, his thrusts were relentless and driving.

Slider wasn't holding back. Not anymore.

And it made Cora's heart sing even as her body threatened another explosive release she wasn't at all sure she could handle.

"Jesus, Cora. A condom. We didn't . . ." He made to pull away.

She grasped his back. "Don't go. Not yet. Just pull out. Pull out and come on me."

Rigid and still, his face was a decadent mask of arousal and need and debate. But then she rolled her hips up, forcing him deeper inside again. Her movement ripped a groan out of his throat and lured him to cave. Hands on the backs of her thighs, he set a fast pace that made her pant and writhe. The lean muscles of his shoulders bunched and his stomach rippled. He was a feast for the eyes, masculine and raw, and he was hers.

God, let him be mine forever. And let me be his.

"Coming. God, I'm coming." On a shudder, he withdrew from her and took himself in hand. Two strokes and he was true to his word, shouting her name and shooting white stripes on her ass and hip and thigh.

Cora went limp with satisfaction, not caring in the least that he messed her up. His come on her skin felt like a claiming. And no one had ever claimed her before. Not really.

Leaning down, Slider kissed her, a soft tug of lips on lips, his hand gentle in her hair. "I see you," he said. "Always."

Four words. And her heart felt too big for her chest.

I love you was so close to the tip of her tongue she didn't know how the words didn't fall out. But he hadn't said them. She knew he was coming to terms with the idea of them. And she didn't want to push.

So Cora just said, "I see you, too."

For now, that was enough. And so much more than she ever thought she'd have.

"HEY, GUYS," CORA said to the boys as they climbed into her red baby in the carpool line at school. She'd picked them up today because she'd been out running errands for Bunny and Haven, who were busy with race night party preparations at the clubhouse.

"Hi, Cora," Ben said brightly, while Sam's "Hey" was more subdued.

As they buckled in, Cora's belly did a little flip. This weekend, Slider planned to at least tell the boys that the two of them were dating. The house wasn't that big, and Sam was old enough—and sensitive enough—to pick up on the change between them. It was important to Slider that they hear it from him, and Cora agreed.

But, God! What if the boys hated the idea? What if they weren't ready for their dad to date another woman? Thus her belly and the flip-flopping.

"You guys excited for race night?" she asked, pulling out of the driveway and heading to the grocery store. At this, Sam, who was as interested in cars as his dad, finally perked up, and both boys launched into an excited discussion of drivers and cars and racing stats that left Cora totally dazed—a feeling that probably wasn't helped by the ambivalence she felt about going.

She'd attended all three nights of the carnival that the Ravens held on the grounds of the track back in June, but had attended only two of the races since, and only because Slider asked her to take the boys while he worked. Both times, they'd attached themselves to Ravens who were more than happy to give Slider's kids a behind-the-scenes experience, allowing Cora to hole up in the brothers' lounge near the ticket and security offices.

Those places, however, she avoided like the plague.

Because the security control room was where she and Haven had been forced to hide from their fathers when they came to kidnap Haven. And the ticket office was where Cora had witnessed Haven's dad shoot Meat point-blank in the gut to prove that he was willing to use violence to regain his daughter. If that hadn't been horrific enough, that room was also where Haven said her good-byes before she fled to sacrifice herself so no one else got hurt.

Just the memory of that moment—Meat bleeding out on the floor as Haven thanked Cora for giving her even the smallest chance at a happiness she wouldn't let herself keep . . . Cora shuddered. She couldn't let herself think about it. Because not knowing if she'd ever see her best friend again had been one of the worst moments of her life.

So the racetrack was *not* her favorite place.

But it was important to the Ravens, and to these boys whom she loved—

The thought stopped her in her tracks, so much so that she didn't immediately notice that the light she'd been sitting at turned green until the car behind her honked its horn.

Glancing into the rearview mirror revealed Sam and Ben playing rock-paper-scissors to determine who got the first turn to push the grocery cart. Awed and amazed, Cora had to acknowledge the truth. She'd spent most of the past nearly five months with these kids . . . and she'd grown to love them. Not just care about them or enjoy them or like them. She loved them as if they were family of her own. The boys had made it so easy that she hadn't even realized it was happening. But now that she saw it, now that she recognized the feeling for what it was, she couldn't ignore it. She couldn't go back.

Cora didn't just love Slider. She loved his boys, too.

And she thought her belly had been jiggly before. It wasn't every day you not only started dating a man, but admitted your feelings to him and realized they were deeper than you even knew.

At the grocery store, Cora found the parking lot to be an absolute madness, Friday afternoon not being the ideal time for any sane person to go to the grocery store. She drove in circles looking for a space without success, and finally had to drive down the sketchy side lot of the store off which the loading-dock area backed to an empty-looking industrial park.

The three of them climbed out, the boys chattering away—goofing around one minute, and bickering the next.

Barking. The sound crept through the mental checklist she'd been running through. But there it was again.

Cora peered at the nearby cars, worried that a dog had been left without enough air on the unusually warm October afternoon. But the barking sounded aggressive and agitated, and way too loud to be coming from inside a car. Something about it made the hairs on the back of her neck stand up.

Frowning, she debated. "Stay right here guys."

She walked to the back of the store building and peered around the corner. Nothing. Just a tractor trailer backed to one of the docks. But the barking was louder, and . . . was that a man shouting?

"Cora?" Sam whispered, worry plain in his voice.

She held up a hand. "Stay right there with Ben, please." Her gut twisting with dread and suspicion, she followed the sound to a fence at the back of the lot. A line of scrubby, overgrown bushes grew haphazardly on the other side, but they weren't so thick that she couldn't make out two men standing behind the open covered cab of an older blue pickup truck facing off with a big black-and-tan dog. Her heart was suddenly a bass drum in her chest.

"Shit, we shouldn't have stopped," one man said. "I told you we shouldn't have stopped."

"You also told me he was out cold, asshole," the second man bit out. Taller than the first, his tone seemed to indicate that he was in charge. "We couldn't drive through town with all that barking. Your grasp of the need to keep things on the down low is surprisingly lacking . . ."

Holy shit! She wasn't sure what she'd stumbled upon, but her gut seemed to have an idea.

"Let's just go before someone hears all this racket."

Cora tried to get a closer look at the men, but they stood a good thirty feet away with their backs to her. Both wore baseball hats. And, damnit, it was too risky to chance moving to a part of the fence where the bushes were thinner. She'd learned that dogfighting carried a felony charge, which meant anyone involved in it—if these guys indeed were—wouldn't want to be found out. And might do all kinds of things to make sure no one did.

Glancing over her shoulder, she found that Sam had come halfway across the wide lot behind the grocery store, a concerned scowl on his face that looked so much like his father. Ben hung back at the corner. She gave Sam a fierce shake of her head, silently pleading for him to stay where he was.

"Fuck it," the taller man said. "And fuck these goddamn piece-of-shit dogs you've been finding me lately."

For a minute, the dog's growls and barking were all she heard, and then the men reached some sort of agreement, one of them turning to close up the truck's rear hatch.

Heart in her throat, Cora scrambled in her purse

and found her phone. Her hand was shaking so bad she wasn't sure how good her pictures were going to be, but she tried to zoom in and take some anyway. Of the men, the truck, its license plate.

And then they were gone, and there was just the terrified dog, barking and whining and making the most pitiful, angry sounds. Cora couldn't get a good look at him through the bushes, but there was something she could do. She had the shelter's number in her contacts, so she placed a call.

"I think I just saw two men drop off a dog in the industrial park behind the Shopper's Way," Cora rushed out when one of the volunteer receptionists answered. "Is Maria there?" When Maria picked up, Cora detailed everything she saw.

"Whatever you do, don't try to approach it, Cora," Maria cautioned.

"I won't. We're behind a fence. But he's really whining now, Maria. I think he's hurt."

"I'm sending animal control to you. Can you wait?"

"Yes. Should I call the cops, too?" she asked.

"Animal control will call it in. Just hang tight."

Cora did, with the boys at her side, a little scared but a lot more angry at those men. Fifteen minutes later, two men in a boxy van arrived, first for the dog, and then to interview her.

Subduing the dog, a Rottweiler, it turned out, was not something she could watch—and she didn't let the boys watch, either. Because it involved shooting him with a tranquilizer, and even though that's what it took to safely get the dog the help it needed, Cora didn't want to see an animal get shot.

Unbidden images of Meat's blood rolled through her mind's eye . . .

By the time she'd recounted what they'd come upon, provided descriptions of the men and truck, and forwarded her pictures, Cora was late. *Really* late. She shot off a quick text to Haven and headed with the boys into the store.

"We'll have to hurry," she said. "Bunny and Haven are waiting on us." The boys were unusually helpful as they speed-shopped throughout the aisles, Ben pushing the cart and Sam running off to find items here and there. Twenty-five minutes later, Cora hoped she hadn't forgotten anything as they loaded up her trunk.

It felt like a whole day had passed by the time they were fastening their seat belts again.

And then Sam leaned up from the backseat. "What you did was really badass, Cora."

"Sam!" she said, trying not to chuckle. Or melt at what looked like admiration in his eyes. "Language, dude."

He rolled his eyes, but she imagined it was hard not to pick up a few bad habits when you grew up around a biker club. "Sorry. But it's true."

"Sam's right. Even his bad word is right."

Cora turned in her seat. "And what do you know

about his bad word, Mr. Bean?" That made both of them laugh, since they'd watched movies with the British actor who'd once played that role and knew who he was.

"I'm just sayin', Coowa. It was bad butt."

That had them all laughing, and it felt good after the stress of having witnessed men who might be involved somehow with all the dogs that'd been appearing in the area. She could only hope that something she'd seen could help even a little.

Being later than planned meant that Bunny and Haven were already neck-deep in cooking and baking for that night's race party, a weekly tradition for the club. About midway through the races, club members started showing up to hang out for the rest of the night, until nearly the whole club, friends and family of members, Hang-Arounds, and women the brothers referred to as Biker Bunnies overran the place, turning it into a loud and rowdy party that was often as crazy as it was fun.

The boys ran off to watch TV in the rec room, and Cora recounted what she'd seen as she unpacked the groceries and got to work in the Ravens' big kitchen, styled in a mix of old mountain inn and new industrial touches. "I still can't believe I saw that," Cora said, washing her hands. "But I really hope something I witnessed might help. The shelter's director said the authorities have been looking into this for a while without much to show for it."

Bunny squeezed her shoulder. "You did good, hon. But please be sure to let the guys know what happened. I don't love the sound of all this."

"I will," Cora said, eager to see Slider later at the races. After spending all day yesterday repairing some equipment at the track, he was actually eager to attend a race for the first time in a long time, so they were meeting after his daytime shift at the shop.

"You sound like you're really enjoying working at the shelter," Haven said, a big smile on her face as she scooped warm cookies off a tray.

"Well, I've only worked two days so far." Cora grinned, pitching in with the cookies. "But it is a lot of fun. I get to walk the dogs and feed them and play with them, and I think Maria is going to let me assist in the clinic, too."

"Wow, I don't think I've ever seen you this excited about something, Cora." Her friend's expression went soft. "And I'm really happy for you. We deserve this."

And that wasn't even all Cora had to be happy for. Her thoughts drifted back to the previous night with Slider. Sharing her secret. Receiving his support. The incredible sex that had felt as emotional as it was really freaking hot. The only problem was that, having told Slider, she really felt like she owed it to Haven to tell her, too.

To tell her all of it.

"We do deserve it," Cora said, dropping balls of raw batter on a cool cookie sheet. The Ravens might be big, scary-looking, tough bikers, but each and every one of them seemed to have a sweet tooth thanks to Haven's recipes. On race nights, they often went through fifteen dozen or more. "And if we can find some time soon, there are a couple other things I want to tell you about, too."

Haven arched a brow and gave her an appraising look, one filled with questions about why Cora couldn't just tell her now. "Okay, of course. You know I'm always here for you."

But they didn't find the time while they were putting the finishing touches on the party food, and then it was time to take the boys down to the track to meet Slider. Ever since the attack on the clubhouse during the summer, Bunny didn't like to stay there on race nights, and so they said their good-byes to the older lady before piling into Cora's car and driving the short distance down the mountain to the track.

The parking lot was a big field that extended out from two sides of the oval track, and it was already hopping. They found a spot at the end of a line and then threaded their way toward the venue, which had a huge mural filling one whole exterior wall. It read, *Green Valley Racing*, the words painted in green over a waving black-and-white checkered flag.

Seeing a few of the Ravens directing traffic, the boys ran ahead.

"Watch the cars!" Cora called as Sam gave a wave of acknowledgment.

"You're such a freaking natural with them, Cora," Haven said. "It's really cute."

Warm affection had her watching them as they did funny handshakes with Phoenix. "I think it's because I'm still a kid myself."

Haven shook her head. "Nope. You may be funny and sarcastic and playful, but you're not a kid anymore. Neither of us are. All kinds of crap forced us to grow up way before we wanted to." She shrugged, the slanted evening sun bringing out the blond highlights in Haven's hair. "But we made it out the other side, and that's what matters."

Cora held up her hand for a high-five. "Amen to that, sister."

Haven returned the high-five with a laugh. Then, maybe a dozen feet away from the boys, she grasped Cora's arm. "Can you tell me whatever it is now?"

"Yo, alligators!"

Coming from one of the side aisles of the lot, Slider's voice caught Cora's attention, and she grinned as she watched the kids barrel right for their dad. Ben nearly tackled him with a hug, hard cast and all, while Sam hung back. What was it between them that kept Sam from showing his dad the same excited affection when he was clearly happy to see him? Or, at least, as happy as he was willing to put on.

"Another time, I guess," Haven said with a wink.

"For sure," Cora said, trying not to give anything away by ogling the way those jeans hung on Slider's lean hips, or the way his Ravens cut emphasized the size of his shoulders. "And it's nothing to worry about, I promise."

It was true. For once, all the problems and all the danger in her life were in the past. Her present and maybe even her future, for once and finally, were looking up.

CHAPTER 17

"D ad! Dad! Cora saw men arguing about a hurt dog and they left it!" Ben exclaimed.

"Yeah, and it was so cool, Dad. She got pictures and everything and then the animal control officers took her statement," Sam said, both of them almost dancing around Slider as they competed to recount the details.

Frowning, Slider's gaze lifted to where Cora stood talking to Haven. And, damnit, there was some magnetic force between him and Cora—had been for weeks, even though he'd been fighting like hell to resist it—that made him want to go to her and hold her and make sure she was okay.

Because if she saw something related to the dogfighting ring that Caine suspected the 301 Crew ran, she had no idea how close she'd come to being in real danger.

Haven headed to the track, in search of Dare no doubt, and Cora turned his way. Jesus, she was pretty. Wavy blond hair framing an angel's face, green eyes happy and mischievous, her curves as enticing as always in a form-fitting navy V-neck sweater, and the jeans and boots she loved to wear together.

"Sounds like you had an adventure," he said, not wanting to come at her with both barrels blazing with his concern.

"Boys told you, huh?" she asked.

Slider nodded, even as Ben tugged at the edge of his cut. "Dad, can we go in?"

"Go ahead, buddy. We'll be right behind you," he said, and then they were alone in the parking lot. Which was to say, they weren't really alone—not with a few of his brothers standing twenty feet away and race-goers making their way inside. Music and announcements blared through the concourse, the atmosphere festive and frenetic. Slider wanted to pretend none of it existed and pull Cora to him for a kiss.

Or something more.

"Hi," he said, staring at her mouth.

She grinned, her cheeks turning a pretty pink. "Hi."

He licked his lips. "I want to kiss you right now."

Her gaze flickered around them, a sure sign of uncertainty even though her expression read as all kinds of interested. Thank fuck they were in this madness together. And how crazy was it that he was in a position to have a thought like that? "Aren't we on a PDA moratorium until you let the boys in on what's happening?"

He chuckled. "Yeah. Remind me what asshole came up with that idea again?"

Her smile lit him up inside. "Well, you know," she said, her taunting tone going right to his cock. "PDA is only a problem if you get caught . . ."

He stepped closer. "Is that right?"

Nodding, she gave him a brazen, challenging look that made him want to bend her over the hood of the nearest car.

"Best be careful what you wish for, Cora Campbell. Because I just might give it to you."

She hugged herself and chuckled. "Now you're just being cruel, Slider. Because that's the most enticing thing I've heard all day."

Grinning, they walked in side by side when what he really wanted was to take her hand. He wanted everyone to know that she was with him now. And he sure as shit wanted to dissuade the motherfuckers whose gazes lingered too long on her body from holding out the slightest hope that they had a chance.

Because they didn't. Not if he had something to say about it.

For fuck's sake.

It was on the tip of Slider's tongue to pull Cora aside

and interrogate her for all the details of what she'd seen earlier. To ask to see the pictures the boys said she took. Or maybe even to find Caine and pester him to see if he'd had a chance to dig into this dogfighting bullshit yet. But Slider didn't want to ruin her fun over something that shouldn't pose them any problem tonight, at least. Especially if he stayed by her side.

Which he intended to do.

It ended up being the best night out Slider had had in a long damn time. A woman he cared for—and who cared for him—at his side. His boys having fun. His brothers all around and the roar of the race in his ears. He ate bad food and survived the torture of Cora licking her way through a strawberry ice cream cone—barely—and laughed more times than he could count. Cora seemed curious about the rules of racing, racing strategies, and the cars themselves, and Slider was only too happy to tell her everything she wanted to know because cars had been his passion even before he'd fallen in love with his first Harley and learned about this club that was . . . Jesus . . . that was more of a family than anything he'd ever had . . .

How had he ever forgotten that? How had he let himself become so lost? He might be able to blame a lot of things on Kim, but that part of it was his to own, wasn't it? He'd *let go* of things he hadn't had to lose, and in the process, he'd defined his world so narrowly that there'd been almost nothing left.

He saw that now. Saw how he'd spiraled. And saw

the truth of the Raven Riders—they *were* his family. They'd always been his family. As surely as if they were blood.

The realization was a total fucking eye-opener. And it made him feel like he'd found something for which he'd been looking for a long damn time.

The only thing that sucked was how hard it was to keep his hands off Cora. Now that he'd acknowledged his feelings—and admitted them to her—he was done playing it cool, playing it safe, playing it like the world didn't matter.

After being disengaged for so long, he didn't want to waste even one more second letting everything pass him by. He'd wasted too many precious seconds already. Having watched his kids' mother die so young, he had no illusions that time was on his side—on *anyone's* side. And he wanted to truly live again before fate made him say his last good-bye.

Sitting beside him in a section of stands reserved for the club, Cora touched his arm and pulled him from his thoughts. "I should head up to the clubhouse soon to help set everything out. I think Haven was planning to go up around nine-thirty and I told her I'd definitely be there by ten."

Slider glanced at the big electronic board at the end of the field. It was nine-thirty now, so he nodded. "Let me find the boys and I'll run you up."

"You don't have to do that, Slider. Stay and have fun. I'll just see you there later."

He appreciated the offer, he really did. But he was enjoying her company more than the races, and that was truly saying something. "No, sweetheart, I'm with you."

She turned toward him, her thigh against his. "This no-kissing thing is hard."

He chuffed out a little laugh and arched a brow. "So hard, Cora. It's *so* fucking hard." She laughed and smiled and blushed at his innuendo, and it lit him up inside to think that maybe he was capable of making another person so happy.

The boys, however, were definitely not happy to go. "Aw, Dad, can't we stay till the end?" Sam asked with Ben's full agreement.

"They're welcome to hang with me. I got a million little jobs they can help with," Phoenix said. The kids had been shadowing him all night, and he was being a really damn good sport to humor them. Slider appreciated it, he really did. But it also made him a little sad, because it was usually Jagger, the club's Race Captain, they stuck to like glue because he was—until recently—the man in charge. And he was really good with them, too. Making them feel important and needed and useful.

Damn, Slider hadn't thought about that in a long time, and it made his gut squeeze that much harder over the injustice keeping Jagger locked up.

"Yeah, Dad, can we?" they asked in unison.

"Okay," Slider said, clasping hands with Phoenix. "Thanks for letting them hang."

"What, are you kidding? These are the coolest munchkins in the whole place."

"Hey, I'm not a munchkin!" Ben yelled, setting off a mini wrestling match that Slider grinned and walked away from.

Out in the parking lot, he asked, "Your car or my truck? We can leave the other parked here and grab it on the way out later."

"I don't care, but I'm only three rows back. You?" Cora's car was closer, so they headed to the end of the aisle near the trees . . . where it was really dark because the overhanging branches filtered out the stadium's light.

Slider frowned. "Sweetheart, is now a bad time to mention that I feel pretty fucking protective of you and therefore the fact that you chose this creepy-ass parking space is making me kinda nuts?"

She chuckled and gave his stomach a swat. "It wasn't dark when I parked."

"Yeah, but that just means you gotta think of it beforehand," he said, his mind unhelpfully imagining a dozen bad scenarios. Not here at the track, necessarily, because after the attack on the club over the summer, they'd buttoned up security all around their property. But in general, he needed her to look out for herself when he wasn't there to do it. And, damn, it had been a long time since he'd had to worry about from which direction bad news might strike his life. He wasn't sure how he felt about that part of reengaging with the world—and with his heart.

And of course, the driver's door was closest to the woods.

"Okay, I will. I wouldn't want you worrying about the boys not being safe anyway."

He followed her around to her door and boxed her up good and tight against the red fiberglass. "Aw, hell, no. This is not about the kids. I have zero worries about their care or safety when they're in your presence. Understand?"

She nodded. "Okay."

"This is about you. And the fact that I care about you. And that I'm already pretty fucking attached over here and don't want anything to happen to you."

She relaxed against the car and put her hands on his chest. "I like Pretty Fucking Attached Slider."

Her tone stirred heat in his veins, heat made easier to ignite by the possessiveness and protectiveness he'd felt from their whole night together. "Do you now?"

She nodded. "Uh-huh. I like him a lot."

Slider leaned in. Slowly, so slowly, until his lips grazed hers, then skated to her cheek, her jaw, her neck, where he licked and nibbled his way back to her ear. "And what might make you like him even more?"

Her exhale was nearly a moan. "Hmm. Anything?"

"Anything."

"If he was making me come."

"Christ," he bit out, his cock turning to steel. "Here? Now?"

"Please?" she asked, her tone edged with desperation. "Not being able to touch you tonight has driven me crazy. I can't wait."

He didn't want her to beg for something he was only too happy to give. "Then push down your jeans and turn around."

ADRENALINE WAS AN aphrodisiac in Cora's blood. It flooded her nerves, her muscles, her senses, even as she complied with Slider's command, unhooking her jeans and sliding them and her panties down over her hips. And then she turned and braced against her car, the mild October night air tingling over her skin.

Suddenly, Slider's heat was gone, and she peered over her shoulder to find that he'd retreated a step or two. He caught her looking. "Don't mind me, Cora. I just needed to make sure I never fucking forget what you look like half naked against that car."

An excited breath rushed out of her, even as the wetness between her legs proved how urgently she needed him there. Stroking her, filling her, driving her wild. "Slider," she finally pleaded.

It was as if his name hauled him to her. His hands were at his jeans, his zipper, his cock. He fished a packet from his wallet, and tore the wrapper to reveal a condom. His fist bumped against her ass as he rolled it on, and it was so damn erotic, that little bit of contact, because it meant it was almost time.

But instead, it was Slider's fingers that plundered

between her legs. "Aw, Jesus. Feel how wet you are for me." His middle finger sank deep, once, twice. Cora tilted her hips back to give him more access, her fingers scrabbling at the roof of her car, her breasts covered by her sweater but pressed against the window. The sensations were arousing as hell— the hard metal and glass of the car in front of her, and him trapping her from behind.

That thought unraveled a tendril of fear through her belly, because the last time she'd had sex from behind, well, *It hadn't freaking been sex, Cora, okay?* Right.

And she refused to let what it *had* been force her to surrender the hot satisfaction of having Slider like this, of sharing this with him, of letting him take her in such a primal way. Especially since a dirty part of her mind, a part she maybe wasn't ready for, got off on imagining Slider taking this encounter to a whole other place—a place where he pinned her arms behind her back and clamped his hand over her mouth and took her hard and relentlessly against the car . . .

"Oh, God," she moaned as he added a second finger and penetrated deep. "I need more."

"Yeah?" he rasped in her ear. "Tell me."

"I need your cock in me, Slider."

"Yeah, ya do." And then his hardness was there, at her entrance and sliding home.

Her moan was high-pitched and tortured, but standing flush against the car as they both were had his cock stroking against a place inside her that made her want to cry and beg. His chest pressed against her back and his arms came around her body, and then he hunched himself around her and took her in a series of fast, hard, grinding strokes.

"Oh, yes, oh, please," she said, so close but hanging there on the edge. Way off in the distance of her awareness, engines roared and fans cheered and people walked out to their cars. But all Cora knew was Slider's grip and his breath and his cock inside her.

"Taking me so good," he growled, his hips smacking hers.

"*Please*," she moaned as the friction wound her higher and higher.

"Please what?" he asked, sucking on her earlobe.

"Put your hand between my legs," she whispered, too desperate to feel any self-consciousness about telling him exactly what she needed.

His fingers were there in a heartbeat, circling her clit and coating her with her own arousal. "That what you need?"

"Yes. God, Slider." Cora ground back against him as much as she could, but he held her so deliciously tight that mostly she had to just take him. And that was everything she wanted to do.

"Want you to come, Cora. 'Cause I'm gonna be right there with you."

The urgency in his voice was what did it. She hung on the knife's edge for one more second, and then she was falling, flying, floating. Moaning his name on the night air, her breath fogged the metal of the roof, an apparition of ecstasy that disappeared way too soon.

"*Fuuuck*," Slider groaned, his jerking cock buried to the hilt inside her. He withdrew most of the way and then filled her up again. And once more. "Jesus, I'm still coming."

"Yeah, give me all of it." And, man, what she wouldn't give to be able to feel the claiming mark of his come inside her, skin against skin . . .

But just then, she soaked in the pleasure they'd shared as his head fell against hers. His grip turned into a warm embrace that felt like love in a touch. For a long moment, they just were. Together.

Cora unleashed a long, satisfied exhale. "I love this car."

Slider chuckled so hard it turned into an outright laugh, and then she was laughing too—at the ridiculousness of what she'd said *and* in delight at his still too-rare laughter. They were still chuckling as they righted their clothes, got in her red baby, and drove up the mountain to the clubhouse.

The lot was already pretty full, but at least she wasn't *too* late. Five after ten didn't seem bad for having had such an earth-shattering orgasm.

Slider grasped her hand as she reached for her

door, tugging her to him for one last contact before they had to try to keep their hands to themselves again. His kiss was a deep, lingering affair that made it clear he was in no hurry to part from her. But more bikes pulled in, and they resolved themselves to a few last hours of being good.

Cora didn't know if it was easier or harder after they'd just been so bad.

Inside, music, voices, and laughter greeted them as they wound through the lounge and the mess hall to find Bunny, Haven, and Alexa in the kitchen. All three looked up when Cora walked in, and then all three did double takes as Slider came in immediately after her.

"Hey, how can I help?" Cora asked.

"Put me to work, too, if you want," Slider said, his voice quiet and a little reserved.

Cora could feel her friends' surprise—and almost hear the million questions pinging around in their heads—but of course they didn't let on a thing with Slider, and happily asked for his help to carry the heavy Crock-Pots of meatballs and chili out to the mess hall tables. Race night parties were always buffet style, as usually there were too many people to try to seat them all.

Soon, beyond the immediate din of the music, the night went quieter, a sign that the races had ended. Within fifteen minutes, the clubhouse was rocking as race-goers filtered in, grabbed food, drank at the bar, and generally raised hell.

Cora loved the atmosphere of this place, even its rowdier, grittier side. Because it seemed so real. People who knew who they were and what they valued and weren't afraid to live their lives by their own rules.

She got the appeal of the Raven Riders. She truly did. And that was to say nothing of how much she admired the protective mission they'd embraced on top of it all.

For the next hour, she and Slider parted as she hung with the girls and he sought out the boys and his brothers. Laughing and talking and teasing and joking, for the first time in her life, Cora felt *normal*. Accepted. A part of something so much bigger than her—friendships, a relationship, a community. She thought about pulling Haven aside to tell her about Slider and what her dad had done, but tonight she just wanted to *be*.

When Slider found her again, she was still with the girls drinking wine around the kitchen table. "Hey Cora, can I steal you away for a minute?"

She didn't miss the way Haven's eyes bugged in a *something's going on and you'll be telling me ALL* look that made Cora bite back a grin, and then she was following Slider through the clubhouse and all the way to Dare's office in the back hallway. "Is everything okay?"

"Yeah," he said. "But I wanted you to share what you witnessed earlier with some of the guys."

"Wow, do you think the Ravens can help find out

something about this dogfighting?" she asked, hope snaking through her belly.

Slider stopped just before opening Dare's door. "Sweetheart, the Ravens have got ears, eyes, and friends just about everywhere. Never forget that."

"Good to know," she said.

He nodded and opened the door.

CHAPTER 18

Cora walked into a room full of the entire Ravens' board. Well, everyone except Jagger.

Dare, Maverick, Phoenix, and Caine waited for them as she and Slider closed themselves inside Dare's small office. The guys were laid back and totally friendly, but Cora didn't think she was imagining the current of tension under the surface.

And then, of all people, Caine McKannon was the one to speak first. "Cora, we need to know exactly what you saw and heard. Don't leave anything out." This wasn't Cora's first interaction with the Ravens' most intimidating member. He'd been her and Haven's point of contact for creating their new identities when they'd at first thought they'd be relocated away from the club. But with each new interaction, Caine never seemed even a little more approachable or knowable. And it wasn't just his pitch-black hair always covered in a black skullcap, or his fathomless ice-blue eyes, or the gauges in his ears, or the miles of ink that covered even his throat.

It was something untouchable *inside* him.

So she rushed to give him exactly what he asked for, starting with hearing the barking dog, and ending with watching the men's blue truck drive away and calling the shelter.

They let her speak without interrupting, Slider right by her side, a silent wall of strength and support. And then Caine traded looks with the other men that made her ask, "Do you know something about this dogfighting ring or these men?"

Caine nodded. "There's a gang up north of the county. Worst of the worst. I'd heard rumors the past few months that they'd gotten into it. Earlier today, I confirmed it." He nodded to a sheet of paper on the corner of Dare's desk, and Cora picked it up.

It was an invitation to something called the Crew's Cross. The details were sparse. Just a town's name, a date, and a time for next Saturday night. "How do you know this is for a dogfight?" she asked.

Dare gave a troubled sigh where he sat in the chair behind his cluttered desk. "Because dogfights aren't widely publicized. No one just happens upon one. You have to seek it out, earn the organizers' trust or be referred, and then get invited. Sometimes they don't even share the location information until the day of because they move around." Cora guessed that's why no street address appeared on the sheet.

Caine nodded. "I found a guy who got me an in, plus two." No doubt there was a very interesting story there, but in typical Caine style, that was all he said.

"You mentioned hearing about this the past few months," Cora said, musing out loud. "My director said the increased incidences of finding these injured dogs has been the past few months, too."

"That's no coincidence," Slider said, and all the other men agreed.

"Cora," Caine said. "Slider said you took pictures. Can I see them?"

She handed over her phone. "I'm sorry they're not that great. I was . . . kinda shaking." She felt a little pitiful admitting that in front of all these big, tough guys. Slider put his hand on her lower back as if to soothe her, and it worked.

Eyeing the images one by one, Caine didn't look up and he didn't miss a beat. "Given that the Crew was involved, that just proves that your fight-or-flight instincts were working."

Coming from a man who seemed scared by absolutely nothing, that felt like some pretty high praise.

"Anything useful?" Maverick asked, leaning against a file cabinet with his arms crossed over his big chest.

Caine gave a single shake. "We're going to need them enhanced."

"Shit," Slider said on a frustrated sigh that was

almost a growl. "With a fight coming up next weekend, we're going to need that work done fast."

"Marz?" Phoenix asked, looking at Dare. Now there was a name Cora hadn't heard in months, but it was one she recalled fondly. Derek "Marz" DiMarzio had been one of the first friendly faces Cora really remembered after she and Haven had been rescued from a gang in Baltimore that had intended to sell them to God only knew who. The car they'd fled Georgia in had broken down, and the repair service that'd shown up hadn't been legit. Not that she and Haven had realized in time . . .

But Marz was part of a small, elite ex-military team that had rescued them and taken them back to their headquarters—a seedy-looking warehouse that housed Baltimore's Hard Ink Tattoo. He'd been kind and compassionate and careful with them, letting them know that they were safe and that no one would hurt them. It was almost hard to believe all that had happened less than six months ago.

Dare nodded at Phoenix's suggestion. "Probably too late tonight, but shoot me copies and I'll call him first thing in the morning."

"You mind me forwarding these?" Caine asked Cora, gesturing to her phone.

"No. Of course not. Whatever I can do I want to do," she said, leaning back into Slider's touch. She was so glad he was at her side.

Phoenix shifted in the chair where he sat, his gaze

settling on Dare. "Why don't you see if Marz can also scan some of the traffic cameras around that industrial park? Maybe he can pick up the vehicle Cora saw."

"That's smart," Maverick said, deep blue eyes flashing. "In fact, if we're getting the Hard Ink team involved again, maybe it's time we brought them in on our other situation, too. Maybe Marz can access information about some of Slater's people that the PI has been investigating and help him piece together relationships and associations. We gotta get our guy some help if we're gonna crack this. Slater was too fucking dirty, which means our investigator is going to get lost in the weeds of all his corruption looking for the one thing we want—the names of who dumped the shit that framed the club and put Jagger in jail."

Frustration rolled off of Mav in a nearly physical wave, and Cora knew exactly why. Alexa. Grant had framed the Ravens to try to blackmail Alexa into marrying him when she'd left him a few weeks before their wedding day. He'd promised that the longer she delayed obeying him, the worse the consequences would be.

Which was how Jagger landed in jail, Alexa had gotten burn scars on her hands, and her mother ended up in a coma. Grant had paid with his life for two of those, and it'd been the result of his own actions. But someone still had to pay for the third. And

Cora didn't blame these men one bit for making sure someone did.

"Okay, I'll talk to them about that, too," Dare said.

"If we're going to this dogfight next weekend, I want in," Slider said, a lethal tone in his voice Cora had never heard before.

"You sure about that?" Dare asked, tilting his head.

Slider stepped forward, shoulders tight, fists clenched, as if bracing for a fight. "Me going makes sense. We can't walk in there as the Ravens, because no way do we want to be on the Crew's radar as dicking around in their business."

Caine's icy eyes flashed. "That right there is for damn sure. Word on the street is that the Crew's events usually run four fights at a time and draw well over a hundred people, but the more down low, the better."

"There you go. Dare and Maverick are too well-known around town, so they're out," Slider continued. "Caine's invitation said he could bring two more. It should be the three of us." He pointed to Caine and Phoenix. "Caine is the master of keeping his shit tight, so they won't know him as a Raven. As Road Captain, Phoenix is out of the area a good amount of time, so that gives him some cover. And, fuck, the only good thing about my shirking off my responsibilities around here the past two years might be there's no chance in hell any outsider would know I'm a member."

"Damn glad that's all over now, man," Maverick said. "'Cause it's good to have you back."

"Hear fucking hear," Phoenix said.

"Slider's got the plan right there," Caine said, his gaze approving.

Cora was so glad to witness Slider reconnecting with his brothers, but she truly hated the idea of them going to something organized and attended by such questionable—not to mention criminal—people, especially if this 301 Crew was as bad as Caine said. "Exactly how dangerous is attending that fight going to be?"

Slider turned to her, his pale gaze more frankly aggressive than she'd ever seen it before. "We can handle ourselves. And we'll just be there to observe, so not very."

Not very seemed like way too much for her taste, but she knew there was no talking them out of this. "Okay, so what can I do?" Cora asked.

They all spoke over each other at once.

"You did your part, Cora," Dare said.

"We'll take it from here," Maverick agreed.

"You can't chance messing with the Crew, Cora," Phoenix said.

"Steer clear of the whole damn thing," Caine growled.

And Slider hammered the point home by taking her by the arms and pulling her close. Even though the words were sweet, his tone was filled with steel.

"You gotta keep out of this, Cora, and trust us to handle it. I didn't find this with you only to chance losing you. We got this."

She nearly held her breath. Did Slider realize what he'd just revealed to his brothers?

As if he'd read her mind, he nodded. "I don't care who's listening right now. I need you to promise. Go to the shelter. Do your job, of course. You hear anything, sure, pass it along. But otherwise, promise me: leave the rest of this to us."

He'd just claimed her in front of his closest friends, and it lodged a knot of emotion so tightly in her throat it took her a moment to answer. Finally, she nodded. "I promise, Slider. I won't go after any of this on my own."

Cora had the house to herself the next morning because Slider had taken the boys out to spend some time with them—and to tell them about their relationship.

She was equally excited and nervous, which meant she needed to keep busy before she drove herself crazy.

Slider had asked her to work on refreshing the house—and he'd even given her a budget for it, so Cora walked through the old farmhouse with an eye toward what she might do. Pad and paper in hand, she made notes. She jotted down new sheer curtains and comfy throw pillows for the living room. Perhaps a new slipcover for the couch and chair? Cora had always loved colored glass, and the front of the house got such amazing light—maybe she'd find some decorative bottles or sun catchers to add color to the room.

There wasn't as much she could do in the kitchen, so she decided to choose a bright accent color and find scatter rugs, placemats, and some other things to add a little fun.

In the family room, she'd just made a note to pick up a soft area rug when there was a knock at the front door. The surprise of it startled her, because in all the time she'd lived here, no one had ever come here who wasn't expected. Slider didn't have friends—or, at least, not before recently, and he didn't order anything that got delivered.

Curious, she opened the front door.

And found a county sheriff standing there.

"Can I help you, Officer?" she asked, her eyes going to the name tag pinned to the shirt of his uniform. *Sheriff Curt Davis.* Medium height, medium build, with brown hair and eyes and an average face, there was nothing especially interesting about him. Except that he'd been the one who arrested Jagger and Dare at the clubhouse that day, and Cora knew the Ravens didn't like him but didn't know much about why. And now he was here.

"Are you Cora Campbell?" he asked.

"Yes," she said, her body filling the gap between the door and the frame.

"I'm with the sheriff's office and I'm following up on the statement you provided to animal control yesterday. Can I come in, Miss Campbell?"

Her gut told her to say no, but that seemed kind of silly when he was doing what she hoped the police would do—investigate the dog abuse and fighting that had been landing way too many injured animals at the shelter. In fact, maybe this was a good thing. So she stepped back and opened the door wider. "Sure, come on in."

He did, removing his hat and peering around as he stepped into the living room. "Isn't this the house of Sam Evans?"

"Uh, yeah. I'm his nanny," she said, not liking something in his tone. "So what did you want to know? I gave a full statement to the officers yesterday and forwarded them all the pictures I took."

He didn't ask to sit, and she didn't offer. Getting out a black leather notebook, he stood poised to take notes. "I'd like to hear it all from the beginning myself, miss."

"Oh, okay. Well . . ." She recounted the story for what was the third or fourth time in the past twenty-four hours, making sure to highlight everything about the men and the truck that she could remember. He took some occasional notes, seemingly all business, but there was something about the way he slanted his gaze at her that made Cora uncomfortable.

That just proves that your fight-or-flight instincts

were working. She heard Caine's words from the night before, and casually took a few steps back.

"So you never saw the dog inside this truck?" he asked.

"No. He'd gotten out by the time I heard the commotion."

"But how do you know he was ever in the truck, Miss Campbell? Isn't it possible these men had come upon a stray?"

She frowned. "No, because I heard them say—"

He held up a hand. "With the distance between you and them that you described, and the volume of the barking, and the road noise around you, how can you be so certain about what these men said?"

Why was he being combative with her? Almost accusatory, even. "I know what I heard, Sheriff. I was right at the fence. I could see and hear them pretty clearly."

He shifted his stance. "Yet you can't describe the suspects' hair or eye color, whether they had any identifying marks, or tell me the license plate number on the vehicle."

Anger stirred in her gut, and she braced her hands on her hips. "No, but—"

"Would you be able to recognize these men in a line-up?" he asked.

Her shoulders fell. "I don't know." Frustratingly, the answer was probably no.

"How about the vehicle? Would you be able to identify it if you saw it?"

She thought she had a better chance at that. "Probably. The old blue color with the white truck bed cap was distinctive enough, I think."

He flipped his notebook closed and stashed it in his pocket. "I think that's all I need, Miss Campbell." His tone was so dismissive she wanted to scream.

"Sheriff, there's a problem around here with these dogs. I volunteer at the animal shelter and I know for a fact how many abused dogs have been showing up with injuries consistent with dogfighting. Please, you have to help."

"An investigation is under way, ma'am. That's why I'm here." He handed her a card, then turned to the door. "If you remember anything else, let me know. And Miss Campbell?"

She glanced up from the card in her hand.

"Men involved in dogfighting can be dangerous. I'd be careful if I were you."

CHAPTER 19

When was the last time Slider spent time with the boys like this? He'd picked up some sub sandwiches and drinks and brought the kids to Frederick's farm park, a big sprawling green space on the outskirts of town that combined playgrounds and picnic areas with an operating farm. Visitors could walk through and see all the animals, and watch the farmhands feed and tend them. Sometimes they offered horseback rides or let the kids hold the baby chicks.

Slider wasn't sure he could name the last time Sam and Ben had been so happy alone with him. But they were. As they ran and climbed and made friends with new kids the way only kids could so easily do, they absolutely exuded happiness.

And so much of that was because of Cora. It was clear that the boys adored her. But man, what if that wasn't enough to make them okay with their dad dating her? The thought that they might not approve—or worse, might be hurt by it—twisted his gut up inside.

Finally, they all got hungry, found a picnic table in the shade, and unpacked their lunch. The boys dove in like they'd never eaten before in their whole lives. And in truth, Slider was famished, too. Years of depression, grief, guilt, and shame had ravaged his body, but the past few months, he'd put on some weight again. His jeans no longer hung on him, and he had more energy than he remembered having in years.

"So, I have something I need to talk to you guys about," he said.

They looked at him as they ate. "What is it, Dad?" Ben asked, not a care in the world despite the cast on his arm.

For two days, Slider had run through a million lines in his head to open this conversation, and in that moment, not one of them came to him. "You guys like Cora, right?"

"Yeah, we love her," Ben said, peering up at him with that sweet little face. "Don't you?"

"Of course we like her, Dad," Sam said, more appraising in his look. Like he was waiting for some kind of bad news. "What's going on?"

Slider wiped his hands on a napkin. "Well, it's just,

I wanted to talk to you guys, because . . . I like her, too."

Ben's expression was totally blank. "Okay, good talk, Daddy."

Slider chuckled, but the smile slid back off his face when his older son's eyes went wide with understanding.

"Are you two, like, *together*?" Sam asked.

"Would it be okay with you if we were?" he asked, his heart pounding harder in his chest each second they didn't answer.

"Wait, like boyfriend and girlfriend?" Ben asked.

"Yeah, Benji. Like boyfriend and girlfriend." Slider looked from one of his mini-mes to the other. "No one will ever replace your mom," he said. "Which Cora would never try to do, of course. But I . . . I miss having another grown-up in my life. And Cora . . ." He shrugged. ". . . I really like her."

Ben popped onto his knees on the bench beside Slider and threw his arms around his neck. The kid nearly beat him in the back of the head with the cast, but Slider didn't mind, not one bit, especially when he said, "I don't mind, Dad. I love Cora. And you should have a person."

Aw, hell. Those words. They just slayed him. Just laid him out flat. "Yeah," he said, choking back emotion. Ben dropped onto his butt and dove back into his food like he hadn't just mowed his old man over.

Sam nodded. "Ben's right. You should." But even

though he agreed, there was something in the boy's tone that felt off. Not anger, and not even disapproval. Slider couldn't put his finger on it. "Just, you know, keep the kissing to a minimum."

"Eww!" Ben said. "I'm eating here."

Chuckling again, Slider arched a brow at Sam. "Oh, yeah? Talk to me in five years, buddy."

"Gross, Dad," Sam said, but there was no heat behind it.

"So are you guys sure you're okay with this?" When they reassured him again, he felt himself relax for the first time in days. "Good. Then any chance you want to help me with a surprise for Cora?"

They were immediately on board with doing something for her, but Slider kept it a secret from them as they packed up, left the park, and drove across town. Fifteen minutes and a million questions from Ben later, Slider pulled into the parking lot of the animal shelter where Cora worked.

"All right! Are we visiting Cora?" Ben asked.

"Nope. Even better. This is where her surprise is." He took them inside, where he'd come the day before to judge just how lovable a certain basset hound truly was. Cora hadn't exaggerated. One look at that droopy face and a wet kiss on his hand, and Slider was a goner, too. Apparently, he was easy like that.

After they checked in, a lady took them to a small visitation room, and a few minutes later, the door opened and Bosco lumbered in.

"Guys, meet Bosco," Slider said, crouching to pet the dog's sagging face.

"Oh, Dad," Ben said, leaning down close. Bosco gave his cast a snuffling sniff and then licked his face, leaving a decent swipe of slobber behind. "Eww!" Ben laughed, falling immediately in love. "He's awesome!"

Sam sat all the way down, and Bosco sniffed him next. But because Sam hadn't leaned down, Bosco took it upon himself to climb into Sam's lap until Sam couldn't help but give in and laugh. "You crazy old dog," he said, almost giggling as that big tongue attacked again.

Slider watched them interact with the dog and felt the rightness of this decision into his bones. He'd never been allowed to have a dog growing up, but he wanted the boys to share in both the responsibility and the unconditional love that came with taking care of one.

And maybe, just maybe, Cora and Bosco would stay around for a long, long time . . . After everything, Slider almost couldn't believe that thought had originated in his own brain, but it didn't make it any less real . . . or less terrifying . . .

Slider sat next to Sam so he could pet Bosco, too. "This is the older dog that had Cora asking that question at dinner the other night."

"So he'd be Cora's, but we'd get to spend time with him, too?" Sam asked.

Nodding, Slider gave the old dog a scratch behind

his ears. "Yeah. Would that be okay? She's sorta fallen in love with him."

"Sure you can stand the competition?" Sam smirked.

Slider nailed him with a stare. "Just for that, you get to clean up any accidents in the house for the next week."

Grinning, Sam smirked harder. But then he pressed his face to Bosco's and closed his eyes. "If he could live with us, I would totally do that." Sam's expression grew more serious. "Cora should have a family, and Bosco could be that for her."

"You mean like when my teacher calls her cat her fur baby?" Ben asked, hugging Bosco next.

Sam nodded. "Something like that." He peered up at Slider. "I think we should get him for her."

Cora should have a family.

Damn if the boy's words didn't hit Slider square in the chest—and unleash a strange longing inside Slider that was as scary as it was strong.

An hour later, they'd completed all the paperwork and sprung Bosco from the joint, and Sam's words were still pinballing around in Slider's head. Still, he could barely contain himself with the excitement of surprising Cora. But first they had about a hundred things to buy at the pet store—something that thrilled the boys to no end. They didn't see a single toy or treat in the whole place they weren't entirely convinced Bosco had to have.

Four hundred dollars later, Slider found himself

glad he owned a pickup truck. While Ben climbed in the cab with Bosco, Slider and Sam loaded up the bags full of treats, toys, bowls, collars, and leashes, not to mention the giant dog bed and a fifty-pound bag of food.

They'd even had a name tag engraved for him:

Bosco T.L.B. Campbell

Slider had had to explain that to the boys, but he hoped Cora got it right away.

"Dad?" Sam asked when they'd loaded everything up.

"Yeah, buddy?"

"We just need to make sure we don't mess anything up." He ducked his chin. "You know, with Cora."

Guilt sloshed like acid in Slider's gut. He hadn't been responsible for Kim's cancer, of course, but their marriage hadn't been everything he'd thought it was, either. Which meant, somewhere along the way, Slider had messed up in that relationship, hadn't he? But what was important was making his son know nothing like that could ever be his fault. He crouched down so he could meet Sam's gaze eye to eye. "Why would you think anything would get messed up? Or that you'd have anything to do with it?"

Sam gave him a troubled shrug, but nothing more.

"Well, I'll promise you this. If Cora and I didn't work out, that could never be your fault. But I'm going to do everything *I* can not to mess up. Because I'd like Cora to stick around a long while." Maybe . . . maybe even forever.

Nodding, Sam said, "Okay."

"Look at me, son." Sam's brown eyes finally met his. "I want you to know that you can talk to me. I know I probably wasn't here for you the way I should've been the past two years, but I'm here now. Anything you need. Anything you just need to get off your chest. You come to me. Always. Understood?"

"Yeah, Dad."

Slider couldn't stand the distance between them for one more second. He hauled Sam against him, the first hug they'd shared in so long it hurt. And, Jesus, when Sam hugged him back, it felt like Slider had been on a journey on foot over impassable mountains these past years, and now he was finally home.

But Slider played it cool. "Now what do you say we go surprise Cora?"

Smiling up at him, Sam nodded.

And then they were on their way, and Slider wasn't sure which of the males in his pickup was most excited to be going home.

RATTLED AFTER SHERIFF DAVIS'S visit, Cora had picked up Haven to go shopping with her, and they'd bought out the home departments in at least three stores with all kinds of things for Slider's house. And even a few things for her own bedroom. Cora had appreciated the company, even though Haven immediately wanted to alert the entire club about Cora's unexpected visitor.

Cora had convinced her that it could wait until they were home, and now that they were again, Haven was giving her the look.

"Wait," Cora said, needing a minute before five badass bikers potentially filled Slider's living room. "Before I do that—and I promise I will—I wanted to talk to you about some things first."

"Okay," Haven said. Leaving all their shopping bags in the living room, they made their way to the family room and sank onto the comfy couch. "Is this about Slider?" she asked, a sly smile on her face.

Cora chuckled. "In part. And, yes, we're, uh, dating."

"Dating? *Officially?*" Haven's bright blue eyes went wide.

"Yeah," Cora said, warm with the excitement of it. "Slider's actually telling Sam and Ben today." Which was why she hadn't wanted to disturb him with the news of Davis's visit. She suspected he wasn't going to be happy with her waiting, but it wasn't like Davis had done anything to her, or even threatened her. Though there was no denying how ominous his parting words had sounded.

"Wow, Cora. He's seemed so much better lately. I think you must really be making him happy."

She smiled, and butterflies whipped through her belly. "I think we're doing that for each other. Assuming the boys don't mind."

"Pfft." Haven waved a hand. "They aren't going to

mind. I'd put money on them being thrilled. I know I am. Can you believe how much good we've found here? And when I think of how scared I was of the Ravens at first . . ." They both laughed.

"It is hard to believe, isn't it?" Cora mused. "And I guess that's the other thing I wanted to talk to you about." Because she didn't feel like she could embrace the future while she was still holding onto any part of the past. And it was time to end that. Now.

Haven shifted closer, as if she sensed not all Cora's news was good. "Something's been going on with you, Cora. I've asked before and you've always played it off. Please tell me what it is."

Nodding, Cora took a deep breath. Haven wasn't wrong. Cora hadn't always done a perfect job at hiding how her father's attack had left her feeling, especially in those earliest days when she vacillated between being a zombie and screaming awake with nightmares—both of which she played off as the stress of their flight, and then their kidnapping by the gang. And even after that, she'd found reason after reason to keep her pain to herself. "So, something happened before we left Georgia. And, I'm okay now, but I wanted you to know."

"Oh, God. Okay," Haven said, taking her hand and shifting closer until they were sitting knee to knee.

"You know that I always wanted to help you get out of there." Silently, she said a little prayer that her best friend wouldn't be mad for all she'd been holding back.

"Of course," Haven said. "We talked about it so many times. Made plans and discarded them. Dreamed of where we might go and what kinds of lives we might have when we got there."

"Yeah," Cora said, her heart kicking up in her chest. "But there was a reason I was so set on finally trying to run when we did. Three nights before I slept over at your house so we'd be together to go, my . . . my dad . . ." Haven squeezed her hand harder, and Cora met her best friend's troubled gaze. *Just say it. Just be done with it.* "He raped me, Haven."

The admission almost made Cora a little dizzy. It was as if she'd held on to the secret so long that it'd developed its own weight, and now she was finally lighter and free.

"Oh, Cora. Oh, no. I'm so sorry," Haven said, her blue eyes filling with tears. "That bastard. What happened? Can you talk about it?"

So tired of holding on to this secret, especially from her best friend, Cora told her everything. She recounted every detail. Every memory. And answered every question. Like a purging of poison from her system that slowly but surely made her well again. "It was only that one time, but no way was I ever letting it happen again."

Haven pulled her into a hug, both of them crying, but Cora was done shedding tears over her past. She was all about her present and her future now.

"God, I was so focused on my own problems that

I didn't see this," Haven said. "I'm so sorry, Cora. What a terrible friend I've been."

"No. Stop that right now. I hid this from you on purpose, and I made up all kinds of reasons why it was a good idea. And you're right. You did ask. I just . . . I wanted to be strong for you, to get us out of all the trouble we were in. And I felt like admitting what'd happened would mess everything up."

"You're the strongest person I know," Haven said. "Seriously, I never would've gotten away without you. Or found Dare, or this place. I just wish I could've been there for you the way you were for me."

"You don't give yourself enough credit," Cora said. "Maybe neither of us do. But it's never too late, and I promise never to keep a secret from you again." Now that she felt the relief of finally coming clean, it was hard to remember why it had ever felt so important to keep her secret in the first place. She should've known Haven would be nothing but supportive, but sometimes your brain was your own worst enemy.

"Me too," Haven said nodding. They both sagged against the couch, as if the conversation had drained them. "Do you think these Raven men have any idea what they're getting into with the two of us?"

Cora grinned, almost giddy at being unburdened by secrets after all these months. "No freaking idea at all."

They were laughing again when the front door

opened a little while later, and there was a sudden commotion of voices and footsteps.

"Oh, sorry," Cora called, remembering the mountain of bags she'd left in the living room. "I'll be right there to clean up that mess."

"Don't worry about it," Slider said. The boys laughed, and then there was an excited round of shushing.

What in the world were they doing? Cora pushed off the couch to investigate when she caught movement from the corner of her eye. A dog—*Bosco?*

"What . . . how? Bosco!" she exclaimed.

Cora sank onto the floor and the height-challenged old man got right into her lap, put his paws on her shoulders, and licked her on the mouth.

Laughter rang out from the doorway, where Slider and the boys had gathered with the happiest, most triumphant expressions on their faces.

Cora hugged Bosco, and Haven chuckled as he licked her hand when she petted his head. "What's happening?" Cora asked, her brain struggling to catch up with this roller coaster of a day.

"Surprise," Slider said, unable to hold back a grin.

"Are you serious? You adopted him?" she asked, so happy she could barely stand it. She hugged and petted and kissed Bosco until he squirmed to get away.

"Look at the name tag," Ben said, coming to his knees beside her.

Cora did, and she couldn't decide which amazingly sweet thing to react to first. *T.L.B.* The Lovable Basset. Or *Campbell.* "Campbell. You adopted him . . . for me?"

Slider nodded, his expression so soft and intense her heart almost melted. "He's yours."

"And we'll help!" Ben said, making them all laugh.

"Wow." Cora could hardly believe they'd done this, but it just showed that Slider Evans had a wide streak of sweetness inside him that he didn't let many people see, but she saw it. Oh, man, how she saw it. She looked up at Slider. "Thank you. I can't believe you did this."

Slider held out a hand and helped her up, and then they were standing face to face. "I did it for you."

Cora couldn't hold back. She threw her arms around Slider's neck, making him laugh. "I love him so much."

"I know," Slider said, his arms coming around her, too.

She let go of him before she wanted to, because she didn't know how his talk had gone with the boys.

Slider wasn't having it. He grasped her face and pulled her close. "They're happy," he whispered. "And so am I." He kissed her then, just one soft press of lips on lips.

"Argh, Dad!" Sam said, as Ben wrapped his arms around both of them and yelled, "I want in on this hug!"

Haven laughed out loud. "Y'all are so sweet you're making my teeth hurt."

Slider slanted her a glance. "Don't mess up my reputation with that sweet crap."

Rising from where she'd been petting Bosco, Haven chuckled. "Too late, Slider Evans. I'm pretty sure everyone who's ever seen you with your boys already knows."

He grunted, making Cora laugh. "She's not wrong."

Haven planted her hands on her hips and gave Cora a loaded look. "Now I think it's time you deal with that *other* thing."

"What other thing?" Slider asked.

Cora groaned, but Haven was right. She couldn't put this off. Slider needed to know. "I had a visitor today. Sheriff Davis."

Slider's brow cranked down. He turned to the boys playing with the dog in the doorway. "Hey guys, why don't you take Bosco out to the kitchen and unpack his new stuff?" The kids couldn't leave fast enough, both of them excited to show their lovable basset his new toys.

"Oh, I want to help," Haven said, very obviously wanting to give her and Slider some privacy.

When they were gone, Slider turned back to her. "What the hell did Davis want?"

"Ostensibly, to go over my statement, but the whole thing was so weird. His tone was combative and dismissive, almost accusatory. He kept discounting what I'd seen and heard. And then he left with this warning about how men involved in dogfighting are dangerous, and that I should be careful."

Slider released a frustrated breath that was almost a growl. "Davis has been a thorn in the side of the club for as long as I can remember. Him coming here about your statement I could almost buy, but the way he talked to you . . . something doesn't add up."

"I can't lie. It felt odd to me, too," she said. It worried Cora all over again as she thought about it. Talking to him had made her want to take a shower afterward. Nothing concrete, just . . . a feeling. A bad feeling.

His hands landed on her shoulders, and his expression was filled with so much emotion. For her. "Why didn't you call me right away? I would've come home."

"I know you would've, and I thought about it. I promise. But I wanted you to have time with the boys. And Davis wasn't even here for fifteen minutes." Cora put her arms around her man, because she could claim him now, right out in the open for everyone to see. And she adored that. "If I'd have really been upset, I promise I would've called."

Slider nodded. "I don't want to be overbearing, Cora, but I care. Some asshole gets up in your face, even an asshole in a uniform, and I want to know."

"Okay," she said, pushing up onto tiptoes to kiss him. "It's nice getting to do this without worrying about getting caught."

"Aw, damn, does that mean no more sex against your car?" he asked with a grin so sexy she wanted to go find her car right now.

She chuckled. "I sure as hell hope not, Slider."

He heaved a deep breath, the smile slipping off his face. "I don't like this thing with Davis. He comes again, don't let him in. You aren't even obligated to answer the door."

"I can do that."

"Good. Because the more I think about it, the more this all feels wrong," Slider said. "But I promise you, Cora, that I'm going to get to the bottom of it."

CHAPTER 20

After lunch at the clubhouse on Sunday afternoon, Slider and his brothers met up in Dare's office to talk about Davis. The evening before, Slider had texted everyone what Cora had said about Davis's visit, and the wrongness of it had been like shrapnel under his skin ever since.

"I have some news from Marz that's pertinent to this Davis thing," Dare said, sitting behind his desk.

Slider hadn't been around to get to know the Hard Ink guys, but he sure as hell appreciated their expertise and assistance now. Because thinking about Davis being inside his house hassling Cora was making him crazy. Last night, the only thing that made him feel any better was slipping over to Cora's room to sleep. Bosco had lifted his head long enough to grunt an acknowledgment, and then gone back to sleep on her floor. *Next* to the dog bed. Go figure.

Maverick sighed and dropped into the chair in front of Dare's desk. "Let's hear it."

Dare opened an e-mail on his desktop computer. "I talked to Marz for a long time yesterday. The guys at Hard Ink are opening a security firm of their own, and they've gotten some new toys that he was only too happy to try out on our behalf. He said he'd dig into both of our situations, and then first thing this morning, he sent me this." He turned the monitor so that they could all get a better look.

Two pictures, side by side. One of them Slider recognized from Cora's phone.

"What's the other picture?" Slider asked.

"Traffic camera about two blocks away from the grocery store. Gives us a nice side view of the vehicle," Dare said. "No good image of the passengers, though."

Slider leaned in. His brother was right. The sun glare on the window obscured the interior. "Is that a Datsun? Late eighties, maybe."

"Yup," Dare said, reading a note on his desk. "A 1985 Datsun 720 4x4 Truck King Cab with a white bed cap."

"I think Datsun might've been practicing some wishful thinking when they used the word *king*,"

Phoenix said, staring at the old truck's image on the screen.

"All right, Dare, what else you got?" Caine folded his arms, a scowl on his face.

Dare nodded. "It's an older vehicle. Unique enough to stand out on traffic cameras if you know what to look for. According to Marz, that makes it useful if you have software which can analyze and compare footage from different cameras and aggregate all the times it hits on a particular image. Which their new company now has."

"Tell me it picked up this truck," Mav said.

"Hell, yeah, it did," Dare said. One by one, he scrolled through the images that Marz snagged off the camera footage. Most of them were from night-time.

"A bunch of those are from the same intersection. Over off of the Golden Mile," Caine said, referring to the big commercial strip that projected out from the center of town. Slider had noticed that, too, and something about it was bugging him.

"Driver always seems to have a baseball hat on. I can't make out his face for shit on any of them," Phoenix said.

"No need to guess who it is." Dare slapped a sheet of paper down in front of them. "When I've got the car's registration."

It listed one Curtis Davis as the owner of a 1985 Datsun pickup.

"Fuck me," Slider said, as Maverick raked his hands through his hair and exclaimed, "Holy shit."

"Car we're looking at is blue," Caine said, leaning in to eyeball the document. "This says the color is rust."

"That's because he covered the color," Slider said pointing at the screen. "The blue on that truck is primer paint."

"So Davis is somehow involved with the 301 Crew, dogfighting, or maybe both," Caine said, his expression thoughtful—and lethal.

"Hot damn." Phoenix said, giving a fist pump. "Let's get Sheriff Martin up here and share the good news that we can get rid of his asshole colleague once and for all."

Jesus, how Slider wanted to do that, too, but he shook his head. "We're not there yet. This is all circumstantial, which means we need more. Sure as shit explains why Davis was in my fucking house, though. *That* shit happens again and we're going to have a problem." Because it meant that Cora was on Davis's radar, and if Davis was as potentially dirty as this made him look, that was exactly the wrong place for Cora to be.

Sonofabitch.

"Slider's right," Dare said.

Maverick groaned. "Then what's our next play? Because this is the closest we've ever gotten to nailing Davis. And I want him. I want him bad. For being Slater's bitch, for his part in the dumping, and for arresting Jagger."

"We go to the fight," Caine said. "We go and we place him there. And if not there, we bide our time until we nail him."

"Agreed," Dare said. "And we hope that Marz brings us more good news, because he's working on the other research we wanted and he's still running this vehicle image through that program."

"In the meantime," Slider said. "I'm worried about Cora now." Fuck, and about the boys too. Because they were also there at the store that day.

Caine nodded. "The only saving grace is that she couldn't identify the men. That's probably what Davis was there to learn. Hell, if it *was* him she saw, he stood right in front of her and she didn't know."

God, the thought churned ice in Slider's gut. "And she told him that, too. *Maybe* that makes her safe, but I'm not hanging my fucking helmet on maybe."

"I don't blame you," Dare said. "Let's come up with a security detail for your house. Something at a distance so it doesn't worry the kids."

"I'll get it in place tonight or first thing tomorrow," Maverick said.

Dare stood up. "And, Slider, anything else you need, don't hesitate to ask. We'll have your whole family's back as long as it takes."

Slider appreciated the hell out of the sentiment, but it didn't make him feel any better. What he needed was Cora and his boys in his sight and in his arms. So he knew for sure that they were safe.

CORA'S FIRST SIGN that something was off was when Slider announced he was taking a week's vacation from work. He shared the news at the dinner table on Sunday night. All his reasons were good—he wanted to do some work around the house, help Phoenix out more at the track, and pitch in with making sure Bosco got settled.

But that didn't explain why Slider kept looking out the windows. Checking that he'd locked the doors. And pacing around the house like a caged animal.

Cora didn't want to ask in front of the boys, so she waited until they were in their beds and she and Slider were tangled up lying side by side in hers.

"Ready to tell me what's going on yet?" Cora asked, her room illuminated only by the small lamp on her nightstand. She'd added a few personal touches over the past few weeks—a jewelry box, a framed print of the ocean at sunrise, a little bowl of sea glass.

Slider scrubbed at his face, and then he turned toward her. "That truck you saw, there's a pretty good chance it belongs to Curt Davis."

It took a few seconds for the news to sink in, and then Cora's jaw dropped open. "How do you know?" Slider explained the information that Marz had sent to Dare, and Cora wasn't sure her jaw could drop any wider. Reaching over, she unplugged her phone from the charging cord and opened the pictures, and then she zoomed in on every one. "God, it could be Davis. I can't tell."

"None of the shots of the truck we managed to grab caught a good image of the driver either," Slider said. "But think, Cora. Davis was standing in front of you. How did their builds compare? Their height?"

Cora ran through her memories. "I can't say for certain, but I can say that there was nothing about the shorter man I saw with the dog that would make me think he *wasn't* the sheriff who stood in your living room yesterday."

"Our."

"What?"

"Our living room, sweetheart." He tossed the phone away and cupped her face in his hand. "I want you to think of this as your home, too."

Oh, this man. "No one has ever made me feel as special as you do, Slider."

He kissed her then, deep and sweet, but flirting with heat. "I'm going to make it my job to ensure you feel that way every day of your life."

Butterflies stirred in her belly as she retrieved a condom from her nightstand and handed it to him. "Then make love to me," she whispered.

They came together slowly, softly, taking their time to explore and linger. Slider's weight pressed her into the mattress as he moved between her thighs, rolling those hips the way he did, filling her so full that all she could do was moan. He worshipped her breasts and she dug her fingers into his ass. They had no reason to rush and nothing to hide from, not anymore.

And that had Cora thinking . . . thinking about how she'd said the way to move on from the past was to make new memories to replace the old, good memories to replace the bad. Cora wanted to try following her own advice, because she didn't want to be afraid of anything, and she refused to let the past have any hold over her. Not anymore.

She pushed at Slider's chest. "I want you to take me . . ." *The way he did.* But the words got stuck in her throat as the adrenaline kicked up in her veins. "Flat on my stomach. You on top. All your weight on me."

His eyes were a sudden pale storm. "Cora—"

"You won't be hurting me. I know you won't. But I need proof."

"Proof of what, sweetheart?" he asked, his voice strained with emotion.

"Proof that he's not still there." The words made no sense, not really, but she couldn't think of a better way to explain it. "Please?"

He eased off her, and she couldn't help but notice how his body had filled out these past weeks. He was still muscular and lean, but the sharpest edges of him were softer now. And it made him appear bigger, broader, even sexier. But what she most noticed was the dark expression on his face.

Cora reached up and kissed him. "I'm sure about this, okay?"

"I'm not," he said. "Fuck, I don't want to hurt you or scare you or—"

"Don't you see though? You never could. I need you, Slider. Make this new memory with me. Make it good." She turned onto her stomach and lay flat.

He shifted above her, his thighs going to the outside of hers, and stroked his hand down her spine from neck to ass. "So fucking beautiful, Cora. Do you hear me?"

"Yes," she whispered.

He guided himself between her thighs, and his cock found her center and sank deep. She moaned at the tightness and the goodness of the sensation, his slow thrusts dragging his head against that delicious place inside her.

But as good as it was, it wasn't enough. "Please," she said. "I need you."

He came down on her then. Not all at once. His legs around her legs, his stomach against her lower back, his arms curled around hers. "It's me, Cora. Loving you. So damn much," he said, and then he lowered his chest against her shoulders, his whole weight pinning her down.

She couldn't deny the jolt of adrenaline, the tendrils of fear, the fingers of the past reaching out for her. And he must've sensed it, because he guided her face to the side so that they were looking eye to eye.

And, Jesus, that look chased the past away, leaving only them—and the fact that Slider had used the word *love*.

"Say it again," she said.

"It's me." His eyes flared with understanding. "It's me, *loving you*. And, Jesus, Cora. I do. I love you so fucking much."

"I love you, too," she said, emotion knotting in her throat so tightly that it brought tears to her eyes. "I love you, Slider."

Their fingers laced, their faces almost touching, Slider fucked her then. Soft and slow at first, harder and faster when neither of them could resist.

"I'm gonna come, Cora," he rasped, his cock driving deep. "Fuck, I'm gonna come."

"Yes, let yourself go," she said, already flying from the triumph of being able to take him this way, of putting the memory of his love in the place of one of her pain. It was the greatest gift anyone had ever given her.

He shouted out his release, his hips plowing into hers on punctuated thrusts that forced her to brace her hands against the headboard. His cock kicked inside her again and again, and his body shuddered above her.

Slider was off her in an instant. But just as she was about to protest, he pulled off the condom and threw it aside, and then he lay down, grasped her by the hips, and pulled her over his mouth. "Ride my face, Cora. Get off on me while I watch."

"Holy shit," she said, the words alone spiraling the

arousal she already felt. And then she centered herself over his mouth and he banded his arms around her thighs, forcing her down.

With one hand on her breast and the other on the headboard, she rocked her core against his mouth. His stubble tormented her. His tongue lashed and licked and penetrated her. His teeth nipped her. Looking down, she found those pale green eyes blazing up at her. He growled against her, a wordless, masculine command. Cora thrust her hips and rolled her nipple and finally, *finally* lost her mind in a release that was so intense she had to slap her hand over her mouth to keep from screaming.

Gently, Slider shifted her off him and sat up, and then he pulled her into his lap. He stroked the hair back off her face and searched her eyes for a long moment. "You okay, sweetheart?"

"The man I love just told me he loves me, too. I've never been more okay than I am at this very moment."

His smile was soft. "I do. I thought it was impossible for me to feel this way, but I do, Cora. I love you, and I would do anything for you."

She wrapped her arms around his neck. "Just be with me. That's all I want."

"Consider it done for, oh, I don't know, the next forty years."

Cora's heart was suddenly a runaway train in her chest. Because Slider Evans was talking about forever. Forever with her. "You know you'll be seventy-five but I'll only be sixty-three then." He chuckled and kissed her, and she moaned at the decadence of tasting herself on his skin. "Your mouth is a deadly weapon," she whispered.

He quirked a grin. "I'm happy to torment you with it any time you like."

"I'll keep that in mind," she said, grinning right back.

"I'm just happy, Cora. For the first time in years, I'm truly happy. And I owe it all to you." His big hand stroked her face, her hair, her shoulder. She felt like she must be glowing with the way his words warmed her up inside, that warmth touching places inside her she'd thought might always be cold and lonely.

"You're the first person who ever truly wanted me, Slider. So don't think I don't feel the same exact way."

He ducked his chin, a little smile on his face.

"What?" she asked.

"Will you . . . will you be my person, Cora?" he asked, somehow making her fall in love with him even more. Because she didn't have to ask what he meant.

When no one had ever wanted you before, ever claimed you, ever valued you, all you craved was that *one person* who would. Who would give you a place to belong, who would love you no matter what, who would be your safe place to land.

"I already am your person, Slider. And you're mine."

For the first time in her life, Cora finally had a family, love, her *person*. And nothing could ever take the specialness of that away.

CHAPTER 21

Slider had taken off work so that he could keep an eye on things until the night of the fight, so he drove Cora to her shift at the animal shelter and was just pulling away when the text came in from Dare.

> PI identified who did the dumping. Meet at the clubhouse in 30 and be ready to ride.

Fucking finally.

He beelined it back to the house and traded out his truck for the Cross Bones, making it to the clubhouse with five minutes to spare. Dare, Maverick, Phoenix, and Caine were already there, sitting on their bikes and ready to go.

"What's the word?" Slider asked as he braced his heels against the pavement.

Straddling his matte black Dyna Street Bob, Dare gave him a nod. "Here's what the PI learned. Our guys are three twenty-something punks with a long list of priors, mostly misdemeanor bullshit, but some drug charges, too. And get this—they're fucking skateboarders."

Caine squinted. "What does that even mean?"

Dare chuffed out a humorless laugh. "It means that's pretty much what they do with their lives. Go around taking dares and doing tricks and skateboarding on and off of shit that wasn't made for skateboarding."

"So, what, on the side, they take on low-level criminal jobs to pay for this lifestyle?" Phoenix asked.

"That and shoplifting, apparently," Dare said. "Fucking skateboarders."

"Jesus, I think I've seen these guys around town," Slider said. "Skating off of railings in front of businesses and over at the park, too."

Dare nodded. "Well, they apparently built some sort of course, and our guy says they're there today."

Maverick's face was set in a deep scowl. "How'd he finally find these assholes?"

Putting on his sunglasses, Dare said, "He was tailing Davis and saw him meet with them. Looked confrontational, so the PI talked to them and threw fifty bucks their way. They folded like a house of cards in a strong windstorm."

"Sonofabitch," Slider said, stunned that they kept finding Davis everywhere they looked. Which made him having hassled Cora that much less acceptable. "All the pieces are just lining up."

"Yeah, they fucking are," Mav said. "And I'm going to bury Davis with them if it's the last thing I do."

Twenty minutes later, they rolled up to a fenced-in concrete course filled with hills, dips, curves, rails, and obstacles. About a dozen guys skated around, music blaring over a loudspeaker.

They dismounted, and Dare said, "We're looking for Bam, Bucky, and Mikey Mo." He gave them a droll stare.

"Seriously?" Phoenix said with a groan, and Slider got it. Because *these* were the lowlifes who'd landed Jagger in jail? "Mikey fucking Mo?"

Inside, Dare asked the first guy they came to and he pointed to the far side of the course. They found who they were looking for without any trouble.

The first of their targets who noticed them scrambled off his board and reared back, his red-rimmed eyes going wide. "Oh, shit," he said, pushing blond dreadlocks out of his eyes. He wore a pair of knee length shorts hanging low on his hips, a pair of sandals, and nothing else.

"We need to talk," Dare said. "And I think you know why."

Luckily, the skate rats read the writing on the wall and didn't try to run. Before long, the Ravens had them lined up against the fence, Slider and his four brothers in their Ravens cuts, a solid wall of muscle and anger.

"Tell us about the dumping on our property. And start at the beginning, from how you got involved to what happened after," Maverick said, his voice tight.

The one named Bam was apparently their leader, and he spoke first. He had tattoos visible through his hair, piercings . . . pretty much everywhere, and wore jeans hanging so low on his hips that Slider wondered how he could skate with them. "Dude, it wasn't our idea. That muthafuckin' sheriff said he'd jack up charges against us if we didn't help him move a bunch of shit."

"And then he promised us payment that he never delivered," Mikey Mo said. He was the one with the dreads.

"Yeah, dudes, we didn't even know what we were moving until the night of the job," the third guy said. When he opened his mouth, Slider understood his name, Bucky. The guy was missing half his teeth. Add to that his holey clothing and he looked like he lived on the streets. "When we realized where we were, we didn't want to do it, but the sheriff got all up in our grill, threatening us and stuff."

"So he was there?" Slider asked, stepping forward. "Curt Davis was there?"

"Muthafucker would only come partway," Bam said. "He took us to this dirt road that led onto your property and then waited there while we unloaded the stuff. Asshole wouldn't even help. Fucking cops, man, you know?"

"Did you ever meet with Grant Slater?" Maverick asked.

"Don't know no Slater," Bam said. "We're telling you everything."

"Look," Mikey Mo said. "We didn't mean no harm. I mean, my dad used to take me to your races, and they were fucking gnarly."

"Yeah, and the demolition derbies are epic," Bucky said with a toothless grin.

Slider traded looks with Dare and Maverick, who rolled his eyes. These guys were just a bunch of loser kids who'd been pulled in by Davis to do Slater's dirty work. Hell, Slider would be surprised if Mikey Mo was even in his twenties. He crossed his arms. "You three need to clean up your fucking acts. And I'm not talking about the skateboarding. What are you? Twenty? With arrest records already the length of my arm. Get your damn lives together because the next time people like us come knocking, it isn't going to be to talk."

Dare nodded and stepped closer, getting right up into Bam's face. "He's right. Which is why I'm going to let you off with a warning—you *ever* do something that interferes in our business again, you even *think* about it, and I catch wind? We'll burn down your whole fucking world—with you in it."

"Yeah, yeah, man. We get it," Bam said. "It's cool."

"And if we ever call on you to do something," Caine said, that icy gaze as intimidating as Slider had ever seen it, "your answer—your only answer—is yes."

Mikey Mo held up his hands. "Sure, sure. Whatever you say."

Slider sighed. Goddamn kids with no idea of consequences. This could've gone so much worse for them, and it still could, now that the Ravens knew how dirty Davis was. "You need to watch your backs around Davis, too," Slider added. "He's not a friend to you. You need help with a police matter, you ask for Sheriff Martin."

"And tell him we told you to," Dare said.

They left the skaters cowering there and headed back to the clubhouse.

In Dare's office again, he said, "We're going after Davis. Someway, somehow, he's going down. The question is, how dirty do we want the club's hands in doing it?"

On a troubled sigh, Maverick shook his head. "This sucks ass. With Jagger in jail, I feel like we're on the radar too damn much to take out a cop ourselves, as much as I'd fucking like to since it's that prick Davis. I say we go after him, not to kill, but to get him put away." Slider nodded. The club had lost too much the past few months to take such a big risk themselves right now.

Caine palmed the cap on his head and let out a

noise like a growl. "If we're building a case that Martin might be able to use then we need more ammunition against Davis. The word of three druggy skateboarder freaks isn't going to cut it."

"Which means that dogfight just became even more valuable," Phoenix said. "We place Davis there, and he's toast. I think Mav's right. It's time to bring Sheriff Martin into this."

Dare's cell phone buzzed against the desk, and his eyebrows shot up. "It's Marz." He answered. "Marz, hey. You're on speaker. The gang's all here."

"Yo," Marz said. "I'm not gonna lie, I'm feeling like Santa Claus today."

Slider stepped closer, the promise of good news luring him in.

"What you got for us, brother?" Dare asked, trading looks with the rest of them. The weight of their collective anticipation was thick in the room.

Marz's voice came down the line. "A hit on that same truck. Two different cameras. Right by the Ravens' property on the night of the dumping."

"Fuckin' A," Maverick said, voicing the excitement they all felt.

"Am I your favorite person right now or what?" Marz said, making them all chuckle.

"There it is," Caine said. "There's the kind of solid physical evidence Martin's going to need."

"I'll shoot it over," Marz said. "And one more thing. I'm not finding anything criminal on the suit your PI talked to at Slater Enterprises, but what I am finding is that the guy is way behind on paying his taxes. Like, six figures kinda behind. And Davis seems to have a gambling problem, because he's on the radar of some of the bookies here in the city. Which is making me think that Slater was in the habit of finding out and exploiting the dirty little secrets of the people around him to get them to do what he needed."

"Or, at the very least, to keep them quiet or get them to look the other way," Slider said.

"Roger that," Marz said. "Anything else, hoss?"

"That's a good haul for a Monday morning, Marz," Dare said. "Thank you."

When they hung up, the five of them erupted into an impromptu celebration. Whoops and *hell yeahs* and clasped hands.

"We just might be able to take Davis down and bring Jagger home all at once," Maverick said. "God, that would be some justice right there."

"And long overdue," Dare said. "So let me tell Martin what's going on and see how he wants to be involved."

Caine jabbed his finger into the desktop. "But you tell him, either way, this is happening. With his help on the up-and-up, or our way without."

Slider nodded, his gut clenching with the need for this to finally be over, and for them to be able to know that the people they cared about would be safe once and for all. "Davis framed the club, arrested Jagger for it, and threatened Cora. We can't let this sonofabitch hurt us even one more time."

CORA CAME OUT of the shelter to find Slider sitting on his bike, legs spread wide, boots braced on the ground. Wearing his cut and a pair of dark sunglasses, he was so freaking sexy she could barely handle him. And then he saw her and smiled.

"Hey, handsome," she said, coming up to his side.

He put his arm around her waist. "Handsome, huh?"

"I just call 'em like I see 'em," she said, pressing a kiss to the scruff on the side of his face.

"As long as you call me 'yours,' anything else is gravy." His hand slid up to her hair and pulled her in for a kiss. Slow, thorough, almost lazy in the way his tongue explored her mouth and curled around hers. He moaned low in his throat, and the sound hit her right between the legs.

"Slider," she whispered. "You're making me wet."

"Jesus," he bit out, handing her a helmet. "Get on. And hold on tight."

He drove them through town, the cool breeze making her chilly and giving her the perfect reason to snuggle in against all Slider's heat. That closeness turned her on even more and sent her hands wandering over his chest and down to his stomach. His muscles clenched under her touch, and that drove her on to torment him more, until finally her fingers found the bulge filling out the front of his jeans.

Slider's hand clamped down on hers. He didn't push her away, but he held her still. And since that meant her hand was full of his denim-covered cock, that was fine by her.

But by the time they pulled into Slider's garage back at the house, she was a needy mess. And what she most needed was to make him fall apart. Cora removed her helmet and was off the bike in a flash, and then took his helmet and hung it on the handlebars.

"What are you up to, sweetheart?" he asked, grinning as he pushed his sunglasses up on his head.

"Pleasing you," she said, planting a hand against his chest and forcing him to lean back.

Watching her with an animalistic glint in his eyes, he braced one hand against the small second seat on his bike.

"I've been wanting to do this," she said, unzipping his jeans and freeing his cock.

"Have you now?" he gritted out as she took him in hand.

"So much." Cora didn't play or tease, she just wet him with her tongue from root to tip before sucking him in deep.

"Fuck," he said, a hand falling on the back of her head. "Fuck, that's good."

Bracing one hand against the gas tank, Cora stroked him with the other as she lifted and lowered her mouth over him. And, oh, man, he was a delicious mouthful, so long she couldn't fit him all in her mouth, but she sure as hell wanted to try. Again and again, she took him to her throat, ringing groans and curses out of him that stole her breath as much as his cock in her mouth.

"Christ, Cora," he said. His hand tightened in her hair, holding her, guiding her, urging her on. "Taking my cock so good."

She moaned around him and debated pushing a hand inside her own jeans, but she was enjoying his pleasure too much to worry about her own. She sucked harder, took him deeper, until he was thrusting his hips and fucking her mouth.

"Gonna come. Oh, hell, gonna come," he said, his fingers twisting in her hair. "*Cora*," he rasped, his cock jerking inside her mouth. She sucked down everything he gave her and licked and mouthed at him long after the last drop. He shuddered and stroked her back. "Damn," he said, his tone so appreciative that she couldn't help but grin.

"You can pick me up on your motorcycle any old time you like, Mr. Evans," she said, wiping at the corner of her mouth.

His smile was immediate—and devastatingly sexy. "You can bet that pretty little ass that's happening every chance I get." Righting his clothes, he dismounted, and then he took her face in both hands and claimed her mouth in a plundering kiss. "Your turn."

"We only have fifteen minutes until the bus," she said, grinning.

Slider arched a brow. "You suggesting I can't have you screaming in ten? 'Cause that's a bet I'll take." He opened the button on her jeans, then the zipper, and then he shoved his big hand down under her clothing until he found her wet heat.

"Oh, God," she said, clutching at his shoulders.

He kicked one of her feet wider, and then his fingers stroked and circled and penetrated deep. His other hand moved to her hair, holding her to him and forcing her to meet his aroused gaze. "That's it," he said. "Chase it, sweetheart. Ride my hand and get it."

Cora tilted her hips and strained against the maddening friction of his fingers and palm. She held her breath and gasped in turns, sensation tightening and spiraling and gathering inside her.

"Yeah, there it is," he gritted out, his fingers moving harder.

"Slider," she said. Her fingers dug harder at his arms as his strokes made her knees feel too soft to hold her. He gave her a nod, his eyes on fire, and then the orgasm was ... almost ... *there* ... She shouted his name before her release stole her breath. Shaking against him, she writhed as her muscles clenched again and again. She clutched at his wrist, his touch suddenly too much. But he wouldn't stop, wouldn't let up, until she was limp against him and only his arm around her waist held her up.

"God, that was beautiful to watch," he said, kissing her forehead.

"I think I'm dead now."

He chuckled and shook his head. "Nope. You'll live to come another day. Count on it."

Cora laughed, because Slider had been hiding an awesome sense of humor all these months, and she was getting to see more of it every day. "I love you," she said.

"Right back atcha, sweetheart." He brought his hand to his mouth and licked his fingers clean.

"Jesus," she whispered, watching him. "Not gonna forget watching you do that any time soon."

He gave her a wink. "By the way, the bus will be here in six minutes. So I got you off with time to spare."

His tone was so smug that she wasn't sure whether she wanted to hit him or kiss him, but she could only laugh. "Duly noted."

When she was buttoned up again, they walked hand in hand toward the house, past her car—

"Oh, no," she said, frowning. "My tire's flat." The front passenger's tire sat flat against the ground. And then she gasped. "That one is, too!"

"Sonofabitch," Slider said, crouching down to inspect it. "That's not flat, that's been cut." He fingered a slit in the black rubber, and then he stalked around the car to find that all four had been sliced.

"Who would do this?" she asked, her belly tossing.

"Davis," he growled. "Making sure you took his warning seriously."

The school bus pulled up and Cora tried to shake the worry off her expression. "Are we telling them?"

"No," Slider said. "Not unless we have to. Take them inside. I'm going to let the club know and get Martin over here to file a report. And then I'm gonna wring somebody's fucking neck."

CHAPTER 22

Slider waited until the boys were in bed, and then he invited his brothers to come over to strategize. Martin had been there hours before to take pictures of the car and get Slider's statement, but he came back again now for the meeting. Because shit was escalating, and they needed a plan.

When they were all gathered in his family room—to reduce the chances of their voices drifting up the stairs and waking the boys—Slider turned to Martin.

"I want to know what you're going to do about this Davis situation. Because this shit is now ten kinds of personal to me. He was at my house, harassed my girlfriend, and now he's sliced her tires to drive home the threat he issued as he left her that day." Cora sat beside him on the couch, and Bosco lay in a big lump right between both of their feet.

Martin was a few years older than Slider and had gone to school with Dare back in the day. The friendship they'd made then was even stronger now, which was why Martin held up his hand and said, "Dare and I have talked and he's shared everything you've learned. I'm on board. Trust me, I'd like nothing more than to put Davis away and get him out of my office and off the streets. But this needs to be airtight, and that means that I've got to minimize the extent to which Raven Rider hands are all over it."

"No way are we stepping aside," Caine said. Slider nodded.

Raking a hand through his wavy brown hair, Martin shook his head. "Gimme a little credit here. I've known you guys for twenty fucking years. You think I don't know that already?" He sighed. "I propose the following. First, I'll have one of my men patrolling by here on a regular basis."

Slider rolled his eyes so hard they nearly fell out of his goddamn head.

"Second," Martin said, clearly sensing their frustration. "I'm going to organize a sting on this dogfighting event Saturday night. I've already reached out to several surrounding jurisdictions for backup. Take out the dogfighting, maybe some Crew members, and Davis all in one fell swoop. Combine that with the other evidence that you've collected about

Davis's activities, and he goes away. For a long time."

That sounded good, but Slider shared the question that Caine voiced: "Are you asking us to sit out of it then?"

"Ideally, yeah," Martin said, eliciting groans all around the room. "But I know you fuckers. I try to box you out, you go in anyway and shit goes fubar. So the three of you can go in like you planned, ID Davis for us and confirm he's there, and then we close in. Obviously, we want to take the dogfighting down, but if our primary target is Davis—"

"And it is," Dare said.

Martin gave a nod. "Then making sure he's there is useful to both of us."

"What about Jagger?" Maverick asked. They all murmured in agreement.

"I can't control the courts," Martin said. "But you can sure as shit bet I'll press the district attorney to review the new evidence. And I'll get Jagger's lawyer working on it, too—but not until after Saturday night's event. We can't let anything tip Davis off. And that includes all of you. Same routines. Same activities. In case he's watching—or has someone else doing it—nothing to alert him that anything's happening. If he was over here interrogating Cora about her statement, then he's already paranoid enough. We don't want him acting—or running."

"He's already escalating things if he's the one behind cutting Cora's tires," Slider said.

"Agreed," Dare said. "Send by your patrol cars all you want, Martin, but we've also got three details around Slider's house now. No one will go up or down this road without us knowing it."

Maverick released a frustrated breath. "Fuck, Slider, I'm sorry I didn't get people in place first thing this morning."

"This isn't your fault, Maverick," Cora said, piping up for the first time. "This is all on Davis."

"She's right," Slider said, appreciating her for defending his brother that way. "And Saturday night, we finish this once and for all."

A plan in place, the week absolutely dragged. But at least there was something fun to celebrate—on Wednesday, Haven started her first day working down at Dutch's, an old-time diner located in the heart of Frederick's old town.

"Let's take the boys and go for dinner," Cora said. "Maybe Dare and some of the brothers will come. We could all go down and support her."

Slider nodded, loving the way his woman always wanted to take care of everyone around her. And getting out of the house would be better than sitting around waiting for the weekend, because they were all going a little crazy doing that. "Yeah, all right. Let's make this happen."

Which was how he and Cora, his boys, and a dozen Ravens ended up filling the joint, one of those hole-in-the-wall-looking places with amazing food. Situated on a street corner, Dutch's was a long, narrow space filled with red-and-white booths, a jukebox, and a Formica counter with a dozen spinning stools. Once, Dutch had opened it only for breakfast and lunch, but now that he'd finally had his hip replaced, he was newly open for dinner a few nights a week.

Standing behind the case of desserts, Haven nearly glowed with happiness and surprise as more Ravens came in until the place was absolutely jumping.

"I should've hired you years ago, Miss Haven," Dutch said to everyone's laughter. A tall, older man with warm brown skin, graying hair, and a manner that always put everyone at ease, Dutch had been a friend to the club for as long as Slider could remember.

"Look at her," Cora said from their place at the counter. "I'm so proud of her I could burst. You don't understand how painfully shy she used to be. Six months ago, this seemed like an impossible dream."

Slider spun his stool toward his own impossible dream. "I know exactly how that feels, Cora. Sometimes things actually do work out right." He couldn't believe those words were coming out of his mouth, of all people, but these days, he was living proof of it. And he was finally going to let himself embrace it, despite all the shit swirling around them.

"Yeah," she said, her smile so pretty. And all for him.

Everyone ate too much and then piled one of Haven's big desserts on top of it. The boys had thick slabs of chocolate cake and vanilla ice cream, while

Cora moaned over a piece of strawberry shortcake, and Slider tried a piece of the pumpkin-apple spice cake with chocolate chips and raisins in it and a sinful creamy icing drizzled over it.

"Jesus," he murmured around his first bite. "This is amazing."

Cora laughed. "Annnd another one bites the dust." She shook her head. "It's impossible not to fall in love with Haven's baking."

He pressed a sticky kiss to her cheek. "It's impossible not to fall in love with you."

"Sweet man," she whispered, her expression so soft and beautiful.

"Aw, come on, Dad. We're *eating*," Sam said.

Cora laughed and ruffled the kid's hair, and then she went in for a sneak attack and nabbed a bite of his cake.

"Hey!" Sam turned to the side, shielding his plate with his body as they all laughed.

Many of them cleared out when they were done in order to make room for other customers, but Slider and Cora hung out with Dare at the counter, and the boys entertained themselves with a stash of comics that Dutch kept under the counter. While Cora chatted with Haven, Slider and Dare shot the shit about everything and anything. And it was fucking nice.

Once, they'd been close. Not as close as Dare and Maverick—who were connected by blood and had grown up together. But Slider and Dare had once hung out a lot, run on road trips together, and generally raised hell together, even after the kids had come along. Dare had seemingly accepted Slider back into the fold, no questions asked, but Slider was suddenly feeling like he owed one of his oldest friends an explanation for the way he'd just dropped off the face of the planet.

His gut squeezed at the idea of coming clean.

And that little niggle of fear was exactly why Slider should do it. It was time to move on. So. Right.

Slider took a deep breath, and let the question fly. "Hey Dare, can I talk to you for a minute? Outside maybe?" A wave of nausea made him regret having finished that whole piece of cake.

Dare gave him a look and a quick nod, and then they were heading out onto the quiet evening street. "Everything okay?"

"Now it is," Slider said. "But I feel like you deserve to know what happened to me all that time."

Eyebrows shooting up, Dare shook his head. "You don't owe me anything. Your wife died, Slider. The mother of your kids. I can't even imagine what that was like."

His stomach was a wreck. "It was more than that, Dare. It was so much fucking more."

His friend's eyes narrowed. "Okay. Whatever it is, brother, I'll have your back. You know that."

Slider sighed, his gaze catching on something down the street. And then he manned up and looked

Dare in the eyes. "Kim was cheating on me. For about a year. Was going to leave me. She told me all this a few weeks before she got sick, and then the asshole she was with refused to care for her when it started getting bad."

"Christ," Dare bit out, his expression solid, no pity to be found. "But you stepped up and took care of her. That took a lot of fucking guts, man."

"I just . . . I couldn't let the boys know that their mother planned to leave them. Not after the way I grew up. I couldn't let them have to live with that." He shook his head. "But it ate at me from the inside out until it felt like there was nothing left to give, not even to my friends and this club I have loved most of my life."

"Jesus, Slider, you're a damn good man. And an even better father. Don't think for a second you owe an explanation for doing the right thing or for being wrecked by having done it. You're here now, and that's what matters." Dare held out his hand. "But know that I appreciate like hell that you trusted me with knowing this. You can count on me to keep it between us."

Slider returned the shake, feeling like a weight he'd been carrying for so long lifted off his shoulders. It was the past, falling away, at long last. "I know I can."

"Everything all right?" Cora asked when they returned.

He slid onto his stool and squeezed her thigh.

"Never better, sweetheart. Never better." And it was true. Somehow, Slider Evans had finally found love, belonging, and peace. That was everything he'd been searching for but thought for sure he'd never be able to have.

Now, just one more fight stood in his way of keeping what he'd found, once and for fucking all.

THE BIG EXCITEMENT at the shelter on Thursday was the arrival of a bunch of new dogs, neglected, but at least not abused. A farm in rural Maryland had been discovered housing—poorly—nearly fifty dogs of all ages, and the local shelter there hadn't been able to take them all. So Cora got to help do intake on the eight dogs they were taking in, including two seven-week-old shepherd-collie mix puppies that were so cute she could hardly stand it.

"We get to name them," Dr. Josh said. "Well, at least give them temporary names until they're adopted. These guys are sure to go quick. Would you like to do the honors?"

"Me? Really?" Cora asked. She picked up the first of the puppies, who was so small he almost fit in her hand. Brown and tan with soulful little brown eyes. "I think this guy should be called Howie."

The doc laughed. "Howie it is. And his brother?"

What went with Howie? She wanted something fun and silly, since he'd probably have another name before too long. "How about Horace."

Dr. Josh pulled a face. "That is quite possibly the worst dog name I've ever heard."

She laughed. "I like it! Howie and Horace. That's cute!"

The names stuck, and Cora was still chuckling about it when she left at the end of her shift. And her smile just got bigger when she found Slider there on his bike to pick her up again. He'd taken her car to his shop and replaced her tires, and her red baby was now locked in his garage to keep it safe. Until the dogfight was over and Davis was finally behind bars, Slider wanted to personally take her wherever she needed to go.

That wasn't much of a hardship.

Except that, unlike on Monday afternoon, Slider wasn't smiling back at her today. "What's wrong?" she asked, sensing it before he even said a word.

He pushed his sunglasses up on his head. "Caine just got a text. The dogfight's been moved up."

Standing beside his bike, her hand on his thigh, Cora frowned. "Okay, to when?"

"Tonight."

Surprise rocked through her, along with a wave of nervous anticipation. "Okay, so . . . What does that mean? Why is that bad?"

Slider sighed. "Because Martin can't get the other jurisdictions in place within the next two hours on this short notice. These dogfights can attract a hundred or more people, so the original plan was for the cops to be in place at least two hours beforehand, maybe more, to set up a perimeter that would contain all the participants without the Crew knowing. There's no way to do that now."

"Does that mean going this time is off then?" she asked, her stomach dropping. She'd so been hoping this would all be behind them sooner rather than later.

"No. Me, Caine, and Phoenix are still going in. Martin and two other sheriffs are going to give us some backup, but it'll be a smaller operation than we initially hoped."

Cora gasped, because that sounded really freaking dangerous. "Slider, I don't like the sound of this."

He grasped her hand against his thigh. "Don't worry. The plan's still the same. Observe. Find out who's running this ring. Get some pictures of Davis there. Get back out. Hopefully we won't even have to be there that long, because I am not looking forward to watching dogs tear each other apart."

Her mind scrambled for an alternative. "Why can't more of the Ravens go so it's not just the three of you?"

"Because, sweetheart, if the 301 Crew perceives us as attacking their territory, it'll start a war that'll only end when a whole bunch of bodies are lying on the ground, and that's the last thing we want. We have to do this low key, and hopefully, they won't even realize we were there."

"But won't Davis recognize you?" she asked, stepping in closer. He put his arm around her waist.

"If we spot him there, we're going to keep our distance. And we're going to borrow a page out of his book. Street clothes. Hats. Phoenix even found an old pair of glasses he's going to wear."

That made her smile, just a little. "I just don't like the idea of you in danger, Slider."

"That's why I gotta do this. It's time to put it behind us." He handed her a helmet, and too soon they were back at the house so Slider could change. He came downstairs fifteen minutes later in the same jeans and boots, but wearing an oversized hooded sweatshirt under a blue and brown flannel jacket. A Ford baseball cap sat low on his head. And he had a clean shave.

"You make redneck look good," Cora said, trying to inject a little humor into the situation. But it fell flat.

"Right?" he asked, crouching at the end of the living room couch where she sat with Bosco at her feet. "The boys will be home in a few, so let me ask you before they get here and want to interject their opinion. Would you prefer to spend the evening at the clubhouse or at Dare and Haven's? Meat had reserved the clubhouse tonight for his fortieth birthday party, so it might be a little crazy there, but of course you can grab one of the rooms upstairs."

"Would Dare be okay with us crashing over there?"

she asked, not sure she was up for pandemonium tonight with the way her head already pounded with tension.

"Yes. He said he and Haven would hang with you wherever you wanted to be."

"Then I'll go there. The boys love Dare anyway."

The bus pulled up just then. "I'll get them," Slider said. And it was such a normal thing. A dad meeting his kids off the school bus. It was hard to believe that in just a few hours, that same dad would be walking into the middle of a bunch of criminals betting on animals attacking each other, all while also trying to nail a dirty cop.

Cora just hoped with all her heart that he'd be walking back out again, too. And coming home to her.

CHAPTER 23

T his ends tonight," Caine said, a beat-up John
Deere baseball hat on his head. In baggy
jeans and a gray hoodie cinched at the neck to hide
his ink, he almost looked like one of the skate rats
they'd seen.

"A-fucking-men," Phoenix said from behind the
wheel. A cowboy hat sat beside his lap.

"In and out, just like we talked about," Slider
added, hoping like hell that nothing diverted them
from the plan.

They rode to the fight in one of the old pickups
used for the Ravens' track business, not wanting
to put anyone's personal vehicle in the 301 Crew's
sights. The address they finally received was located

about forty-five minutes away, and luckily the early sunset of the season meant they'd get to go in under the cover of darkness. Martin and two of his officers followed in unmarked cars, giving them at least a little backup in case shit went south.

As shit was wont to do.

Which was why they were all riding hot. Slider fucking hated it—hated the risk of it—but they'd be stupid to go in unarmed with the Crew involved.

The address led them to a long gravel driveway that cut through a stand of woods and emptied out into a big field. A barn sat at the center with maybe forty cars and trucks parked all around, many of them with trailers attached—likely belonging to people who'd brought their own dogs to fight.

They could hear the barking and howling before they even got out of the truck.

"This is going to suck ass," Phoenix said.

Slider thought about Bosco back at home. Bosco, who would roll over onto his back to get a belly scratch, and who came running every time Slider opened the freezer door because he loved to chew ice cubes, and who often fell asleep with his droopy head propped on a stuffed animal squirrel the boys had picked out for him. Yeah, this was going to suck. The last thing Slider wanted to see was an animal getting hurt.

They piled out, Caine and Slider in baseball hats and Phoenix wearing a brown cowboy hat that hid the scar on the side of his face, cowboy boots, and a pair of black-framed glasses. They weren't perfect disguises, but none of them looked like they normally did, and Slider hoped that would be enough.

Even as they made their way toward the barn, a few more cars pulled into the field, and the noise coming from inside made it seem like this was going to be a decent-sized event. That suited Slider just fine, because it meant a bigger crowd to get lost in.

A blue pickup—a blue Datsun—sat at the end of one row. Satisfaction rolled through Slider as he nudged Caine's arm and pointed. "Heads-up." Curt Davis was here, just like they hoped he'd be. Now they'd just have to be careful about being spotted by him.

"Fucking perfect," Caine said, his tone like ice.

Two men stopped them at the door, small *301* tattoos on their necks identifying them as part of the Crew. "Name?"

"Chuck Mason," Caine said. Their master of new identities for their protective clients no doubt had a few set up for himself as well.

The men gave the three of them a once-over and waved them in.

"Jesus," Slider bit out under his breath. It was as bad inside as he feared. Fighting pits filled the barn's four corners. Maybe twenty square feet, there was nothing fancy about them—they were constructed simply out of plywood fencing that stood about three feet high. A pair of dogs fought in three of the pits, and thirty or forty spectators stood around each one, cheering and yelling and booing. A betting booth stood at the center, and a concession stand filled the far wall. People milled around both and wandered up the center aisle.

"Who could eat?" Phoenix said. He wasn't wrong—the stench of animal blood and other bodily fluids hung in the air.

"Come on," Caine said, leading them to stand at the railing of the closest fighting pit where it appeared a fight was about to begin. Blending in necessitated acting interested, so Slider braced his arms on the edge and paid close attention to the two pit bulls being restrained on leashes in opposite corners. Deep lines had been scratched diagonally into the dirt in front of each corner.

As they watched, a referee supervised each dog getting washed down with sudsy water from the same bucket. Listening to the chatter of other spectators, Slider learned that was to remove any chemicals or poisons that a dog's owner might put on the coat to make the opposing dog sick, which just proved how truly twisted this whole thing was.

"Okay," the referee called out, his voice drawing new attendees. "We're playing by Cajun Rules, gentlemen. Let the show begin. And may the best dog win."

Slider assumed the men holding the leashes were the dogs' owners, and as they released the pit bulls into the ring, both men stepped back into their corners but stayed in the pit. The dogs went at each other so hard it made Slider sick. They bit, snarled, tackled, and jumped. As their attacks landed, new bloodstains soon joined older, faded ones on the floor. The owners in the corner shouted commands and encouragements, and it was clear that one dog was a favorite among the gathering crowd.

Something caught Slider's eye on the opposite side of the fighting pit—a kid. Maybe Sam's age. Watching the fight. "Who the hell would bring a kid to this?" he asked Phoenix.

"That's some messed-up shit." Phoenix leaned in closer, so his words wouldn't carry to the other spectators. "I'm gonna wander. Take some pics. I'll text if I see Davis and get what we need."

Slider nodded and watched as Phoenix moved away, his hat tilted down low. Turning to Caine, he said, "No one of interest here. Wanna move on?"

At the next fighting pit, the dogs appeared in bad shape. "How long's this been going on?" Caine asked a man at the fence.

"Thirty minutes," the guy said. "They have great fucking stamina, don't they?"

"Yeah, man, they do," Caine said, leaning over the fence a little like he was interested. Slider scanned the crowd around this pit, but still didn't see who they were looking for. His phone vibrated in his pocket.

Surprisingly, the text was from Martin.

More backup en route. Text when departing.
We're going in after.

That was the best news Slider had heard all day.
When the date changed, they'd resolved themselves
to having to walk away and leave these fuckers to
fight another day, but maybe now the authorities
would break up this ring once and for all.

Caine arched a brow at him, but Slider just shook
his head. He'd fill the others in when they were out
the door.

At the third pit, a fight had just ended, and people
were moving away from the fence in search of new
action. Surreptitiously, Slider scanned the faces. But
still no Davis. Where the hell was he?

Slider's phone vibrated again. And Caine's must
have, too, because, he pulled his cell out at the same
time. The text was from Phoenix.

Found Davis. Took pix. Bigger problem: that fucker
Dominic from the Iron Cross is here. Head out.

Caine turned to him, eyes wide. "Crew's *Cross*.
Sonofabitch."

They turned and made for the nearest door as
Caine's meaning sank in.

Though Slider hadn't dealt with them personally,
he knew who the Iron Cross were—they were the
Baltimore gang who'd worked with Haven's father

to try to kidnap her. The Raven Riders had first interacted with the Iron Cross when the Ravens reluctantly sold them some arms the club was trying to unload, but that'd blown back in their faces, proving the wisdom of why the Ravens usually stayed out of the dirtier shit like guns and drugs. Next thing the club knew, the Iron Cross had learned that Haven and Cora were under the Ravens' protection and were threatening to tell Haven's father if they didn't pay up.

But the Iron Cross had gotten theirs in the end when the Ravens had helped the authorities take out their Baltimore headquarters. Their contacts had told them that all the Iron Cross were either dead or in custody, but clearly they'd missed one. And not just *any* one, but their fucking leader.

Phoenix caught up with them at the door. And then they were out in the night, and heading for their—

"Leaving so soon, gentlemen?" came a voice from behind them. "I don't think you placed any bets."

Ice formed in Slider's gut as they turned. The man was tall, bald, and had bright blue eyes that glinted dangerously in the barn's exterior lights. "Got a sick fucking kid at home," Slider said. "My only night out. Figures." Keeping his body loose and relaxed, he stepped forward, sensing his friends' tension.

Slider hadn't ever interacted with this Iron Cross asshole, but Phoenix and Caine had. At that arms deal. What kind of luck was it that they'd managed to steer clear of Davis but gotten nabbed by an old enemy they hadn't even known to look out for?

Dominic crossed his arms over his broad chest. "It's not really good form to leave without supporting the operation, if you know what I mean."

Slider inhaled to respond when he noticed a series of puncture wounds on the guy's left wrist. And then it was like being sucked back in time. To the hospital, the day that Ben broke his arm. The tall, bald man with the dog bite injury, bleeding all over the desk . . .

Jesus, he'd seen this man before after all. He'd seen him, but because of all his baggage and bullshit, Slider hadn't known *who* he was seeing, or the kind of danger he represented. His gut twisted. That night, if Dominic had turned and seen Cora, who he'd conspired to sell back to Haven's father . . .

He scrambled to respond normally. "Look, man, we don't want any trouble. I'd like to stay, but when the wife calls because your kid needs to go to urgent care, what are you supposed to do?"

Dominic stepped closer, and Slider made sure to make easy eye contact with him. *Nothing to hide here. Nothing to hide here at all, motherfucker.*

"And what about you two? You got nagging wives and sick kids, too?" he said, suspicion and agitation rolling off him. Slider didn't know whether those were directed specifically at them, or were simply the result of his previous gang having been obliterated. No doubt being the sole survivor of a once powerful organization could lead to some serious paranoia, paranoia likely compounded by being an Iron Cross island in the middle of the Dead Men's violent sea.

"Naw, man," Phoenix said, peering up from under his hat and laying on a thick Southern accent. "But he's our damn ride." Caine nodded.

Dominic eyeballed Phoenix and Caine for a long minute, then shook his head. "I don't want to see you assholes here again. I do and I'll throw you in one of the pits. Now get the fuck out of here."

Just as he spat the words, Slider spotted Davis over Dominic's shoulder, wearing civilian clothes and heading toward the door. Straight toward them. "Yeah, man. Okay. We're out." Slider turned and hustled his friends ahead of him.

And then they were through the parking lot, inside their truck, and pulling out—fast. "Holy shit, do you think he recognized us?" Phoenix asked.

"Dominic or Davis?" Caine said, slapping his baseball hat against his leg.

"Neither," Slider said. "I don't think either one did. Davis was too far away. And no way Dominic would've let us walk out of there like that if he recognized either one of you."

"No, because there's no way he wouldn't have heard the word on the street that the Ravens were involved in talking out his club," Phoenix said, speeding out the long gravel driveway to the road beyond. "Jesus. *Jesus.* That was some unexpected shit right there."

Guilt sloshed in Slider's gut. "I fucking saw that guy at the hospital. The day Ben broke his arm. But I'd never seen him before and didn't know who he was."

"No reason you would've known," Caine said. "But you're right, he wouldn't have let us go, so let's all fucking breathe."

"Yeah, and anyway, Martin texted while we were in there. He managed to round up some backup. They're raiding the fight after all. Speaking of which . . ." Slider tugged his phone from his pocket and pecked out a text.

We left. Got over 100 people in there, including Davis and the fucking leader of the former Iron Cross gang. And some kids. We got pix. Be careful.

Less than a minute later, Martin replied: Roger that. We're going in.

Within another three minutes, a line of police vehicles whizzed past them, lights flashing but sirens off.

"Woohoo!" Phoenix yelled. "Go get 'em, boys!"

Slider grinned, some of the tension bleeding out of his shoulders. "I'm too fucking old for this shit."

That earned him some laughter, and Slider didn't mind. Because they'd gotten the evidence on Davis, helped set up a raid on the dogfighting ring, and even managed to learn that an old enemy remained—though he was about to be taken down once and for all.

That was about as much as they could've hoped for. And now all Slider wanted to do was go home to his woman and his boys and live their lives free from the pull of the past, their eyes set firmly on the future.

EVEN THOUGH THE others had done their best to distract her, Cora was strung tight waiting for some word from Slider.

Dare had invited Maverick and Alexa to come over, so Cora and Haven had made a big, hearty dinner of chicken pot pie. They'd sat for a long time around the table, everyone talking and laughing, and the men even shared some funny stories about a much younger Slider that made Cora and the boys laugh. Like the one where a female park ranger caught Slider skinny-dipping at night up at the South Mountain lake, the rest of them having run into the woods in time. Unable to find his clothes in the dark, he'd simply walked bare-assed through the woods to the parking lot while the ranger followed him out, her flashlight guiding the way and throwing a spotlight on his behind.

Cora almost couldn't imagine such a ridiculously carefree version of Slider, but it all just made her realize how deeply she loved him, and how much he already felt like family. She couldn't lose that. Not when she hadn't thought she'd ever find it in the first place.

At some point, Ben slid into her lap to listen to everyone talk, but when he started yawning, she suggested he grab some sleep in Dare's bed until his dad got back.

"Okay, Cora," he said, yawning again.

She took him by the hand. "You good, Sam?"

The older boy nodded. They hadn't told him what was going on, but he was old enough and had been around Dare and Maverick long enough to sense that something wasn't right. "I don't want to sleep yet."

She read the concern on his face loud and clear, so she just nodded and led Ben upstairs. She turned on the lamp on the nightstand and tucked him in, then sat on the edge of the bed. "Okay, Mr. Bean, close those peepers and get a little sleep. Your dad will be back before you know it and then we'll go home."

"I love you, Cora," he said.

The words made her throat go tight and her chest feel too small for her heart. "Oh, Ben, I love you, too."

He threw his good arm around her neck, and then he turned onto his side. "Wake me up when Dad comes."

She nodded and smoothed the cover over his shoulder, then closed the door on her way out.

"Did he get settled down okay?" Haven asked, when she returned downstairs.

"Yeah," Cora said, hugging herself. "And he told me he loved me."

Haven's expression went so soft as she pulled Cora into a hug. "Of course he loves you, sweetie."

"I want Slider to come home," she whispered, trying so hard to keep her worry in check. She didn't want Sam to see it, not when his worry was already so clear on his little face.

"I know. Soon. Just hang on a little longer," Haven whispered back. They'd been through this before, but in the past, Cora had been the one comforting Haven while Dare was away.

Finally, Cora's phone rang. "It's Slider!" she called out, and everyone gathered around. She pressed the cell to her ear. "Are you okay? What's happening?"

"Yeah, we're all fine. Put me on speaker?"

She did, but her gaze went to Sam. "You're on, but Sam's here."

The boy shook his head. "I know something's going on. I'm not leaving, Dad." Cora traded glances with Dare and Maverick.

Slider's voice came through the cell. "Sam, everything's okay—"

"*Something's* not okay, and you're out there in it, so I deserve to know," he said, giving more than a hint of the man he was going to become. Slider's son, through and through.

Nodding, Dare finally asked, "How'd it go?"

"We got in and out. Phoenix got the pictures. And we just passed Martin leading a raid on the location after all," Slider said, his words breaking up a little. "But we hit a complication, too."

Cora's belly threatened to fall to the floor.

"What's that?" Dare asked, his expression fierce.

It was Phoenix who answered. "You're not going to like this, Dare. But Dominic Hauer was there. He's the one who's running these fights on behalf of the Crew. That's why it's so new."

Haven gasped, and Cora clutched her hand. The guy who'd blackmailed the Ravens over them was still alive?

"Aw, Christ," Dare said, and then he grimaced as he looked at Slider's boy sitting there taking it all in. "Sorry, Sam."

Maverick met Dare's stormy gaze. "But you said Martin's raiding the place, right? So that should take care of him?"

"That's our read." Caine's voice now. "Listen, you're breaking up . . . storming . . . bad here . . ."

Beep beep beep. Cora's phone dropped the call.

Dare raked at his hair and paced the room, agitation rolling off him.

"You really don't have to censor what you say around me, you know," Sam said, crossing his arms.

Dare and Maverick chuckled. "You say that, but we'd prefer your father didn't want to kick our butts for teaching you bad habits," Maverick said with a wink.

Just in case Slider might be able to receive it, Cora shot off a text. I can't wait to hold you in my arms and look in your eyes so I can tell you in person how much I love you. Because I do. xo

The storm they must've been driving through finally hit Dare's house, and he and Haven went around lowering some of the windows where the rain came in. But the sound was soothing and almost lulling, and Cora enjoyed it as she sat in a big comfy chair by the front window.

Headlights swung across the front of the house a moment before the sound of an engine drifted in on the breeze. Cora was up out of her chair in a flash, her face pressed to the window. "It's them. They're back," she said, and then she ran out onto the front porch just as Slider was jogging up the sidewalk. She rushed out into the soft rain and jumped into his arms.

He held her to him so tight, and his mouth found hers. It felt like the first time she'd been able to take a deep breath in hours, the relief of holding him again was so strong. "I missed you. I love you," she said.

"God, sweetheart, I love you, too," he said. "Come on, let's get in out of the rain."

"I'm so proud of you," she said as they jogged up the steps. "You guys really did it."

Inside, they all gathered around Dare's living room as Slider, Phoenix, and Caine spent the next half hour recounting what they'd seen. Cora's belly flip-flopped to think of what they witnessed in that place, and she'd gasped out loud when they described how Dominic cut them off as they were leaving. Would the past never stop coming for them?

"You're sure neither Davis nor Dominic recognized you?" Dare asked.

"We went over this ourselves," Phoenix said. "No way Dominic would've let us leave if he had, and none of us ever got close enough to Davis for him to have any reason to notice us."

Caine nodded. "It was as clean as it could be, considering."

"I texted Martin on the way home," Slider said, "but not surprisingly he hasn't replied yet."

"No doubt he's got his hands full after the raid," Maverick said, "but let's keep trying him. I want the full details."

Dare nodded and sagged in his chair. "I need some whiskey." The men chuckled and agreed, then relocated to the kitchen at the back of the big open space.

"Can we go home soon, Dad?" Sam asked, his voice tired.

"Yeah, buddy. In just a little bit," Slider said from where he stood at the big island.

Cora stretched and got up out of her seat. "We're gonna sleep good tonight, aren't we, Sam?"

"Yeah, I guess," he said.

"I hope the rain lasts all night," she said, going to the front window and leaning against the sill. Sam joined her, and she smiled at his reflection in the glass. "I want to open our windows at home . . . and . . ."

As she watched, a truck passed the house, hit its

brakes, and backed up. A blue truck. Dread rolled through her, sudden and sharp. "You guys!" Cora yelled. "Davis is here!"

Which was the last thing she knew as the bullets shattered the world around her.

CHAPTER 24

Slider saw it all unfold in slow motion. As in a dream, or a nightmare.

Him turning as Cora called out.

A voice shouting in the night. "This is for the Iron Cross, you Raven pieces of shit!"

A hail of automatic gunfire hitting the front of the house, shattering glass, ricocheting around the room.

Slider yelling Cora's name. Oh, Jesus, she was right in front of the window.

She turned, grabbed Sam, pushed him to the floor.

And then all of a sudden, time was a runaway train, speeding so fast Slider could hardly keep up. Screaming, crying, shouting, diving. Were they still shooting? Slider couldn't tell for the buzzing in his head. He pulled his weapon from the small of his back and went to the edge of the window, but the brake lights were already moving away, and Caine was running across Dare's front yard, firing as their attackers retreated.

Seconds had passed at most, but Slider couldn't breathe for needing to get to Cora and Sam. He went to the floor next to where she was curled around his son. "Cora, are you okay?" Ignoring the glass under his knees, he put his hand on her back. "Sweetheart, are you okay? Sam?"

"Christ, who's hurt?" Dare yelled, all kinds of commotion happening around Slider that he couldn't even track.

Because Cora and Sam weren't responding. Why weren't they responding? Slider turned Cora over . . . and found the whole left side of her sweater soaked with blood. He couldn't tell where she'd been hit through the thick fabric, but his hands went to her anyway. "Jesus, Cora! Oh, God. Oh, no. Somebody call nine-one-one!" Slider didn't even know what he was saying, he was horror and devastation personified, especially when she still didn't respond.

Sam moaned. "Dad?"

"Sam, thank God!" Slider cried, torn between these two people he loved. He reached for him before he noticed the blood covering his own hand. Cora's blood.

"I got Sam," Alexa said, crawling up to them and examining the boy. "It's his arm."

"Dad? Is it over?" Sam said, his voice a raw scrape, his shirt streaked red.

Lifting Cora's sweater, Slider tried to assess her wounds, but the material was so fucking thick and he feared jostling her too much trying to take it off. "Yeah, buddy," he managed. "Hang in there. You're gonna be okay. I promise." When his brave little boy gave a shaky nod through his shock and tears, Slider called, "Scissors. I need scissors. And towels."

"Is Cora okay?" Sam asked, panic lacing into his voice for the first time.

"Yeah," Slider managed. "She's strong. She's a fighter. You hear me, sweetheart? You're a fighter. *Damnit.*" His own voice cracked, because he wasn't sure which of them he was trying to convince.

"That's right," Alexa said, the words wobbly as she pressed her hands to Sam's arm. "She is. She's gonna be okay."

After what was probably seconds but seemed like hours, someone finally brought him everything he needed, and Slider didn't even know who. And then he was cutting off Cora's sweater to find two gunshots to her left arm, a shot to her side, and a fourth through her upper chest, high enough to almost be her shoulder. Shaking and pleading, he pressed towels to the most serious wounds. Because, Jesus fuck, she had more of them than he could even address. *Nonono this is not happening. Please, God. I just found her.*

"Sam's arm is bandaged," Alexa said, grasping a clean towel. "Is it okay if I put pressure on Cora's?"

God, Alexa was his angel tonight. "Please," he rasped. The word wasn't even all the way out of his mouth before Al was right there, her hands helping to staunch the flow.

Maverick crouched beside him, his face a mask of rage and shock. "Ambulances are ten minutes out. Can I help here?"

"I . . . I don't know," Slider said, his mind reeling. Ten minutes felt like a lifetime. "I don't know what else to do." The admission was like a knife to the heart.

Mav's blue eyes burned. "Just hang in there and keep doing what you're doing. Haven and Caine are also hit. But we're going to get everyone the help they need."

"Haven, too?" Slider rasped, knowing how much that would tear Cora up. But before he let Mav respond, he gasped. "Ben! Where's Ben?" How the hell had it taken his head so long to think to ask?

Grasping his shoulder, Maverick looked him in the eye. "Phoenix has him upstairs. He's fine. And the club's on its way." Dark meaning hung on the words. They were going to fix this. And thank fuck the clubhouse was so close.

But Slider shook his head, grief raging inside him. "Go. Go now. Go get those fuckers before they get away, Maverick. This does *not* get to happen!" he shouted, Cora's blood starting to soak through the towels. "You know they'll just keep coming if you don't."

"I know, man, but I'm not leaving you all unprotected."

As if Mav's words beckoned their brothers, a monstrous roar sounded out in the night. The sound of two dozen motorcycles descending like the hounds of hell.

"We're covered. Now, *go*," Slider growled, part of him wishing he could be the one to wring the life from Dominic's and Davis's necks with his bare hands. But if he couldn't do it, his brothers would. "And make them pay, Maverick! Make them fucking pay."

People came and went. Voices shouted and talked. But Slider had a hard time keeping track of anything besides Cora and Sam after that. Cora, who lay far too still. And Sam, who'd pulled himself into a sitting position as he held the towel tied around his left arm.

"Cora," he cried. "She saved me."

"I know, buddy," Slider said, his hands pressed to Cora's worst wounds as if he could maybe hold her in this world with his skin and his bones alone. "I know. How you doing? You're being so damn brave, Sam."

"I don't feel brave," the boy said, shaking his head and trying to rein in his tears.

"That just proves how brave you really are," Slider said, filled with a tragic, wrenching pride in his son's courage in the face of all this chaos. "And we're gonna save Cora. Don't you worry." But Slider didn't know if he believed the words. There was so much blood. And she was so still. And her skin was so pale. How did this happen? How the fuck did this happen? Martin *had* them. They saw the police turn into the road that led to that barn. How the fuck did this happen?

A small moan. Then another. Cora's head turned and her eyelids fluttered.

"Cora!" Sam cried. "She's moving!"

"Can you hear me?" Slider asked, dangerous hope flaring through him. "Oh, God, Cora. Tell me you hear me."

Her lips barely moved. "Sli . . ."

"Yeah, I'm here," he said, leaning close, his heart torn between breaking and flying. "I'm right here."

Her eyelids lifted heavily, her gaze not tracking. Still, seeing that beautiful green again nearly slayed him. "S-Sam. O-kay?"

Aw, God, his heart. His heart was never going to survive this. She'd been hit four times, and her first thought was for Slider's son. "Yeah, sweetheart, he's right here. He's gonna be fine."

Sam came closer. "I'm here, too, Cora. It's okay," he said through silent tears. "Everything's okay. I love you, Cora." Alexa gently squeezed Sam's good shoulder and he sagged into her embrace. "She has to be okay."

"She will," Alexa managed. "She's one of the strongest people I know."

And it was true, except . . . the blood, and the stillness, and the paleness. But at least she was awake. "Keep talking to me, Cora. Keep talking."

But she didn't say any more.

"Ambulance is here," someone yelled, making Slider realize for the first time that colored lights from outside flashed on the ruined interior walls of Dare's living room and kitchen. "Make way."

The paramedics came in with their big kits. Multiple teams. And cops, too. The house was crawling with people. When had all of them even gotten there?

A man and a woman knelt down next to Slider. The woman examined Sam's arm, and Slider said, "That's my son, Sam. He's almost eleven. Take good care of him."

"I will," the woman said with a small smile.

"Sir," the man said. "Let me take over now. I'll take good care of her, too, I promise."

"She's everything," Slider said.

"I know, sir. Let me assess her so I can help."

Slider sat back and removed his hands from her, and it felt so fucking wrong not to be touching her, not to feel her heat, not to feel her pulse against his skin. What if he never got to feel any of that again? He scrambled to her other side, out of the way but still close, so he could tell her over and over. "I love you, Cora. I love you. Fight this. Fight for us. I love you."

THEY TOOK CORA straight into surgery. Haven, too. Yet Slider felt like he must be the one whose heart was open on the table. The only thing that kept him sane at all was being with Sam in his little room in the ER.

The bullet had gone straight through the meat of Sam's bicep, missing the bone entirely. It was good news, and the doctor assured Slider that Sam would make a full recovery.

"You were very brave tonight, Sam," Slider said, trying to give him the attention he deserved, trying to force his focus to remain right here in the moment with his son. "I'm only sorry you ever had to experience something like that."

Sam shook his head. "Cora was the brave one. She warned us. She knocked me down. It would've been so much worse without what she did."

The kid wasn't wrong, and it made Slider's heart clench so hard he couldn't catch his breath, so he just nodded.

"Everything would be so much worse without Cora," Sam said, his voice cracking on her name and tears falling. "*Dad*, I love her." Sam's whole face crumpled and a sob ripped out of him.

Slider sat on the bed and pulled his son into his arms. "I know, Sam. I know. We just gotta stay strong for her now. She needs us, you know?"

Crying, Sam clutched at Slider's shoulder with his good hand and nodded his head. "I know. This is m-my f-fault," he wailed.

The sound of the boy's pain threatened to break what was left of Slider's heart. "No, Sam. Nothing about this was your fault."

"If she hadn't tried to protect me . . ."

"That was all Cora," Slider said, feeling the truth of it down deep. "That's just who she is. You couldn't have kept her from protecting you."

"But Mom was my fault," Sam rasped.

The shock of the subject change was so abrupt, Slider almost felt like he'd walked into a pole. "What?"

"Mom . . . you're gonna *hate* me." Sam heaved a shaky breath, then another, and another, trying to calm his tears.

Coming from his son, and knowing how his own father had felt about him, that word was like a kick in the gut. Slider leaned down to look his son in the eyes, needing him to know, needing him to *believe*. "I could never, ever hate you. What would I possibly have to be mad at you about? Your mom had cancer, Sammy." He hadn't used the nickname in years, since before Kim died, but it felt right, just then.

"I . . . I knew . . . about Mom," he said, his voice shaking so much his teeth almost chattered.

"Knew what . . . ?" Slider's gut twisted as realization dawned. "What did you know? You can tell me. I promise I won't get mad."

Sam's eyes were so shattered when he looked up. "I knew about the man she saw. I caught them, once. And once after that she took me to see him."

White-hot rage curled in Slider's chest. Not at Sam, but at Kim. For her infidelity, for the years he'd lost to his shame and grief, for her planning to leave their kids. And now for this—for putting the knowledge of her betrayal on her son's too-small, too-young, too-innocent shoulders. Slider blew out a breath. "None of that was your fault, either, Sam. Those were choices your mom made that she never should've laid on you."

"B-but I . . . I should've told you, Dad. And I'm so, so sorry I didn't." His tears started again.

Slider gently cradled Sam's head against his chest and pressed a kiss to his hair. "You listen to me, Sam. I love you. Nothing could ever change that. You don't owe me any apologies, and you never should've felt like you had to choose between us. I'm sorry."

Sam's good arm came around him tight. "I love you, Dad, so much."

When was the last time Sam had hugged him, talked to him about how he felt, or told him he loved him? It was like some wall had come down between them, and Slider was going to make sure it never, ever went back up.

"I love you, too." God, how light Slider's heart would be if only Cora were okay, too.

"Did you know I interviewed Cora for school?" Sam whispered after a long while.

"Oh yeah?"

"Know what she told me?"

Slider forced a deep breath. "What's that, Sammy?"

"That in five years she hoped she'd be in college, married, own a dog, and maybe even be a mom." Sam lifted his gaze to Slider's, and those little brown eyes were entirely open with want. "If she . . . if she's okay, after this . . . maybe we could be the ones . . ." He shrugged with his good shoulder.

Slider heard what Sam didn't say just then, because he'd said it once before.

Cora should have a family.

Slider gave a quick nod and blinked away the sudden sting behind his eyes. Because his boys wanted Cora Campbell in their lives as much as Slider did. "Yeah," he managed, his heart torn between hope and despair. "Yeah, maybe we could."

Drained and drowsy from the pain meds, Sam fell asleep not much later.

So Slider slipped out and stopped at the nurses' station. "Any word on Cora Campbell in surgery yet?" But there wasn't. "How about Haven Randall?" No news on her, either. Slider had learned that Haven had been hit in the shoulder, too, so the two best friends were going to have matching scars. Someday, a long, long time from now, he might find some humor in that. Hell, Cora would probably find the humor even sooner.

But not him. Not today.

A few rooms down, he knocked on a door, and found Caine sitting in bed, his left arm bandaged from wrist to elbow, Phoenix at his side. A bullet had passed straight through Caine's wrist, yet Slider distinctly recalled seeing him run after the truck in the seconds after the shooting. It was one of the few clear memories he had that wasn't directly associated with Cora and Sam.

"Hey," Slider said. "How are you feeling?"

"It's not serious," Caine said. "How are Cora and Sam?"

"Sam's fine. Sleeping. No word on Cora and Haven." Slider blew out a breath, his every movement like walking through molasses. "What happened after?"

Phoenix rose, his expression more serious than Slider had ever seen it during all the years they'd known each other. "Maverick, Caine, and I took care of it. It's over. It's done. We made it look like Dominic and Davis turned on each other, and Martin will make sure that's how the scene report reads, too."

It was a hollow sort of satisfaction. Slider couldn't take any pleasure from it. But he did at least draw a measure of relief. "Good."

"Fuck, Slider," Phoenix said, gripping the rail of Caine's bed. "This is all my goddamn fault. Dominic *made* me. The fucker. He made me and I didn't know it."

Caine cleared his throat. "That's how Dominic and Davis got out before the police arrived. They were already leaving before the shit hit the fan at the fight."

Slider's brow cranked down, confusion swamping him. "But we didn't have a tail. We looked. Repeatedly."

Shaking his head, Caine grimaced. "They didn't follow us. They wanted to catch us off guard. Davis was drowning in gambling debt to Dominic and had been for years, so when the guy recognized us, Davis bargained to show him where we live. He tried your house, and then Phoenix's, and then finally Dare's, figuring we might come back to report."

"He told you all this?" Slider asked.

"Men say a lot of things when it's their time to die." Caine nailed him with a lethal stare. "Including that Dominic was the last of the Iron Cross fuckers to survive." Slider nodded. At least there was that.

Phoenix hung his head, his shoulders tight with anger. "I'm just so fucking sorry."

Slider rubbed the back of his neck and blew out an exhausted breath. He wasn't letting one more person he cared about live with guilt and grief for things that weren't their fault. So he went to Phoenix and put an arm around his brother's shoulders, even though he had so very little solace left to give. "You don't have anything to apologize for. We didn't know. None of us did. With Dominic in play, if it hadn't have been tonight, it would've been another time. Or it would've been Davis instead. Either way, this disaster had our name on it no matter what we did. It was a matter of when, not if."

Slider believed that, he did, but he didn't feel remotely okay about it with Cora still fighting for her life. What the hell was taking so long anyway?

Besides the four fucking gunshot wounds.

Sonofabitch.

Caine nodded. "He's right, Creed. This wasn't your fault."

Phoenix scrubbed his hands over his face, not refuting, but not accepting, either.

Slider ground the heels of his hands against his eyes. He felt ancient. What the hell time was it anyway? Not that he'd be able to sleep until he knew Cora was okay. Still, he retrieved his phone from his back pocket to see that it was just after midnight—and that he had a text.

He almost ignored it. Until he saw who it was from.

Cora.

I can't wait to hold you in my arms and look in your eyes so I can tell you in person how much I love you. Because I do. xo

Fist to his mouth, he was barely able to restrain a sob. "I'm, uh, I'm gonna head out to the waiting room. See who's there. See if I can find Dare. Need anything?" Slider managed. Both men shook their heads, and Phoenix dropped back into his chair on a troubled sigh.

On the way out, he read Cora's message again. And again. *God, Cora. Pull through this and tell me now. To my face. So I can say it back. But please don't leave me with this text and nothing else.* He forced a deep breath and swallowed down the agony of his fear as he made his way through the maze of the emergency department.

Pushing through the double doors, Slider came to a halt. Because the waiting room was absolutely packed. There was a sea of men in Ravens cuts, and dozens of other people besides. Dare and Bunny and Maverick and Alexa and Ben, sweet Ben, who ran into his arms as Slider lifted him to his chest and held him so damn tight.

"Sam's sleeping," he said to Ben, to everyone. "He's doing okay."

"No word on the girls," Dare said, his voice like sandpaper, his whole demeanor like he was a breath away from being wrecked. And Slider got it, he really fucking did.

"I know," Slider said. "But they're gonna get through this." They hugged each other then, two old friends sharing the same unbearable pain and facing the same impossible loss.

"Yes, they are," Bunny said. "Those two are fighters. So don't you do anything but plan how you're going to take care of them when they're out of here. That goes for both of you," Bunny said, her eyes so glassy she was hard to look at. Because Slider was hanging on by a very thin thread.

But he nodded, appreciating the hell out of the sentiment, and praying to God with everything that he had that Bunny was right.

"Everything else is taken care of," Maverick said, his eyes raw, blue fire.

Slider nodded, too gutted to care the way he should. "I know. Thank you for handling it."

"Families of Cora Campbell and Haven Randall?" a woman's voice called.

About fifty people stood up.

And, damn, how Cora would've loved seeing that. *Please let me be able to tell her.*

Slider and Dare rushed to where two doctors stood side by side, one woman and one man. A few others came with them, but Slider was too focused to care who heard the news as long as it was good.

"We're all here for both of them," Dare said. "Please just tell us."

The woman started. "Haven's surgery went entirely by the book. Her clavicle was broken, and we were able to repair it and the soft tissue around it. She's in recovery and resting comfortably."

Dare braced his hands against his knees. "Thank God," he said. And Slider shared the sentiment down deep.

"And Cora?" he asked.

Nodding, the male doctor said, "They're just finishing up now, but we knew we had a waiting room anxious to hear. All in all, she was very lucky. The most serious of the wounds were the two in her chest and abdomen. She suffered a broken rib and a punctured lung, which we were able to repair. The shot to her upper chest broke another rib and fractured her scapula, all of which we stabilized. The gunshot wounds on her arm were less serious, but we've repaired the damage as much as we can and have her on a course of antibiotics to treat for any infection. But we expect a full recovery."

The room spun around Slider until he stumbled. Someone caught him, and someone else pulled Ben from his arms. "She's okay?" he asked, his brain not quite grasping what he was hearing.

"She's going to have a long road in front of her and she'll need physical therapy on that arm and shoulder, but she's going to be fine," the doctor said. "And, oh, one more thing." The doctor hesitated, and it nearly killed Slider. "Perhaps we should discuss this in private?"

"Say what you have to say, Doc," Slider gritted out.

The man eyed their little group and nodded. "We detected trace HCG in Cora's blood." When Slider shook his head, the doctor elaborated. "The pregnancy hormone. The levels indicate it's very new, maybe not even two weeks since conception."

Slider went to his knees. Just flat-out went to his knees in wonder and thanks and sheer amazement. Cora was pregnant. Cora was *pregnant* . . . with his child.

"She's okay?" he asked, looking up. The doctor nodded. "And she's pregnant?"

"It appears so. But a lot depends on her condition over the next couple days," he cautioned.

Slider nodded. He heard what the man was saying, and he got it. Still, he'd been so prepared for the worst that part of him couldn't process the good news—or not want to embrace it even if it might be tenuous. "Jesus, thank you," he said, hands clapping him on the shoulders. Someone held out a hand and helped him to his feet amid words of cautious celebration. "Can I see her?"

"As soon as she's ready."

It felt like an eternity, but finally someone called his name. "Mr. Evans, we can take you to see Cora now."

CHAPTER 25

Slider nearly held his breath as he stepped up to Cora's bedside. The joy of seeing her and knowing that she was alive was tarnished by knowing what she'd been through, and everything she would still have to go through. An oxygen mask rested on her face, and IVs protruded from her good arm. Little bandages covered a few places on the right side of her face, and a thick wad of gauze was wrapped around her left shoulder and arm, propped up on a set of pillows.

And yet, she was the most beautiful woman Slider had ever seen.

The truest, the most loyal, the bravest.

He eased into the chair beside her and clutched

her hand, careful of the second IV above her thumb. "Hey, it's me," he said, just needing to talk to her. Just *needing her.* "I'm here. And everyone is going to be okay. Sam's right, you know. You were so fucking brave. God, Cora, you saved Sam's life. I'll never be able to thank you enough for that. And sweetheart . . . Jesus, Cora. We made a baby. It's early. *So* early. I have no idea what'll happen or even if you'll want it. But, God, I hope you do."

The wonder of that still hit him on so many levels. He thought about what Sam had confided in him earlier, how Cora wanted to be a mom. Now she would be. And he remembered how, from the first second he'd held Sam as a newborn baby, Slider had loved being a father. Now he was going to have that privilege all over again. And the boys were going to have a new brother or sister, a new life that would bond the four of them together in yet another way.

And, Jesus. How many times had he tried to tell himself that he'd be best off defining family by blood? Even though he now realized it'd been a defense mechanism he'd built to block out the pain of Kim's lies and betrayals, Slider couldn't help but shake his head. Because here, Cora shared his blood. Through the baby struggling to grow inside her.

Cora *was* family. Cora was family in every way he'd ever defined it. Or ever would.

Which meant . . .

"You have to wake up now, Cora. I need you. I

need your eyes and your voice and your touch. I need your humor and your silly names and your love of animals. Please wake up for me."

But he couldn't will her awake. And anyway, he'd wait for her as long as it took for her to recover. So he laid his head down on the edge of her bed, still holding her hand, and talked and talked to her, so she knew that she wasn't alone, and that he wanted her, and that he always would.

He talked so much and so long that he didn't remember stopping. But the next thing he knew was a soft weight in his hair.

For a moment, he moaned and settled back into sleep, and then his brain jolted him awake.

Bright green eyes stared at him, and then a smile eked onto Cora's face beneath the oxygen mask. "Hi."

"Hi," he said, emotion knotting in his throat. "Hi." Slider stood up, needing to be closer, and leaned in over her, careful not to put any weight on her body.

"Wha' happened?" she said, her words a little slurred as she brushed away the mask.

He gently stroked her face. "All you need to know for right now is that everyone is going to be okay." She needed to know the details, and in time she would, but not right now. Not while she was still so weak. "And the other thing you need to know is that I love you so much I don't know how to be without you."

One side of her lips lifted in a little smile. "Love you, too." Her eyes went wide. "Sam?"

Aw, Jesus, the way she cared for him and his. "Downstairs resting and doing good."

"Okay," she said, her eyelids falling shut again.

Relief. Sheer and total. It was like a tidal wave inside him, one that took his knees out from under him until he sagged back into the chair.

And then Slider wept. Wept like he hadn't in years. Not even after Kim died had he cried, given everything that had led up to that terrible moment. But now he wept. It cleansed his soul of so much of the pain he'd been holding onto, and it healed his heart of so many of the breaks caused by abandonment in his life, and it removed the poison of shame from Kim's betrayals from his mind. He wept.

And then it was as if his brain just needed to shut down, because he fell asleep again, his head against her hip, their hands laced together. Because he knew now—knew with *clarity*.

Slider never wanted to let Cora go.

THE FIRST THING Cora was aware of was the warm weight of Slider's head against her, and it made her smile before she managed to force open her eyes. Even a little fuzzy, he was the sexiest man she'd ever seen, not that she was really in any shape to be thinking about sex. Apparently.

Her head lolled as she tried to take it all in. Lots of things hurt. Her face, her side, her shoulder, her arm. But she had an odd floaty feeling that told her she had drugs on board, and that was good.

"Hi, there, hon," a nurse wearing pink scrubs and a black Afro said. "How are you feeling?"

"Okay I think. A little sore," Cora said as the woman checked her vitals.

"Do you need pain medicine?"

Cora nodded. "Maybe."

"Okay, hon, I'll get that ready for you."

On a sudden inhale, Slider blinked awake, his gaze going from Cora to the nurse and back again. "Hey, is everything okay?"

"Yep," the lady said. "Just checking in."

"What's wrong with me?" Cora managed. She remembered the truck, and the popping sound of gunfire, and then . . . Nothing.

"The doctor will be by within the hour to talk to you, but you suffered four gunshot wounds. They patched you back up real good though," she said with a friendly smile. "Let me go get that pain medicine."

Wow, that was a freaking lot to take in. "Four," she said.

"Yeah," Slider said, leaning closer, those pale green eyes intense and clear. "I talked to the doctor earlier, and he said they were able to repair everything. You had a few broken bones and a punctured lung, but they put you back together again."

"What about the others?" she said, having a vague recollection of Slider saying everyone was okay before. But still, there were a lot of kinds of okay. And Cora needed to know.

"Wait, sweetheart, there's something else you need to know," he said.

"What is it?"

"It turns out . . . Cora, you're pregnant," he said, his expression so full of love.

The room went spinny around them, and then his words really sank in. "I'm pregnant. They said that?" He nodded. "They're sure?" she asked, awe and disbelief and wonder shaking the ground beneath her. Because . . . because she was going to be a mom. And Slider was going to be a dad again—with her.

"It showed up in your bloodwork," he said. A tentative smile played around his mouth and just brought out the hint of his dimple.

Then Cora gasped. Four gunshot wounds. *Four.* "Oh, God, do they know if the pregnancy will be okay?" Panic shot through her, and the pulse monitor spiked.

"Ssh," he said, stroking her face. "Don't worry. It's very new but so far it's fine. You just worry about healing you and the rest will work out the way it's meant to be."

Love and desire rushed through her because she wanted this baby to live. God, she wanted it so much, this child that she and Slider had made. But did Slider want it, too? "Does that mean you'd be okay if I had this baby?"

"Oh, Cora. I would be fucking ecstatic if you had

this baby," he said, so much emotion in his voice that it choked her up. He kissed her cheek, just a light brush of skin on skin. "For something so beautiful to come out of so much pain would be an amazing gift."

"I'm so glad, because I want it, too." She couldn't stop the tears from falling no matter how hard she tried. Tears of hope and fear and love. She was going to be someone's *mom*. She and Slider were having a baby together. And they were going to love this child—and Sam and Ben, too—so much that none of them would ever wonder if they were wanted or cherished or loved.

"You're gonna be the best mama," Slider whispered, catching every one of her tears.

And then the nurse returned with a syringe of pain medicine. "This will make it better," she said, sliding the needle into the line.

The next time Cora woke up, she had the sense that it was daytime. The room was brighter, noise filtered in from the hallway, and flowers lined her windowsill. Oh! And she had more visitors. "Boys," she said. "Hi."

They rushed to her, one on each side.

"Watch her arm, Sam," Slider said.

Almost reverently, Sam nodded. "Hi, Cora," he said, a little shyly.

"Hi yourself." Her gaze went to the thick gauze on his bicep, and her belly clenched. She'd tried so hard to protect him, but he'd still gotten hit. "You too, huh?"

"Yeah," he said, not taking the bait of her humor. "But you more."

"I guess we'll have to help each other get better then," she said.

"I will, Cora. I promise. I . . . I love you," Sam said.

The words absolutely filled her chest. Here she was in a hospital, in more pain than she wanted to admit and recovering from getting shot, and yet she felt lucky. "Oh, Sam. I love you, too. Both of you guys." She smiled at Ben. "So much."

"And Daddy, too," Ben said.

She peered up at Slider where he stood next to Sam. "And your daddy, too."

An aide came in with a lunch tray and settled it on a rolling table. "Good afternoon," she said, in almost a sing-songy voice. "How are you today?"

"Thank you, okay so far," Cora managed. But she wasn't interested in the food, because she still didn't know who else had been hurt. So when the lady left, she met Slider's gaze. "Who else?"

His shoulders fell, which meant the news wasn't good.

"Who else?" she asked again.

"They're both okay," he hedged. *Both?* Cora's belly rolled as Slider finally told her. "Caine was discharged in the middle of the night with a single shot through his wrist." Slider pressed his lips together for a long moment. "And Haven will be released within the next few hours. She took one in her shoulder, too."

"Haven? Oh, God," she gasped, her stomach dropping to the floor and tears immediately flooding her eyes. "She's okay? You promise me?"

Slider eased onto the bed by her knee, and his hand went to her thigh. "I promise you. In fact, she's going to come see you as soon as she can."

Cora sighed, impatient to see her now. "And what about Davis?" She was almost afraid to ask.

He squeezed her thigh. "He's gone, Cora. And so is the man who shot at the house. That guy ran the dog-fighting ring, too, and that's all over now. All of it." It felt weird to celebrate such macabre news, but Cora was glad these men were gone. There were too many people in the world who thought it was okay to hurt, abuse, or exploit others, and Cora was happy to see a win for the good guys, for once. If that made her a bad person, she could live with that.

But what she couldn't live with was waiting to see Haven. The two hours until she was finally discharged felt like a million. But then Haven was sitting there in the doorway, Dare pushing her in a wheelchair.

"Hi, Cora," Dare said. "Brought you a visitor."

"They won't let me walk," Haven said as Dare rolled her closer.

A little chuckle spilled out of Cora, and she groaned. "Don't make me laugh."

Haven took her hand, and her blue-eyed gaze ran over all Cora's bandages. "I'm sorry. God, Cora. I'm *so* sorry."

"Don't be. I'm just glad you're okay. I would never want to be without you," Cora said.

"I feel the very same way. You're like a sister to me. And we're going to survive this just like we've survived everything else." Haven gave her a watery smile.

But her best friend was right. "Yes, we will. We all will." Her gaze went to Slider then. "And we'll be stronger for it."

He gave her a nod and a look full of so much love it had to have healed some part of her.

And that night, when it was just the two of them again, Slider made Cora even stronger by telling her just how much he wanted her. "I couldn't live without you, Cora. Or, at least, I wouldn't want to. Along with the boys, you're the best thing that's ever happened to my life. I know we have a lot going on right now, and you'll need time to heal. And I'm going to give that to you, that and everything else you need. But I just want you to know. You're my forever, Cora. And when you're ready, I'm going to be asking you a question and hoping you'll say yes."

She exhaled a long breath that released every bit of the loneliness and abandonment she'd ever felt. "God, I love you, Slider, and I already know what my answer will be. So just know I'll be waiting for you to ask."

CHAPTER 26

Thanksgiving dinner at the Raven Riders' clubhouse was bound to be a pretty huge affair in a regular year, but this year's celebration was special.

Because every single one of them had something to be grateful for.

Cora sure knew she did. Nearly six weeks had passed since she'd been shot, and though she still had some pain, she was recovering even faster than the doctors expected, which was probably explained by the fact that Slider and the boys wouldn't let her pick up a single thing around the house. Here she'd been hired to be their nanny, and they'd spent almost every day since taking care of her.

Not that she was complaining. Because the Evans

men knew how to dispense some serious TLC. Especially the oldest Evans man. With his mouth and hands and cock. It had been a joyous day indeed when she first felt well enough again to enjoy each of those . . .

In the kitchen, Cora helped Haven, Alexa, and Bunny put everything they'd been cooking for the past two days into all the pretty serving bowls and platters they'd bought just for the occasion. The girls laughed and talked and joked as they always did, but it felt different now, deeper. Because all these crises they'd been through, all these challenges, had forged them into a sisterhood. And when Cora thought of all the ways she now belonged to the people around her, it almost made her want to cry with the sheer goodness of it.

The door swung open and a hand wrapped around her still-flat belly as lips pressed to her neck. And those were two more things Cora had to be grateful for. The eight-week-old baby in her belly, almost old enough for *his* very first sonogram—because Cora was sure he was another Evans man—and the father of her child who loved them both. None of which was a secret anymore, not after the doctor had apparently shared the news of Cora's pregnancy in front of Ben. Luckily, the boys were thrilled about the possibility of a new little Evans. So much so that when, a few weeks ago, Ben had crawled into her bed and asked her if he could call her *Mom* like the baby would one day do, Cora had been absolutely floored—and immediately said yes.

"There's my sweetheart," Slider said against her throat.

"Mmm, I'm feeling a little more grateful already," she teased.

Slider chuckled and nipped her neck. "I'll be happy to make sure you're *very* grateful later. How're you feeling? You're not overdoing it, are you?"

She turned in his arms. "I'm fine. It's a good day," she said, not willing to think about any of the bad ones. Not today. "The best."

"Yes, it is."

"You going to share your news?" she whispered, because she knew he'd been keeping something he'd been working on under wraps from the guys until the details were final.

Slider grinned, and he was so damn handsome with some scruff back on his jaw again. "I think today would be a good time, don't you?"

"I really do."

"What are you two whispering about over there?" Haven asked, winking.

"World domination," Slider deadpanned. Cora threw her head back and laughed.

"Sounds about right," Bunny said. "Now, Slider Evans, go recruit some help to start carting everything out to the tables, if you would."

He snagged a piece of stuffing from a bowl. "Yes, ma'am."

Cora swatted at him but missed, and she rolled her eyes at the smug expression he wore.

"You realize," Alexa said, "that you are literally glowing."

Her three friends lined up, all of them nodding.

"Yup," Haven said, grinning.

"She's right," Bunny said. "That's what the magical peen does to a girl."

They all burst out laughing. Just stupid, snorting, can't-stand-up laughing.

Slider, Dare, and Maverick stopped in the doorway and traded looks like they wondered what the heck they'd just walked into. And it made Cora start laughing all over again . . . since they were the owners of some of the magical peens in question.

From the mouth of a sixty-year-old!

How very much Cora hoped she grew up to be just like Bunny.

When the girls managed to pull themselves together again, they supervised everything getting taken out to the tables, and then they all gathered in the mess hall.

Everyone.

Including Jagger, who sat at the head of the main table. His freedom was the biggest thing the club was celebrating today. After an arduous and frustrating set of legal delays, he'd finally been released—and exonerated—three weeks ago. His wavy mess of brown hair had been cut off in jail, but otherwise, the time in hadn't seemed to change him. At least,

364 · **Laura Kaye**

not much. He still smiled easily and talked freely and constantly played guitar chords with his fingers, whether he was holding a guitar or not. And he'd jumped right back into his work at the track. But it seemed to Cora that something inside Jagger shined just a little less brightly than before. And they were all determined to help him get it back.

But for now, he was free, and home where he belonged. Justice, at long last, had finally been served.

Cora sat next to Slider on her right and Haven on her left, and the boys sat right across from them. No one had dressed the slightest bit differently for the meal, and all the brothers wore their cuts. That felt right. Because they were being exactly who they were.

The tables were laden with turkey, ham, stuffing, mashed potatoes, sweet potatoes, cranberry sauce, gravy, cornbread, and so much more—not including Haven's desserts, of course—and everyone filled their plates and dug in.

One giant family of choice and of blood, of friendship and of love. One where Cora finally fit in. One that finally claimed Cora right back. One that she'd have forever. For the first time in her life, she had no doubts about that.

And the fact that it was a legacy she'd be able to pass on to her *own* child made it that much more special. The newest little Evans was never going to know what it was like to want for love.

"So, I have some news to share," Slider said, catching the attention of everyone around them. Cora squeezed his thigh, a silent encouragement to remind him how proud she was.

Maverick tapped his spoon against a glass, gathering the rest of the room's attention, too. "Hold up, Slider has some news."

"Stand up, brother," someone said.

"Oh, well, okay." Slider rose, and Cora could feel the excitement rolling off him. "You all know I've worked at Frederick Auto Body for years. Well, you're looking at its new owner, effective the first of the year." Cora nearly burst to hear him say it, and the club was enthusiastic for him, too, clapping and calling out words of congratulations. In the weeks while she'd healed, when Slider had spent so many days at her side, they'd talked about dreams and futures. And the minute Slider had talked about wanting to own his own shop, maybe make a name for himself with custom paint and remodeling jobs, she'd pushed him to do it. Cora hadn't known that he had decent savings consisting in part of money from Kim's life insurance, but she was entirely supportive of him using it to build his future.

Their future.

"I love you, Slider, and I'm so proud of you," she said when he sat back down.

"You make me want to build a life I can be proud of, sweetheart. For all of us." He kissed her there, in front of everyone. And didn't even care when the boys groaned and Phoenix teased and Maverick declared that Slider and Cora were the worst PDA offenders among them.

He wasn't wrong . . .

When people had nearly finished their dinners, Dare stood up and raised his glass. "I'm not sure I've ever had as much to be grateful for as I do this year. This club—and every member in it—has stepped up again and again, and I've never been prouder to wear these colors." Murmurs of approval circled the room. "So today, I want us to count our blessings. First and foremost, that Jagger is free, his name has been cleared, and he's back where he belongs, with all of us."

A cheer rose up, and everyone raised their glasses. "To Jagger!"

The guy blushed to the tips of his ears, and it was the most endearing thing, especially as his sister and her boyfriend were sitting right there with him, and his sister got a little teary and took his hand. It was so sweet it almost made Cora cry, but then she seemed to get weepy over TV commercials these days. Stupid hormones.

Dare continued, "Next, I'd like us to raise a glass to Caine, Haven, Cora, and Sam, who are all healthy again after some pretty hard fights." Another round of toasts went up, and Slider pressed a kiss to her cheek. "We also have a special gift for Sam and Ben, too." Dare pulled two boxes out from under the table and passed them down to the boys.

"Did you know about this?" Cora asked.

Grinning, Slider shook his head.

"Whoa!" Sam said, his eyes going huge as he opened one of the boxes. It was a sentiment Ben echoed a few seconds later. Both of them jumped up holding cutoff jackets, denim and leather, not with full colors, of course, but with the word *Prospect* on the back. For prospective member.

A huge round of applause and hoots and hollers went up as the boys put on their miniature cuts. Sam looked so much like a younger Slider that Cora could only shake her head. Some girl was already in so much trouble in another ten years, and she didn't even know it. What an amazing gesture it was for the club to make to these boys who had witnessed so much these past months. Teary again, she met Haven's smiling gaze and nodded. *Thank you, my friend.* Because Cora had no doubt that Haven had had a hand in this.

"And the last blessing I'd like to count is a more personal one." Dare reached out a hand. "Haven, would you join me?"

A grin came immediately to Cora's face as she watched her friend stand by her man in front of the entire club.

And then Dare Kenyon went down on one knee.

Cora sucked in a breath as Haven's mouth dropped

open, and you could've heard a pin drop in the room as the club's president began to talk.

"Haven, you have literally saved my life. But even before you did that, you'd saved me in a different way—you made me face that I was only ghosting through the life I had and dared me to want more. And even more than that, you made me believe I deserved it. For a man who spent most of his life certain he didn't deserve anything, you've given me everything. And so, I want to give you everything back. My heart, my love, my name. I don't want to ride alone anymore. I want you in my saddle and at my side, always. So, Haven Randall, will you do me the greatest honor of my life and be my wife?"

Cora pressed a hand to her mouth, her heart so full she had no chance of keeping her emotions in.

"Nothing would make me happier, or prouder, than marrying you, Dare," Haven said.

Grinning bigger than Cora had ever seen before, Dare slipped a ring on Haven's finger, then rose and took her in his arms. While the club clapped and cheered, their friends kissed and laughed and started a life together.

Just like the life Cora and Slider were starting. Just like the little life growing in Cora's belly.

"Someday soon that's gonna be us," Slider whispered in her ear.

Cora smiled and wiped happy tears from her eyes. "Yes, it is, Mr. Evans. Yes, it is." But Cora wasn't in any rush.

For all the craziness, she'd only been together with Slider for less than three months, and they had the boys to consider. So she and Slider were focusing on settling in together, adjusting to having a new family member arrive soon, and helping Slider start a new business. Not to mention spending time as a family with the boys—and with Bosco the Lovable Basset. Whose nametag now read *Bosco T.L.B. Campbell-Evans.*

The rest? It would come when they were all ready.

In the meantime, Cora already knew where she belonged. And Slider already knew she was his forever. And they both knew love. *So much* love.

And in this life, what more was there?

They all brought out the desserts, and then Dare raised his glass one more time. "To brotherhood, club, family!" he called out, his arm around his new fiancée's waist.

"To brotherhood, club, family," they all cheered back, bringing to a close the best Thanksgiving Cora had ever celebrated.

But that was just a start to the celebrations that brightened her life these days.

Because Slider proposed at Christmastime, and baby Jackson Dare Evans was born in June, and Cora Campbell became Mrs. Slider Evans in September. And for the first time in her life, the girl who nobody wanted learned to believe in happily-ever-afters, and found hers, too . . .

A NOTE FROM
THE AUTHOR

One of the most challenging things about writing this book was researching dogfighting and the abuse and neglect that animals face every day. I'm a huge animal lover and a dog owner, and reading about (and seeing) how so many dogs are treated and what they endure—especially those involved in dogfighting—truly broke my heart. That is why I'm donating a portion of the proceeds from *Ride Wild* to Noah's Arks Rescue, a real nonprofit organization that supplies emergency medical, surgical, and rehabilitation services to abused animals. The injured dog Cora witnesses on her first day at the animal shelter, whom I named Otto, is in memory of Noah's Arks' Otto, whose story you can find on their site, www.noahs-arks.net.

ACKNOWLEDGMENTS

S ome books are a trial by fire, and this was definitely one. Of necessity, this book had to be
written fast. But the most amazing thing happened—
Slider and Cora were so right for each other that the
words often flowed faster than I could get them down.
This couple surprised me at every turn—with the
depth of their emotion, their profound connection,
their amazing humor, the way they loved the boys.
And I found myself falling in love with the Raven
Riders all over again. They have certainly come to
feel like my home, too.

I have a couple of people who absolutely must receive my words of appreciation, because when life
made finishing *Ride Wild* difficult, these people

helped make sure it could happen. My first thanks must go to my editor, Nicole Fischer, for the incredible support she gave me in letting me finish on a less-than-ideal schedule. Knowing an editor has your back that way means the world, and I really appreciated it. Similarly, a huge thanks to my agent, Kevan Lyon, who was my biggest cheerleader—and my reality check—throughout the entire process. It's amazing to work with such supportive women every day.

Next, I have to thank my bestie, Lea Nolan, for always being available to plot and brainstorm, including at least one midnight phone call when I'm convinced she got back out of bed to help me. That's true friendship, and I couldn't have finished without her. Also, an incredible thanks to another amazing friend, Christi Barth, who put her polishing touches on the book, posing probing questions that made me go deeper right when it counted, and giving me the confidence in a crazy writing situation to know that Slider and Cora were as awesome as I hoped. These two ladies made this book possible, and to have them as my bestest friends makes me the luckiest girl ever.

I can't miss thanking my amazing husband and daughters, who really sacrificed to support Mom on the world's craziest deadline ever. I couldn't do any of this without their constant love and support, and it means the world to me.

Finally, I must thank my Heroes and my Reader Girls for being constant sources of encouragement and motivation. And I have to thank each of you for taking my characters into your hearts and letting them tell their stories again and again.

~LK

Wrong to Need You by Alisha Rai
Accused of a crime he didn't commit, Jackson Kane fled his home, his name, and his family. Ten years later, he's come back to town: older, wiser, richer, tougher—and still helpless to turn away the one woman he could never stop loving, even after she married his brother. Sadia Ahmed can't deal with the feelings her former brother-in-law stirs, but she also can't turn down his offer of help with the cafe she's inherited.

Cajun Crazy by Sandra Hill
Former Chicago cop Simone LeDeux is back home in the bayou, and she has one rule: no Cajun men. Loved and left by too many double-crossing Cajuns, Simone puts bad experience to good use by opening Legal Belles: an agency that uncovers cheating spouses. But Adam Lanier learns of the dangerous game Simone is playing . . . and the sexy single dad comes to her aid.

REL 1117

*G*ive in to your Impulses!

These unforgettable stories only take a second to buy and give you hours of reading pleasure!

Go to *www.AvonImpulse.com* and see what we have to offer.

Available wherever e-books are sold.

AVONIMPULSE

IMP 0811